"Do you have any idea how good you feel to me right now?"

"I've got some idea, yeah."

"I'm not going to let you go until you promise that I can see you tomorrow. You can't disappear on me for another six months. Okay?"

"You're the genius who told me to take some time."

"I wouldn't have said it if I'd known how I'd feel when you were gone."

With dizzying speed, her heart skittered to a stop and then sprinted into the thousand-beats-a-minute range. "And how is that?"

"Lost," he said, lowering his head.

It was a slow and thorough kiss, unbearably gentle, their lips fitting together and sliding against each other in every wondrous combination possible. He kissed her senseless, until her bones melted into the purest spun gold and her skin shivered with readiness, and then there was more.

Also by Ann Christopher

Deadly Pursuit

Risk

Trouble

Published by Kensington Publishing Corp.

DEADLY DESIRES

ANN CHRISTOPHER

Dafina
BOOKS

Kensington Publishing Corp.

http://www.kensingtonbooks.com

DAFINA BOOKS are published by

Kensington Publishing Corp.
119 West 40th Street
New York, NY 10018

All Kensington Titles, Imprints, and Distributed Lines are available at special quantity discounts for bulk purchases for sales promotions, premiums, fund-raising, and educational or institutional use. Special book excerpts or customized printings can also be created to fit specific needs. For details, write or phone the office of the Kensington special sales manager: Kensington Publishing Corp., 119 West 40th Street, New York, NY 10018, attn: Special Sales Department, Phone: 1-800-221-2647.

Dafina and the Dafina logo Reg. U.S. Pat. & TM Off.

ISBN-13: 978-0-7582-3545-9
ISBN-10: 0-7582-3545-3

First Dafina mass market printing: October 2011

10 9 8 7 6 5 4 3 2 1

Printed in the United States of America

To Richard, always.

Acknowledgments

Thanks, once again, to Assistant US Attorney Kenneth L. Parker and retired Assistant US Attorney Robyn Hahnert, for not blocking my e-mails when I wrote with additional questions. To my old friend Kevin Schad, Esq., I send eternal gratitude for his tips on making my villain as devious as possible.

Thanks to Navkaran B. Singh, MD, who answered my medical questions with good humor and steered me in the right direction.

Any mistakes are, of course, mine.

A million thanks to my editor, Selena James, who agreed that Kira's story wasn't finished quite yet, and let me tell it.

Finally, to Eve Silver, for brainstorming and handholding, and to Eve, Kristi Cook, Lori Devoti, Laura Drewry, Caroline Linden, and Sally MacKenzie, for helping this writer stay as sane as any writer can ever hope to be. I couldn't do this without my pals.

Chapter 1

Cincinnati

Kareem Gregory didn't know who he wanted to punish first: his wife or his lieutenant.

The bitch. Or the snitch.

In a world full of liars and cheats, he'd relied on a handful of people, and this was the thanks he got for his faith and trust. His wife, Kira, had walked out on him, and his right-hand man, Kerry Randolph, the man—the one fucking man on earth—who'd seen the naked underbelly of Kareem's drug empire, had flipped on him.

Was that undying loyalty? No. Was that till death do us part? Hell no.

That was betrayal, the worst possible crime against him.

The punishments would reflect that.

"We need you to empty your pockets and put your jewelry in here, Mr. Gregory."

The voice interrupted his thoughts and cut through his rage and bewilderment, putting him squarely back in the here and now, which was the last place he wanted to be. Here was the US Marshal's office, where the DEA brought you for after-hours processing when you had the misfortune of being arrested for possession of approximately two hundred and fifty kilos of coke and horse with intent to distribute. Now it was about eleven o'clock on the night that should have been the greatest of his life.

Oh, yes. Just this afternoon, he'd been acquitted at his retrial on money-laundering charges and, better than that, one of his men had hit the DEA agent responsible for Kareem's entrapment and conviction in the first place. Just this evening, he'd been hosting a little celebration dinner and toasting his success with the finest champagne his world-class wine cellar had to offer. Just a few short hours ago, he'd been free and clear, with his entire life ahead of him, his wife by his side and everything to live for.

But that was before Kerry flipped and led the feds to the drug warehouse, where they'd found about seven million dollars' worth of his shit. Before the DEA broke down his front door and raided his house. Before his beautiful wife packed her little bags and walked out. Before Special Agent Dexter Brady knocked Kareem to the polished floor of his own damn house, put his booted foot in the middle of his back, and handcuffed him like a street-level dealer.

Now here he was, once again at the mercy of these little government fuckers who didn't have the slightest idea who they were dealing with. Once again reliant upon the nonexistent skills of Jacob Radcliffe, the high-priced lawyer bitch who was standing right there, watching the proceedings with his aw-shucks, Howdy Doody red hair, blue eyes, and freckles, useless to prevent Kareem from spending tonight at the Justice Center with the common criminals. Once again being searched, fingerprinted, photographed from all sides and numbered like a cattle farmer's prize bull.

"Mr. Gregory?" the DEA youngster, or marshal, or whoever the fuck he was, slid the blue plastic box across the table toward him and tried again. "Your personal items?"

Kareem glared at the punk, enjoying the slow drain of color from his face and the way he tried to jerk up his chin in front of his superiors, acting all brave and shit when really he was beginning to understand the situation here.

Here was the situation.

Kareem was like a Siberian tiger. Siberian tigers didn't belong in cages. You could catch one, yeah, and throw it in a cage, and sometimes you could even keep it there for a while. The tiger might sit quietly and eat his three squares a day. But the thing about both tigers and Kareem was this: they had fangs, claws, and unholy power. They chose the right moment to strike, and then they tore their captors to shreds and ate their flesh when everyone least expected it.

Kareem channeled all of this into his silent gaze, and he stared the youngster down until finally the kid looked over his shoulder and shot Brady a *What should I do now, boss?* look.

Brady edged forward, ready with a smirk and a taunt. "What's wrong, Kareem? Afraid to trust us with your sparklies?"

"That's unnecessary," Radcliffe told Brady.

Wow. Two words out of his lawyer's mouth. What was that—a thousand dollars or so tacked onto Kareem's legal fees?

Kareem ignored Radcliffe—he'd deal with him later—and focused some of his fury on Brady because there was plenty to go around. Brady was the DEA bloodhound who'd been sniffing after Kareem for years. Brady was the one who'd been working with Kerry and got him to flip on Kareem; he could feel it in his gut. Brady was the one who'd led the raid tonight and riffled through all of Kareem's precious belongings.

Brady needed to be brought down.

Later for that.

For now, he had to show the feds that they couldn't rattle his cage, no matter how they tried. So he shrugged, ignored the slight shake in his hands, and reached up to unscrew the first of his three-carat diamond studs. Then he tossed it into the box and went to work on the other one.

"I'm not worried. Who can you trust if not the United States government?"

"Funny," Brady said. "Don't forget the Rolex."

Kareem unhooked the heavy clasp, slid the watch off his wrist, and dropped it into the box with a satisfying clunk. Fifty thousand dollars' worth of gold and diamonds had a nice weight to it, and he'd miss the watch. Especially if, as was looking pretty likely, the feds seized it along with his house, his cars, and every damn thing he owned down to his dirty drawers and used toothbrush.

Ah, well. Possessions could be replaced.

Except . . .

The plain platinum band on his ring finger, the one he'd never taken off.

That was priceless, even if his wife was a faithless bitch.

He wasn't a fan of plain when it came to jewelry, but Kira picked the bands, and he'd made it a habit to buy

Kira whatever she wanted. At least he had. Before she walked out on him.

He grabbed the shining band, meaning to slide it off, but it didn't want to budge and he didn't really put his heart into pulling it over his knuckle. These rings bound them together, him and Kira, and when they put them on, he'd meant it to be for life. Oh, sure, there'd been other women, but he'd only ever have one wife. One partner. One Mrs. Gregory.

"That too, Kareem," Brady said. "We haven't got all day."

Kareem looked up from his hands to find Brady still watching him, but with sharper eyes that put Kareem's instincts on alert even if he wasn't sure why. He tugged the ring off and polished it between his fingers, his heart oddly tight. Kira always did that to him—trapped him between emotions like pride and exasperation, love and hate, fury and longing.

Much as he wanted to hurt Kira for walking out on him, punish her, to teach her a lesson she'd never forget, to show her that he was in charge and always would be, he wanted something else more.

Why couldn't she just love him the way she once did?

"You know what this says on the inside, Brady?" he asked, holding the ring up.

Brady's eyes narrowed with clear annoyance and banked curiosity. "Do tell. Since we don't have any-thing else to do tonight but listen to your stories from memory lane."

"It says *Forever and a Day*. That's how long she'll be my wife."

Brady's lips curled with amusement. "Looks like she didn't get the memo on that. Judging from the way she packed her bags and walked out while you yelled for her to come back. Just saying."

They watched each other, he and Brady, and the fine hairs rose all up and down Kareem's arms, probably because Brady didn't flinch or turn away. He had the unwelcome feeling that if he so much as blinked too loud, Brady, despite his Boy Scout soul, would cheerfully pump a round or twenty into him and then talk his way out of it with a judge and be home by dinner.

This animosity between them—it was as personal as Kareem's taste in condoms.

Brady was, therefore, a serious problem. Maybe the most serious one Kareem had ever faced. But he wasn't going to punk Kareem. Not tonight, or ever. So Kareem rolled his shoulders and matched Brady's unconcerned smile with one of his own.

"Kira knows it'll take more than a packed bag for me to let her go," he said.

And watched the color drain out of Brady's face.

Chapter 2

The ancient Tercel spluttered and lurched, clearly trying to give up the ghost and take its place in the great junkyard in the sky. "Come on." Kira Gregory shot a quick prayer up to God, who surely wouldn't bring her this far and then leave her stranded. "Come on."

With rising desperation, she stomped the brake pedal and hoped for the best, which would be something other than the car slamming into the SUV parked just ahead. The car halted, which was great, but the pedal refused to unstick itself from the floorboard, and a freshly acrid wave of burning oil hit her nostrils.

Worthless piece of junk.

One day, when she wasn't consumed with the bare necessities of life—like finding a safe place to stay for the night and trying to divorce her husband without getting killed in the process—she'd spend a little time cursing the used car bastard who sold this so-called vehicle to her, the mechanic who'd examined it and reassured her it was in decent shape, and herself for being desperate and gullible enough to fall for the shiny coat of navy paint and believe either of them.

So this was the freedom she'd fought and prayed for these last months: scared spitless, driving around in the middle of a black and frigid night, protected only by her frayed wits and the negligible body of a car that should be crushed and recycled at the first opportunity, with only her year-old beagle, Max, for company.

Nice.

And well worth all the risks she'd taken to get to this point.

A burst of hysterical laughter shot out of her mouth before she could control it, earning her a surprised sideways glance from Max, who sat in the passenger seat. It got worse when she thought of her previous car, a brand-new Mercedes S-Class sedan that would die of shame before it did anything as tacky as leak a fluid.

The laughing might have gone on forever, but another wave of light-headedness hit her, making the parking lot do a crazy swirl at the edges of her vision. Unconsciousness beckoned—it had been beckoning a lot in the forty-eight hours since Kareem attacked her—but she did everything she could to fight it off. If she passed out in this neighborhood, there'd be nothing left when she woke except for the seat she was sitting in and the car's frame up on cinder blocks.

God, she was tired.

Giving herself a quick second to pull her sanity back together, she leaned against the seat and closed her eyes. Deep breath. Another deep breath.

Okay. Better.

No self-pity, she reminded herself. At least she had a car that was hers, free and clear. The car she'd left behind when she walked out on Kareem earlier tonight was a) bought and paid for with drug money; b) Kareem's; and

c) probably being seized and impounded by the DEA right this very second. The Tercel wasn't new, pretty, or reliable, but she'd paid for it with the honest proceeds from her grandmother's ruby ring (and God knew pawnbrokers never gave you real money for anything), so that was something to be proud of.

Besides. Oprah never wasted time feeling sorry for herself.

Oprah would say something like, "What I know for sure is: My slave ancestors didn't have time to feel sorry for themselves when they were working in the cotton fields, so what do I have to complain about?"

Words to live by.

Well, what Kira knew for sure was that she couldn't sit here on her butt all night. "Wish me luck," she told Max, who yawned with the startling unfurling of a pink tongue that seemed a yard long. "You stay here and be quiet. Okay?"

Max whined, then dropped to a curled ball with his chin on his front paws.

Right.

Pausing only to grab her purse and do a sweeping 360-degree glance in all her mirrors, making sure there were no signs of movement, she got out and immediately felt as vulnerable as a pig in a sausage factory. Pitiful as the car's protection was, it was better than nothing. Out here, there was nothing but the frigid sting of winter air in her lungs, the prickly feeling of unseen eyes, and a thousand and one places for someone to hide, to stalk her before lunging.

Crazy? Probably.

Kareem was downtown being processed right now.

So he couldn't be stalking her right now . . . yeah, sure.

But what about his legion of minions, any one of whom was ready to answer his beck and call and do anything from wipe his ass to stalk his wife for him?

That was a whole 'nother story.

Squaring her shoulders, she strode across the parking lot, through the double glass doors and into the sorry excuse for a lobby/registration area. Just to lift her spirits, it had weathered orange carpeting, brown vinyl chairs, a plywood coffee table, and, honest to God, a condom-vending machine wedged between the snack- and cigarette-vending machines. Wow.

Behind the counter sat a white-haired man who'd last seen young about the time Lincoln was elected president. Rubbing his bleary eyes with weathered hands, he gave her a quick but appreciative once-over, then nailed her with a stare that would only be considered welcoming if you were an escapee from the seventh ring of hell, and waited for her to speak.

"Hello." Infusing her voice with cheer and light, she reached into her purse and pulled out some cash. "I'd like a room for the night, please. Nonsmoking." The last part was probably pushing her luck, but, hey, a girl could hope.

It was no surprise that his voice sounded like Louis Armstrong with laryngitis. "Seventy dollars," he informed her.

This place would need to be razed, burned, and rebuilt from the ground up before it was worth even thirty-five a night, but Kira quashed her outrage and counted out the bills. This was further than she'd gotten at the other two motels, and she was almost home free—

"Oh." Yawning, her charming host scratched at the four inches of gut that hung over his peeling belt and treated her to a glimpse of his cavernous mouth. "And I'll need to swipe your card."

Kira froze, struggling to keep her pleasant smile in place.

Shit.

"Of course," she said, and reached for her wallet, which was what a person did when they had a credit card. She did not have a credit card. Well, that wasn't entirely true, was it? In her old life, the one she'd left mere hours ago, where her husband, the sociopathic drug kingpin, kept her short leash in his fisted hand, she had every platinum card under the sun. And Kareem tracked her spending the way marine biologists track tagged killer whales.

Kareem would find her eventually. But she wouldn't make the job easier for him by leaving a trail of bread crumbs to her motel door.

Shit, shit, SHIT.

"Oh, no." Making a show of it, she rummaged through the wallet, and then through the pockets of her purse. "I can't find . . . Oh, no. Oh, man. I think I left it at the quickie mart at the gas station. I got snacks. Oh, man."

Mr. Friendly wasn't moved by either her keen acting skills or her plight. Staring at her with indifferent eyes and looking like he was anxious to resume his nap, he said the dreaded words: "I need to swipe your card. In case of property damage."

Right. Because if she, say, spilled coffee on the disgusting carpet in this dump, God knew it would be up there with a fire in the Sistine Chapel in terms of human tragedy.

"I understand." She smiled to show there were no

hard feelings. "Why don't I give you cash for two nights? Will that cover it?"

Another yawn. "We need to swipe the card. It's policy."

This had been the end of the matter at the last two motels. The insurmountable brick wall that sent her scurrying back to the Tercel with her tail between her legs. But not this time, buddy.

She was at the end of her rope. In the last twenty-four hours, she'd taken her final nursing exam, tapped into her precious secret savings and bought the lemon that passed for a car, driven and hidden said car near campus, then walked back to the used car lot and driven her Mercedes home. There, she'd stayed in her room while Kareem threw himself an impromptu and celebratory dinner party following his acquittal on money-laundering charges, stayed in her room a little while longer while the DEA raided and tossed the house, left her husband for good, and spent the last couple of hours driving around, trying to find a motel that didn't require a credit card and also wouldn't subject her to devouring by bedbugs.

It was late, and she was beyond exhausted, physically and emotionally.

This fool was not going to keep her from getting a room.

Anyway, he was only a man who had no idea who he was dealing with. Kira was a pro. Hadn't she just spent the last several months matching wits with a sociopath?

So, she planted her elbows on the counter, leaned in, smiled ruefully, and turned on the charm, calling on an inner light that didn't much feel like shining at the moment. He noticed.

A telltale flush crept over his cheeks, and his watery

hazel eyes brightened with interest before dipping to where her coat gaped open over her chest. She could have told him she didn't have any cleavage worth ogling, but why bother?.

"I'm really sorry," she murmured. "I know it's late, and you've probably had a long day, and you're only doing your job." Here she paused to fix him with a look of worshipful hope, as though only he and, possibly, Jesus himself, could save her now. "But I'm really in a tight spot here, and I swear I won't be any trouble. Please help me. Please."

As luck would have it, another wave of dizziness hit, forcing her to close her eyes and hang on until it passed.

"You okay?"

"I need to eat something," she lied. "Can I stay?"

A touch of dimples bracketed his mouth, but he didn't flash the whole smile, because he knew he'd been managed. "Yeah. You can stay. Just don't make me regret it. Last time I bent the rules, a crazy woman let her Chihuahua poop all over the floor."

"You won't. I promise," Kira swore.

And she handed over the money, already wondering how she could keep Max from barking long enough to smuggle him up to her room.

Chapter 3

"This is your room, Randolph."

Kerry Randolph followed the marshal across the suite and peered over his shoulder into the second bedroom. Bed, dual nightstands, desk, dresser, corner chair.

Home sweet home.

Nothing but the best for protected witnesses like him, no siree.

"Everything look okay?" Assistant US attorney Jayne Morrison, his new BFF, waited in the living room, watching as he dumped his duffel bag on the bed and came back. "Need anything before I leave?"

Huh. Funny. He had a comedienne on his hands.

"Yeah." With so many other battles to fight these days, he didn't bother trying to keep the bitterness out of his voice. "I need some branch of the feds to assassinate Kareem Gregory for me. So I don't have to spend the rest of my life in hiding with the marshals." He shot an apologetic glance at the nearest marshal; was that Seth or Joel? Pretty soon he'd have to trouble himself to learn their names, especially since they'd be spending so much quality time together. Seth was the brother. That was it. Joel was the blond. "No offense."

Seth pulled a hurt face that was as fake as the so-called crab they'd had in the Chinese food they'd eaten for dinner tonight. For dramatic effect, he put his hand over his heart as though he'd been gravely wounded. "Gee. You really know how to hurt a guy. We can't think of anything we'd rather do than spend the rest of our lives with you, keeping you safe from harm and making sure you're tucked in bed nice and cozy at night, Randolph. Or do you prefer 'doctor'?"

Joel, who was over at the minibar examining the candy bars with clear disappointment, snorted.

Doctor. Right. Like Kerry wanted the reminder of the chance he'd squandered.

"I'd prefer for you to go fuck yourself, my brother," Kerry said.

"Oh, no." Joel selected a Baby Ruth candy bar, tore off the wrapper, and bit it in half. "The witness is mad at you, Seth. How will you live with the pain?"

"Can you clowns play nice for three seconds, please?" Jayne, now looking as surly as she did exhausted, shot them all a warning glance. "You don't get paid if you kill the witness you're supposed to be protecting. And for future reference, Randolph, I work for the government. So when I ask you if everything looks okay, the only correct answers are *yes* or *can you please bring me a magazine?* Anything else is above my pay grade. Got it?"

Kerry had to smile. He liked Jayne, even if she had grilled the hell out of him at their meeting earlier. Kerry just prayed he'd produced enough useful information about Kareem Gregory's empire to earn himself immunity from prosecution and a permanent place in WITSEC, somewhere far, far away from Cincinnati and Kareem Gregory.

"Got it," Kerry told Jayne. "What now?"

"Well, since it's damn near two in the morning, how about I go home and go to bed, and you three get some sleep. Tomorrow, assuming the three of you make it through the night without bloodshed, we reconvene and continue our fascinating discussion of all things Kareem Gregory. Get you ready for your grand jury testimony. We covered this."

"Right."

The hesitation was not lost on Jayne, who seemed to know he had something else on his mind. With a quick glance at Seth and Joel, who were in the middle of an animated discussion about who deserved the single package of nacho-cheese-flavored Doritos on the mini-bar, she took Kerry's elbow and steered him over to the window for a private word.

"What's up? Don't tell me the accommodations aren't up to your normal five-star standards."

Actually, they weren't. This perfectly nice hotel was a dump, relatively speaking. His bachelor's paradise apartment, on the other hand, with its black leather furniture, floor-to-ceiling windows, and chrome, was heaven, but heaven was gone forever, at least for him. Oh, but there was more. The modern art he'd studied and collected: also gone. Buh-bye. The luxury sheets, computer gadgets, and designer shoes—man, he liked nice shoes. Lost forever, all of them.

Adios. Sayonara. Aloha.

He'd tried to make peace with all of that when he made the phone call and snitched on his boss. There was nothing tricky about it: if you tattle on your boss, and your boss is a drug kingpin, you go into WITSEC and pray the marshals are good at their jobs, which is keeping you alive. Actually, he needed to back up and look at it from the beginning: when you're stupid enough to sign away your soul, lie down with the devil, and sell drugs to your people, you're a parasite whose life and possessions are forfeit.

Simple, right?

But it was still hard, man. The loss of control. The uncertainty. The fear.

"It's fine," he told Jayne.

If the crease between her brows was any indication, she didn't believe him for a second, but a distraction arrived in the form of his favorite DEA agent, Dexter Brady, whom one of the marshals let into the suite. Brady was his contact. He was Brady's confidential informant, affectionately known as *snitch*. They were a team of sorts, like Sonny and Cher or gas and diarrhea. And it was his fondest wish, once he'd testified and disappeared into the WITSEC woodwork forever, to never see the sanctimonious and judgmental bitch again.

For now, though, they needed each other.

After saying hellos all around, Brady walked over. The brother was looking the worse for the wear, no question. Eyes bleary and bloodshot, the scruff of a beard that didn't want to wait until morning to appear, the feral alertness of a man obsessed with a single goal and willing to go to extreme lengths, like not eating or sleeping ever again, to achieve it.

Kareem Gregory.

It was all about getting Kareem Gregory—for good—no matter what it took.

The two men stared at each other while Jayne slipped away, giving them a minute. There was no need for preamble or yackety-yack, not when Kerry's entire life hung in the balance. If things had gone well, Kerry had the protection of the US government backing him up. If they hadn't, he was shit out of luck. Simple.

"How'd it go?" Kerry asked with the scratchy remainder of his voice.

There was only one *it* in question: the raid of one of Kareem's warehouses based on a tip that Kerry had phoned in that morning. Before making the call, Kerry had personally seen kilos and kilos of the Mexicans' finest there, just waiting to be distributed, but Kareem was a sneaky bastard, so there was no telling what tricks he'd pull. For all Kerry knew, Kareem had pulled another rabbit out of his hat and smuggled the shit out the back door while the DEA was breaking down the front.

By way of answer, Brady cracked the beginnings of a smile and held out his hand, something he'd never done before. Kerry liked to think of himself as a cool cat in any situation, but he blinked down at those fingers, wondering if maybe there were explosive devices embedded under the nails.

The gesture would need some clarification, and Brady complied.

"Two hundred fifty kilos," he said.

Kerry blinked again, his mind racing. "Don't fuck with me," he warned.

Brady kept that hand out there, insistent now. "Thank you."

Stunned, he reached out and shook. Brady slapped him on the back with his free hand, and then, the next thing he knew, they were hugging with the fearsome grip

of two soldiers who'd made it off the battlefield alive.
This time.

Pulling back, Kerry tried to wrap his mind around
this much good fortune and asked a few more outstanding questions.

"Did you pick him up?"

"Oh yeah." Brady grinned with wicked delight. "Your
old boss Kareem was throwing himself a little dinner
party celebration. We hated to break down the front door
and ruin the festivities, but that's the way the cookie
crumbles."

"Did he go quietly?"

That killed Brady's grin. "Not exactly. And he suspects you were the one who flipped."

Kerry popped his mouth open in a disbelieving look
as exaggerated as he could make it. "Holy cluster fuck,
Batman! You don't say!"

Brady ignored the sarcasm. "Apparently your absence
from the dinner party made him a little suspicious. So
our friend Kareem is not a happy camper right now."

"Where is he?"

"I just came from his processing downtown. He's
cooling his heels in a cell until his arraignment in the
morning."

"What, with the regular criminals? Poor Kareem.
What if someone barfs on his wingtips? He's not used to
mingling."

"True."

It would have been nice to revel in poor Kareem images
for a while longer—Kareem using the communal toilet
in front of an avid audience, for example—but the full
impact of the situation was beginning to hit Kerry in all
its sickening clarity.

Kareem now realized that Kerry, the man who knew where all the skeletons were hidden, had flipped on him. And, swear to God, Kerry could almost feel the gathering clouds of rage, as though the worst Category 5 known to man, Hurricane Kareem, was gaining strength and heading straight for him.

Kareem's retribution, or at least a mighty attempt at retribution, was inevitable. Why? Well, Kerry had watched Kareem shoot Yogi, another lieutenant, in the back of the head on account of an imagined betrayal. Hmm . . . what else? Oh, yeah. He'd seen Kareem at his weakest, drunk and sniveling among the designer clothes in his walk-in closet, doing a whole lot of woe-is-me because he wanted his wife to love him, and she didn't.

Memories of that ugly interlude two nights ago knotted and congealed in Kerry's gut. He remembered the tears, yeah, and his own rage and shame, because he had, once again, let Kareem get away with the unspeakable.

Most of all, he remembered the blood. . . .

"How is Kira?" he blurted before he could think to stop himself.

It didn't take long for the third degree to begin. "Mrs. Gregory?" Brady's expression was about what Kerry expected to see on a tiger lunging for a monkey in a tree, and his shrewd gaze locked tighter on his face. "Why do you ask about her?"

With difficulty, Kerry yanked back his straining emotions and put them on a reinforced leash, where they belonged. "She's a nice lady. I don't think she deserves what she's gotten in the husband department—you know what I mean?"

This perfectly logical explanation seemed to do a big fat zero in terms of quashing Brady's interest. "True. But Wanda Gregory was there, too, and I don't hear you asking about her. She didn't deserve to see her son dragged away in handcuffs—"

"Actually," Kerry interrupted, "I think she did. I think she knows exactly what kind of son she raised, and I think she deserved this as much as he did."

"Maybe." Brady shrugged, showing negligible interest in Kareem's dear old mom. "But you didn't ask about her. You asked about Mrs. Gregory. And I'm wondering why."

Kerry hit his limit. It was late, he was exhausted, and he didn't have to submit to this verbal equivalent of a prostate exam. Not from Brady. Not from anyone, come to think of it, which was pretty funny. He supposed the one good thing that came out of his association with Kareem Gregory was that everyone else in the world seemed like a teddy bear in comparison.

"It's an easy question, Brady." He didn't bother keeping the rough edge of annoyance out of his voice. "How's she doing? What happened to her?"

Brady studied him long. Hard. Took his sweet time about answering, then took a little longer. "Funny you should ask. She packed her bag and walked out on our friend."

In a day full of extraordinary events, this was the cherry on top, and Kerry couldn't stop his jaw from dropping. Brady was still up in his grill, though, and he needed to take a minute. So he turned and walked to the window. Stared at the closed curtain. Came back and tried to think of a question that wouldn't be a dead giveaway to things that needed to stay hidden forever.

"You serious?"

"As a federal indictment on major distribution charges, yeah."

"I never thought that would happen," Kerry said, another one of those ill-conceived admissions he really wished he hadn't said.

Brady's eyes went flat. Dark. Impenetrable. "You don't say."

"Where'd she go?"

"I have no idea." Brady's jaw tightened with grim determination. "But I intend to find out."

Chapter 4

"I need a minute." Brady walked into the second bedroom of the suite and shut the door in the bemused faces of the marshals, feeling unaccountably surly, which was ridiculous. After years of hard work and sacrifice on the part of his team, they finally had Kareem Gregory dead to rights on major federal charges. He was in jail, where he belonged, and would hopefully stay there for the indefinite future. Forfeiture proceedings were already in the works. They'd seized several of Kareem's cars already, and could soon have his million-dollar house as well.

Even better, one of Brady's men, Jackson Parker, had escaped Gregory's vengeance and would soon be relocated to Panama City, where he'd be safe from the long arms of Kareem's organization. Best of all, Brady had had the intense, orgasmic, euphoric pleasure of seeing fear in Kareem's face for the first time ever. He'd seen reluctant respect in Gregory's eyes tonight, and it was a beautiful thing.

His world should be wall-to-wall roses, rainbows, and dancing ponies.

So why did he want to smash his fist through the nearest wall?

The truth was, something about the way Kerry Randolph asked about Mrs. Gregory just now rubbed him the wrong way. Looked like the snitch had a thing for the drug lord's wife. Wasn't that . . . fascinating? And wasn't Kerry stupid? Having a thing for your boss's wife is always a stupid idea, but when your boss is a major drug kingpin, it's downright suicidal.

Still, he could understand Kerry's infatuation with the beautiful Mrs. Gregory. She was really . . . really . . . Nah. He wouldn't go there.

Didn't want to go there.

The thing was, though, he didn't like the idea of Kerry sniffing around Mrs. Gregory. Which had nothing to do with the case and everything to do with the snarling, seething, primal mass of feeling in his gut.

Oh, yes. Mrs. Gregory had an undeniable effect on men. Yes siree.

Not that her effect on Kerry was any of his business. So he'd let that go.

There. See? He'd forgotten her already.

The issue of her whereabouts was still outstanding, though.

To his utter astonishment, she'd walked out on Kareem earlier tonight, just as Brady and his team were finishing their search of Kareem's *Architectural Digest*–worthy mansion. Well, he wasn't entirely surprised she was leaving Gregory. Hadn't she come to Brady for help on several occasions? Hadn't she told him she wanted to leave her maniac of a husband but was afraid of what he'd do when she did? So, yeah, the Gregorys' pending separation wasn't a surprise to him even if it had been to Kareem.

He just hadn't known she'd do it like *that*.

She just walked out with a single suitcase. Where did she go? She'd asked for government protection, but she didn't have it. He'd hoped to get her into WITSEC, but she'd never been able to find any information about Kareem that could help them frame a case against him. The thing about WITSEC was: if you wanted to be a protected witness, you had to witness something useful to the government and then be willing to testify about it. Kira had never witnessed a damn thing, other than Kareem's morning cereal selection process.

But she left Kareem anyway. Just walked out. Why did she do that? She had to know it wasn't safe. She had to know that Kareem would soon have one of his goons on her tail, trying to drag her back to the mansion, kicking and screaming. If Kareem didn't kill her outright for having the temerity to walk out on him, that was.

So big freaking deal, right? If Mrs. Gregory wanted to get herself killed, then that was her business, wasn't it? No skin off his nose. The domestic situation between a drug kingpin and his trophy wife had nothing to do with the government, the DEA, or Dexter Brady, and he needed to remember that.

Except that something inside him demanded that he check in with her. Make sure she was safe, at least for now.

God damn it.

Why would he stick his neck out for her, though? He had more than enough people to keep track of, what with the assorted agents, snitches, and strays for which he was responsible. His plate was full. Period.

On the other hand, this nagging . . . concern (and it

was only a mild concern, nothing as serious as, say, a worry) about Mrs. Gregory's whereabouts was like the annoying prick of a needle between his shoulder blades.

Unfortunately, he knew himself well enough to know that he'd never sleep until he verified that she was, in fact, still alive. So far. Beyond that, he didn't give a flying fuck because, as he'd told her on numerous occasions, Mrs. Gregory wasn't his problem, never had been his problem, and never would be his problem.

Absolutely not.

Grumbling at his own idiocy, he pulled out his cell and thumbed in the number of her secret cell phone, which he had on speed dial from her efforts to keep him posted about Kareem's illegal activities. It was late, yeah, but if she was keeping him from sleeping, then her ass didn't need to be asleep either.

The phone rang. And rang. And rang some more. Every second that went by without an answer sharpened his desire to punch that wall and/or smash the nearest lamp.

"Pick up the phone," he muttered. "Now, dammit. Pick up the—"

The ringing abruptly stopped. Several beats passed, and then there was rustling, shallow breathing, and then, finally, her voice.

"Hello?"

Thank God. "It's Brady," he barked, because he had other stuff to do and sleep to get, and he didn't have time for this nonsense. "Where you at?"

More breathing. More silence. And then a faint and groggy, "Brady?"

"Yeah. Brady. And I asked you a—"

"I don't . . . feel so good."

She didn't sound so good, and that nagging little voice

that usually steered him in the right direction told him that it had nothing to do with being woken from a sound sleep. For the first time ever, an ugly thought occurred to him, one that had ice coursing through his veins: what if the drug dealer's wife was a druggie? There'd never been any sign of an addiction, no glazed eyes or fidgeting, no clammy sweat, but who the hell knew?

"Are you on something? Don't lie to me."

The question seemed to give her some trouble, and her pause before answering was so long, he wondered if she'd passed out. "What?" Jesus. Was it his imagination, or was her voice fading on him? "No. I'm just . . ."

Just what? *What?*

"I'll be okay."

Fine. Good. Great. She was alive, she'd be fine, and his responsibilities as a humanitarian were fully discharged. Mission accomplished. Nothing to do now except wish her a good life and hang up.

Only he couldn't do it.

"You don't sound okay." Rising fear made his voice gruff. "Why don't you tell me where you are, and I'll come—are you still there? Hello? *Hello?*"

"Brady-yyy." His name was a sigh now, the merest breath, and he felt her slipping away, going somewhere that she didn't need to go. "You always tell me I'm not your problem. I don't need . . . to be rescued."

At some point during their conversation, the adrenaline spike had made him start pacing—what the hell had happened to her?—and now a wave of frustration roared up his throat. How would he find her if she didn't tell him where she was? What if she passed out? What if—

Trying to be rational, he gripped the phone hard enough to make it splinter in his shaking hand. He focused on not scaring her the way she was scaring him. "You don't want to be rescued? Fine. I'll bring you a pizza. Just tell me where the fuck you are, Kira. Please."

"I'm at the Star . . . the Starlight . . . the Star—"

The Starlight Motel? Now there was a fine establishment, fondly known among college students and hookers for its cheap rates.

"Great." He was already in motion, walking for the door. "I'll be there in—Kira? Kira?"

She didn't answer.

"Fuck," he said, and banged out of the suite at a dead run, ignoring his colleagues gaping after him.

"Open the door." Resisting the violent urge to snatch the keys from the man's hand, shove him aside, and unlock the door himself made Dexter vibrate with frustration. "Now."

The motel manager, or whatever he was, looked around and tried to get indignant on him. As though he'd never dream of such rude behavior in a fine establishment like this one.

"Now wait a minute," he began. "We need to knock first. I can't just barge—"

Screw it. So much for not being a barbarian. Grabbing the keys, he edged past Mr. Ethical and went to work on the lock.

"You weren't so worried about manners when I slipped you that fifty, were you?" he barked.

The guy grumbled some half-assed protest, which Dexter ignored.

He turned the knob and encountered a chain lock,

which rattled on the other side. More of an irritation than an actual barrier, the thing gave way without protest when he shouldered through the door.

Christ. If it was this easy for him to get to Kira, and he was one of the good guys, he could only imagine how quickly Kareem or one of his goons could find her. But he'd have to contemplate that nightmare scenario some other time, because he had enough terrors and boogeymen to deal with just now, thanks.

There she was. Sprawled, face down, across the white sheets of the bed, as though she'd collapsed before she could actually get into the bed. The cell phone, he saw at a quick glance, was still gripped in one hand.

Sitting next to her head, whining softly, was an anxious-looking beagle with a red collar. At the arrival of these new humans, he stood, gave one sharp, urgent bark, and wagged his tail, which was as close to *Timmy's fallen into the well!* as Dexter had ever seen in real life.

"Wait a minute." The motel idiot seemed to be working on a fresh batch of outrage. "She told me she didn't have a dog."

Brilliant. Ignore the sick woman and focus on the dog.

With murder in his heart and fear thick in his throat, Dexter paused long enough to glance back and nail the bastard with a look that had him shrinking inside his splotchy skin.

"Get. The fuck. Out."

The guy didn't wait to be told twice. Wheeling around, he scrambled into the dark hallway as fast as his squat little legs would carry him, slamming the door as he went.

And Dexter focused on Kira. Skimming the fine skin of her throat, he felt for a pulse. She had one, thank God, but it felt weak. She was also a little cool to the touch, but what the hell did he know? All the medical knowledge he had came from watching snippets of *Grey's Anatomy* here and there.

"Kira?" Taking all the care in the world, he eased her onto her back and got the shock of his life. Her face, normally caramel smooth, her sleek cheekbones flush with excitement, outrage, and the fierce energy that was Kira, was a horrible chalky color that he only ever saw on trick-or-treating kids at Halloween. Gray tinged her full lips, and her keen brown eyes fluttered but couldn't seem to open all the way. "*Kira?*"

With a labored breath, she roused herself enough to peer up at him and frown. "Brady?"

Relief surged through him, strong enough to make him wet his pants. Sitting on the bed, he eased one of his arms under her neck to support her lolling head. "Hey," he murmured. "What's happened to you? Do you have the flu, or—"

"My head," she said.

"Your head?" The law enforcement officer in him immediately shifted to guns, knives, and life-threatening wounds, but he hadn't seen any—

"I'm going to run you to the emergency room. Okay?"

"Max," she said.

Huh? "Max?"

Beside them, the dog yapped once. Translation: *I'm Max, dummy.*

A lightbulb went off over his head. "Right. I'll bring the dog."

"Don't let Kareem find me." Each word seemed to take a little bit more out of her, and Dexter wanted to beg her to save her energy, but she was determined. With great effort, she opened her eyes all the way and nailed him with a look that dared him to challenge her. "Okay?"

Something powerful gripped him in that moment, something big and bewildering that went way beyond any Good Samaritan moves like helping a sick acquaintance and then sending her on her way while he went on his. Primal and dark, it pumped through his blood with a steady and undeniable beat.

Help Kira. Protect Kira. No matter what.

Nothing was going to happen to this woman. Not one damn thing.

"Don't you worry," he told her, and the fervency in his own voice scared him to death, but he didn't have to think about that now.

This reassurance, apparently, was all she needed to hear. Some of the tension eased out of her body. Either that, or she passed out, a possibility he didn't want to consider. Lifting her into his arms—though he'd always thought of her as fine-boned and willowy, she was unexpectedly solid and strong—he swung her around and headed for the door. The jangling of tags behind him told him that Max was on his heels. Smart dog. He liked that little guy.

As she raised her arms to hold on to his neck, he gave in to an urge, which was an annoying new habit he seemed to be developing where she was concerned.

Lowering his head, and his defenses, just this once, he brushed her forehead with a soft kiss.

Chapter 5

"This way," said Dr. Chang, leading Dexter out of the godforsaken waiting area, past the nurses' station and down the long hallway of patient rooms. "She asked for some food, so we're letting her have a tray."

These fun facts about Kira's appetite were all well and good, but he still didn't know what the hell was wrong with her. The whole time he was sitting there, cooling his heels in the shadow of a blaring TV, while Kira was being prepped for "the tests," going into "the tests," coming out of "the tests" and going into a room after the fucking "tests," everyone, from the various nurses and techs to Dr. Chang here, refused to tell him what "the tests" were. What the hell happened to her? Brain tumor? Stroke? Why were they acting like he needed an FBI check and CIA security clearance before they told him what was going on?

"But what's wrong with her?" It was too late and he was too tired and worried to try to keep the rough edge of frustrated irritation out of his voice. "No one has bothered to tell me—"

Dr. Chang stopped walking and faced him, her lips

twisting with her own annoyance. "We covered this ground already, Mr. Brady. We have privacy regulations, and unless the patient gives permission—"

"I don't think you understand. She doesn't have any family here. I'm the only one she's got—"

"I don't care if you're the president. If Kira wants to tell you about her personal medical condition, then she will. In the meantime, if you can't stop badgering people, then I'm going to have security escort you out." She gave him a sour smile. "Your choice."

Stifling a few prime words for the good doctor here, Dexter ran through his options. He could whip out his badge and try to pull rank on her, but another glance at her blazing brown eyes told him that would end badly. Snatching Kira's medical file and sprinting down the hallway with it would end worse. Plus, then he wouldn't get to see Kira, and his driving need to make sure she was okay still had him by the throat.

That left playing nice and hoping someone slipped up.

The decision made, he mirrored Dr. Chang's sour smile right back at her and held his arm wide to indicate that she should resume walking. "Let's go."

They'd arrived. Dr. Chang knocked quietly on the nearest ajar door and poked her head inside. "You have a visitor, Kira. If he tries to bully you or take your Jell-O, let me know and I'll have him kicked out, okay?"

With a last warning glance that promised dire retribution if he misbehaved, Dr. Chang left. And Dexter edged into the darkened room.

Kira, wearing the obligatory tie-in-the-back hospital gown, was in a bed over by the window, a small bowl in one hand and a raised spoon filled with green Jell-O in the other. The light of the nightstand lamp showed a lot more color in her face, as though she'd officially reentered the land of the living. An IV line of some clear something-or-other, probably fluids, snaked into the back of her left hand. As though frozen, she watched him with wide eyes.

"Hi," he said.

"Hi."

At the side of the bed now, he rested his hands on the rails and looked down at her. She, meanwhile, took another bite of Jell-O with absolute focus, and then, as though she'd lost her taste for it, put the bowl and spoon on the tray table and shoved it away.

"How're you doing?"

Nodding, she worked on a smile that never quite got off the ground. "Good. Better." After a quick swipe at a crease in the sheet, she risked a glance up at him. The contact was brief, though, like a pinball connecting with a lever and skittering away, and it didn't tell him anything he needed to know. "Where's Max?"

"He's in my car in the parking garage, asleep on my jacket, getting hair all over it. I just checked him a little while ago. Don't worry."

Another nod and another attempt at a smile. "Thanks. And thanks for, ah, finding me."

Staring down at the gleaming black hair on her curly head, he wanted to smooth it. To comfort her and reassure himself. He managed not to do it, which was a personal triumph. But then he confessed something he'd never meant to say.

"You scared me."

This time, he got the full Monty: a glittering glare and a smile filled with such bitterness that seeing it was like chewing on burned coffee beans. "Don't tell me that the great and powerful Special Agent Brady ever feels fear. Especially over a woman he doesn't even like."

Some of her bitterness must have transferred to him, because it swelled inside him, erupting in a little snort that left a bad taste on his tongue. His lips twisted.

Yeah. He deserved that. He wasn't one to spare time for touchy-kissy feelings, and, as far as he was concerned, rules were rules, never to be broken. But lots of people didn't see life that way. He got that. He also got why she thought he didn't like her. She was wrong, but he got it.

"Mrs. Gregory," he began, because the best way to keep himself at a distance from this woman was to remind himself who she was married to, but before he could finish his elusive thought, whatever it was going to be, there was a knock at the door and a new woman came in.

Looking very brisk and cheerful in her dark pantsuit and badge, she was halfway through her introductory speech before she realized Dexter was there. "Mrs. Gregory? How are you? I'm Shauna Carter and I—oh! I'm sorry to interrupt."

"Ms. Carter?" Kira seemed wary, probably because she'd had more than enough poking and prodding for one day. "Are you another nurse, or—?"

"Ah, no, dear." The woman darted a look at Dexter. Apparently she didn't want to talk in front of him, and the right thing to do would be for him to excuse himself and let the women have a private conversation. Unfortunately, he wasn't in a gentlemanly mood. He stayed where he was. "Let me give you my card. And I'll stop back in the morning, before you leave. Maybe we can talk then, if you're up to it."

More secrecy. More talking in code. What the hell
was going on?

Years of special agent training hadn't been wasted on
Dexter. No siree. Employing keen detective skills that
would make Sherlock Holmes weep with envy, he
leaned forward as discreetly as possible and squinted at
the woman's badge.

Shauna Carter, LISW, it said. Licensed social worker.
And below that:

Crisis Counselor.

"Thank you." Kira took the card, shot another furtive
glace at Dexter, and ended the conversation as quickly as
she could short of planting her foot on the woman's ass
and booting her out the door. "I'll call you if I need you."

Ms. Carter took the hint. "Have a good night," she
said over her shoulder as she left.

Dexter watched her go, mentally rearranging puzzle
pieces in his mind. Crisis Counselor . . . dizziness . . .
tests . . . extreme secrecy.

He stared at Kira; she resolutely stared in the other direction, refusing to meet his gaze as though she was
ashamed of something and wanted to crawl into a hole in
the ground and never come out; between them, the utter
silence mushroomed and reverberated, hurting his ears.

Blinking, he struggled against it, hoping for another
solution, desperate for a different answer.

He had a tough time finding one.

He thought of Kira's determined attempts to escape
Kareem. He thought of all the times she'd asked Dexter
for help, and all the times he'd said no. He thought of the
wild fear he'd seen in her eyes on more than one occasion,
and how he'd told her, on more than one occasion, that
she wasn't his problem.

"You don't know what it's like," she'd said, and he'd sensed her rising panic.

What had he done then?

The guilt nearly doubled him up, but he forced himself to remember and, worse, to examine the kind of man he really was, which bore no relation to the kind of man he'd thought he was.

What had he done then?

He'd sent this brave, strong, fighter of a woman back home, to her crazed monster of a husband, and that monster had . . .

Face it, Brady. Be a man.

Attacked her.

The sudden certainty hit him like a lightning strike directly from God, or maybe that was the white-hot flash of his consuming rage. Whatever it was, it threatened to choke him.

He felt the seductive pull of several possible reactions, all of them wrong. He wanted to tip his head back and roar like the Hulk, to let the fury swell until it made his muscles bulge and his clothes split down the seams and fall off his body in tatters. He wanted to swipe all her food to the floor, and then use the heavy tray table as a bat to shatter the window. Most of all, he wanted to march down to the Justice Center and use his service pistol to pump a few dozen holes into Kareem Gregory's forehead before putting the pistol in his own mouth and giving the trigger a nice hard pull.

Because Kareem Gregory was the attacker, yeah, but Dexter was the unforgivably judgmental genius who'd handed her over to him on a silver platter, and neither he nor Kareem deserved to live another day.

Except that none of those reactions would help Kira

now, and she was the only thing that mattered in this whole sorry mess.

So he swallowed as much of the bloodlust as he could, which was not, unfortunately, all of it. The best he could do was turn his back on her while he paced over to the far wall, screamed like a silent gargoyle, and tried as hard as he could to crush his skull between his hands. Five good seconds of this wasn't enough, but it was all he allowed himself. Taking ten years off his life in the process, he slammed his snarling emotions in a locked and reinforced cage, wiped his expression clean, and turned back to Kira.

She hadn't moved. Her face, blank as a poker-playing professional's, was still turned away. If he hadn't seen the sparkling track of one tear as it traced down her cheek, he might have thought she'd suffered complete spontaneous petrifaction.

All the stupid things he could say right now crossed through his mind, one lie after another.

You'll be fine.

You're safe now.

Kareem can never hurt you again.

Why bother with any of it? It wasn't like some magic combination of words would heal her.

So he did the only thing he could do. Walking to the bed, taking care not to look her in the face—not now, anyway, because something told him she couldn't handle it now—he laid his hand over hers where it rested on the blanket, twined his fingers with hers, and squeezed.

Chapter 6

The good thing about being raped, Kira supposed, was that it put lesser humiliations in perspective. That being the case, she clung to the solid warmth of Brady's hand, gathering strength from him and not caring, in that one weak moment, that he didn't like her. This was a pity touch for the poor sickling. She knew that. Brady had never deigned to voluntarily touch her before now. Oh, no. In fact, when she let her enthusiasm get the better of her the other day and gave him a thank-you hug, he immediately pulled away with revulsion, as though he'd been served a steaming plate of vomit.

The regular, prerape Kira would have thrown off his hand and let him have it big-time for feeling sorry for her. This new Kira was just grateful for a moment of human contact and compassion, even if it was from Special Agent Perfect and Unsullied himself.

But then she caught herself. Kareem had taken her body against her will, yeah, but he couldn't steal her pride. She wouldn't let him steal her pride.

Yanking her hand free, she swiped that stupid tear off

her face (she hated being weak and emotional) and pretended the last several minutes hadn't happened.

"Where—" Her hoarse voice wasn't up to speed on the show-no-weakness thing, so she paused to clear her throat. "Where is he now?"

"The Justice Center," Brady said.

Since they were now back in safe waters, Kira risked a glance up into the brown blaze of his eyes. "He needs to be arraigned, though, right? When is that?"

"Nine A.M."

"He won't get bail, will he?"

Whoa. A shadow crossed over Brady's face, a dark flash of murderous intent come and gone so quickly she could barely register its presence. Maybe Kareem should try to stay in jail. It might be the safest place for him, at least while Brady looked like that.

"Not if I have anything to say about it."

It was tempting to let this be some comfort to her, but she'd spent far too much of her life doing an ostrich imitation with her head deep in the sand, and she needed to break that habit.

"But you don't have anything to say about it, do you, Brady?"

His lips twisted. If there was one thing she knew about Brady, it was this: he didn't like not being in charge. Funny, wasn't it? He and Kareem had that in common. "The US attorney knows how I feel about the need to keep Kareem off the street. So I'm hoping for the best."

"He set me up, you know." For some reason, it seemed important for Brady to know the whole story, or at least as much of the whole story as she could bear to tell him. "The personal ad in the paper that I thought was from his supplier? It was a fake. He wanted to see what I'd do with the information. A test of my loyalty, I guess you could say. I failed, just in case you're wondering."

Brady's expression was now so dark and fathomless it was like looking into a shadow. "I see."

"I'm confused, though. Since the information I gave you was a false lead that led to the search of an empty warehouse, how did you find out about the real warehouse?"

"I can't tell you that," he said mildly.

He couldn't tell her. Please. Like that would stop her from asking now that all kinds of exciting possibilities were sparking in her brain. "Someone flipped on him, didn't they? You have another confidential informant besides me, don't you? Or should I say a *real* confidential informant, since the information I gave you didn't amount to anything. That's it, isn't it, Brady?"

Unfortunately, he had his poker face firmly in place.

"As I just said, I can't tell you that."

They stared at each other, and the final dot connected for her when she remembered who'd been absent from Kareem's celebration dinner. "Oh, my God. It was Kerry, wasn't it? He's your informant, isn't he?"

A funny thing happened then: Brady blinked.

And that little give was answer enough for her even though he stuck to his script. "I can't tell you that."

"You won't tell me that," she clarified.

"Yeah." His voice was hard now, a titanium rod surrounded by four feet of steel encased in concrete. "I. Won't. Tell. You. That."

But she already knew, and understanding began to sink in. If Kerry was the snitch, then he was a dead man. Simple as that. The DEA would try to protect him, sure, and they'd go through the motions. They'd put him in WITSEC, and they'd post a guard outside his door, and they'd smuggle him to some new city, but it wouldn't matter in the end. Even if Kerry was given twelve new identities, underwent facial reconstruction, and flew off to live with monks atop a Tibetan mountain, it wouldn't matter.

Wow. And here she'd thought she had the shortest life expectancy of anyone in Kareem's circle.

The ache from all this unnecessary loss pulsed in time with her heartbeat. "Oh, Kerry," she murmured, forgetting that she wasn't alone.

Brady shifted closer, and suddenly he wasn't just standing there—he was looming. Those dark eyes, piercing on a good day, now cut through her with a scalpel's sharp edge. It felt as though there was something inside her that he wanted to see, and he wouldn't stop slicing until he revealed it.

"You're awfully concerned about your husband's lieutenant, Mrs. Gregory. Is there a story there?"

God. This man was so intuitive, he really should hang out a shingle and start a career reading palms or crystal balls or some such. He could make a fortune and retire by the end of the year. That was another thing he had in common with her husband: they both had an eerie ability to see things they shouldn't.

Still, when you were married to a sociopath, you learned how to hold your cards close to the vest, and there was nothing like a good deflection to catch people off guard. "That's funny, Brady. I know I was a little out of it, but I could've sworn you called me Kira back in my motel room."

Bull's-eye.

The good special agent dropped his gaze, and just before he turned to grab a chair and set it by her bed, she thought she saw a flush creep up the hard planes of his jaw.

She watched while he spun the chair around and

straddled it, and she felt like a boxer sitting in her corner during a championship bout, waiting for the bell to signal the beginning of the next round.

It didn't take long.

"We need to talk."

She didn't care for the new solemnity in his voice, or for the way he wasn't meeting her eyes again. His utter focus on her blankets made dread skitter up her spine.

"We've been talking," she said flatly.

"You could go to the police." His gentle voice unraveled her defenses and made her feel more exposed than if she'd paraded naked through Times Square at noon. "You could press charges—"

"No."

"—and you know there are resources available for battered women—"

"No."

"Maybe you should think about it."

One arrested moment passed, and then, without warning, she burst into laughter. Ugly, hysterical, uncontrollable laughter.

Brady looked alarmed, probably because he was afraid all the commotion would bring the nurses running. "Mrs. Gregory—"

Tears streamed down her cheeks now, and she spent a couple of seconds swiping at them and trying to get it together. She had a better chance of walking to the moon, but, hey, a girl had to try.

"Call the police, Brady? Really? Press charges? *Really?* This is your best advice after all your years of law enforcement training? And you're basing this on—what? You think a domestic violence charge or maybe a restraining order will stop Kareem Gregory in his tracks even though the DEA, the IRS, and pretty much the entire federal government can't? Brilliant idea. Thanks so much for the advice. All my problems are solved."

Weariness crept over Brady's expression, aging him ten years right before her eyes. Resting his elbows on the tall back of the chair, he rubbed his face so hard she was surprised his features didn't fall to the floor.

Finally, he lifted his head and spoke again, in a tender voice that just ripped her apart. "I know testifying against him would be hard, but you could do it. You're strong. You can do anything you set your mind to."

That was the thing, though. She wasn't. She couldn't. If she got up there on the witness stand, she would open a whole Pandora's box of shameful secrets about herself. Like how she and Kareem had had the most varied and exciting sex life imaginable back when they first got married. Like how she'd been leading Kareem on, kissing and touching him and letting him touch her as though they could heal their marriage, when she knew all along that she wanted a divorce. Like how ambivalent she'd been, even up until the moment things spun out of control on that terrible night. How she'd wanted Kareem. How her body had hungered for him.

How she deserved what happened to her.

How the rape was no one's fault but hers.

"I can't testify," she told Brady. "Don't ask me again."

Thankfully, he recognized a brick wall when he saw one. "Okay."

"Okay."

They sat in companionable silence for a minute, until her exhaustion began to take hold. Lying back against the pillows, she turned on her side and smoothed the blankets, almost wishing he would take her hand again.

"Tired?" he asked.

"Yeah. I have a concussion, so . . . "

"Ah. The mystery is finally solved."

Brady eased closer, now resting his arms on the bed's side rail rather than the back of his chair. Some of the harshness bled out of his expression, making him less formidable. Almost human, like the rest of the mere mortals in the world.

"How are we going to keep you safe, Mrs. Gregory?"

What a nice idea. Doomed, but nice. "We can't."

His lips twisted with what looked like disagreement, but he didn't argue. "What are your plans?"

She smiled, fighting against the approaching sleep that made her eyelids heavy. "Now I take my boards and find a job as a nurse. I took my last final yesterday, which makes me a graduate. Did you know that?"

"I thought you looked different." She had her eyes closed now, but she could hear the amusement in his voice. "Congratulations."

"Thank you."

A pause, then he said, "And then what happens?"

"Then I live my life. Because Kareem has taken the last thing from me that he's ever going to get."

It took him longer to speak this time, as though his thoughts didn't want to be corralled and organized. "Good for you. But what does that look like?"

"Hell if I know, Brady. I'm making this up as I go along."

Just before she fell asleep, she imagined a light touch along the side of her face, as if he'd skimmed her cheek with gentle fingers.

Chapter 7

Kira had no idea how long Brady stayed, but he was gone well before the doctor woke her up to give her a final once-over. After a particularly disgusting breakfast of runny oatmeal, fake scrambled eggs, and cold toast, the nurse gave her a stack of discharge instructions and she was wheeled through the sliding glass doors to the curb, where several cabs idled. She took one back to the motel.

Her car was still in the parking lot, which was something of a disappointment. In a neighborhood that was surely overrun with thieves in all shapes and sizes, her little vehicle had been rejected and she could not, alas, report it missing and try for the insurance money.

Ah, well.

A quick prayer seemed appropriate. "Please, God," she said to the blue sky overhead as she unlocked the door, climbed inside, and tried the ignition. After a discouraging rumble or two, the engine actually turned over—it worked, it really worked!—making her feel guilty for her lack of faith.

"Thank you." Feeling an unexpected surge of affection, she rubbed the dashboard. "Thank you so much."

Then she pulled out of the parking lot, drove several blocks to the address she'd found in the Yellow Pages before she left the hospital, and parked outside a glass storefront, above which hovered one of those rolling steel security gates.

Joe's Gun World.

Ah, yes. This neighborhood was full of fine establishments, wasn't it?

She got out of the car, but loitered on the curb for a minute, having a tough time making her feet walk inside. Though Kareem had guns, and his bodyguards carried guns, and she knew he kept guns somewhere in their house, she wasn't comfortable around guns. She'd never touched a gun, held a gun, or even passed through the rifle section at Walmart.

There was another regret to add to the long list of regrets she had about her marriage: she should have asked the bastard to take her to target practice. He'd have been thrilled with her interest in something so near and dear to his twisted heart.

Well. Enough procrastinating.

Taking a deep breath, she went through the door, which had a jingling overhead bell just like the one at her favorite bakery. The place was, to her surprise, well lit, clean, and uncluttered. The walls were lined with rifles, yeah, but there were racks of clothes for the well-dressed gun owner, including orange hunting vests, various Elmer Fudd hats, and a huge section of what looked like safari jackets, just in case you were headed to Tanzania to hunt lions and elephants.

"Can I help you?" said a voice to her right.

This must be Joe. He was not the Joe of her imagination, a bristled, overweight guy with a military haircut and tobacco stains on his plaid shirt. No. This guy reminded her of Fred and George from the Harry Potter series: young, tall, red-haired and friendly.

"Ah, hi," she said. "I'm, ah, looking for a pistol."

"Great. Let me show you a few things." Just like the guy at Tiffany who'd shown diamond earrings to her and Kareem a few years back, he led her to a gleaming glass case. "Any idea what you have in mind? We've got some nice ones that could fit in your purse—"

She could see where he was going with this. There was a whole row of silver pistols—nickel-plated, weren't they?—that were way too cutesy for what she had in mind. Did those things have the firepower to actually hurt anyone? Why not just throw a brick instead?

"Let me get this straight." Time to interrupt this spiel before it really got going; the next thing she knew, he'd be showing her pistols in pink and lavender with matching rhinestone-studded purses and shoes. "If I get one chance at protecting myself in the middle of the night, say, or one shot at an intruder, or, I don't know, one chance to hit a rapist over the head with my gun before I try to run away and escape—this is the gun you want me to have? Is this the gun your mother has? Or your sister?"

Joe's wide-eyed, drop-jawed expression eased into a wry smile. "Something tells me you have a weapon in mind already."

"You're damn right I do."

"A thousand apologies. What can I show you?"

Thankfully, she'd done some research a while back.

"A Glock," she told him. "Isn't that the gun that most law enforcement officials use?" Dexter Brady, who'd developed the annoying habit of sneaking into her thoughts when she least expected it, tiptoed into her brain and waved hello. Brady had a Glock, if she wasn't mistaken, and there was something comforting about having the same model that he relied upon. "I want a Glock. Forty caliber, right? Semiautomatic?"

Joe's smile widened with unmistakable respect. "You didn't tell me you were a player. I have a couple of them right here to show you. Now this one—"

He reached for a deadly black model with sharp edges that looked as though it could kill a person who simply stared at it too hard. It said 36 on the side, but a memory was coming back to her.

"No," she said. "Isn't the thirty-nine the most powerful? I want the thirty-nine."

"You've got good taste."

"And I'll need magazines, bullets . . . the whole deal."

"You got it. Will you be taking target practice?"

He handed the pistol to her, and she took it. It was solid, but not as heavy as she'd expected. Cool. Comforting, as twisted as that sounded, because this gun, once she learned to use it properly, might just be the thing that saved her life one day.

"Target practice? Absolutely."

"And did you want to apply for a permit today?"

"Permit? Hang on. I don't need to apply for a permit to buy the gun today—"

"No, no—the concealed carry permit."

Oh, thank God. The sudden alarm loosened its hold on her, letting her breathe again. In Ohio, she already knew, you didn't need to register or anything to buy a gun. If you woke up that morning, yawned, stretched, and decided, hmmm . . . I think I'd like a forty-five to put under my pillow, you could get one that day. As long as you were eighteen or older, weren't a felon, and had the money to pay for it, you were pretty much good.

Strange how life worked, though. Married to a drug kingpin and she didn't like guns. Her whole life up until now, she'd been pro-gun control and thought members of the NRA and their ilk were crazed fanatics whose stance on gun ownership was outrageous and dangerous.

Now she thought they were freaking geniuses.

"Yeah. Do you have the paperwork for that? Because I want to keep the gun with me all the time."

"No problem. How will you be paying today?"

That brought a smile to her face. This little weapons purchase was going to cost an arm and a leg, and she wasn't planning to tap into her meager savings to finance it. No way. For this one special purchase, where there was no need for secrecy, she thought it was only appropriate that the money from Kareem's illustrious illegal activities be used.

So she pulled out the platinum card that he'd given her, prayed the feds hadn't somehow suspended the account since Kareem's arrest, and imagined, with great pleasure, the look on Kareem's face when he reviewed the bill and saw the charges from Joe's Gun World.

"I think I'll charge it," she said.

The shocked disbelief was like a Plexiglas shield that protected Kareem Gregory from his surroundings and the proceedings. Sitting in the same uncomfortable-ass chair at the same table, in the same wood-paneled federal courtroom, with the same lineup of lawyers and judge (Roberta Shelton) that he'd had during his trial a few days ago was like taking an all-expenses-paid, first-class trip into *The Twilight Zone,* and wasn't that a bitch?

Yesterday—and it was just yesterday, even though it felt like ten lifetimes plus a million years ago—a jury acquitted him of money-laundering charges in this very same courtroom. He'd walked out of here as a triumphant and free man, with his entire life before him, and all the trouble behind him.

Now here he was again.

Again.

Once again, he was not free to go where he wanted to go or do what he wanted to do. Once again, he'd spent the night locked up, surrounded by the snores, yells, cries, and farts of other men, rather than in the luxurious comfort of his own bed. Once again, he'd trusted the wrong person and paid for it with a knife right through his heart. Which meant that, once again, he'd have to make someone pay for his or her crimes against him.

If they let him out on bond, that was.

It wasn't looking too good at the moment, but his boy Jacob Radcliffe was still on his feet and still swinging, so he wouldn't count him out just yet.

"My client has not been accused of a violent offense," Jacob was saying to the judge. "He's not a danger to society—"

"Anyone in possession of two hundred fifty kilos is a threat to society," interjected assistant US attorney Jayne Morrison, shooting Kareem a disgusted look, as though he'd just rolled through a field of cow shit. Government bitch. "And the presumption is that Mr. Gregory should be detained until trial."

Jacob didn't bother to acknowledge this interruption.

"He has strong family ties in the community, because his wife and mother are here—"

That was only partially true. There was no need to inform the judge that Kira, his precious and most beloved wife (there was that bitterness again, threatening to choke him), had left last night, heading for parts unknown. Mama was still there, though. Glancing over his shoulder, he caught her eye and gave her a tiny wink. Sitting behind him, in the gallery, she perked up at this attention and smiled back, always waiting for the slightest sign that he needed something. Good old Mama.

"—and he's not a flight risk. He can surrender his passport, wear an anklet for monitoring, and submit to house arrest until the trial."

"Your honor," Jayne began, swelling dramatically with outrage, but the judge held up a hand, stopping her.

"I'm inclined to agree with Mr. Radcliffe."

"Your honor." Jayne wasn't acting now, was she? She looked seriously pissed, which made Kareem's day. "This is a complete departure from—"

Judge Shelton kept that one hand up and scribbled something on her pad with the other, looking as though she wanted to wrap this up and get on to the important part of her day. "I've made my decision, Ms. Morrison. The only thing we need to talk about now is the amount."

"One million," Jane said flatly.

This time it was Jacob's turn for the outrage. "In a case like this, your honor—"

"One million is appropriate." Judge Shelton finished scribbling and gave everyone in the courtroom a last sweeping glance. "Is there anything else for this morning?"

"No, your honor," grumbled the lawyers, both of

whom looked equally unhappy at this point, but Kareem didn't care.

He was going home.

After that, they did the "all rise" thing while the judge left the courtroom, and Kareem was about to pat Jacob on the back for a job well done for once, when he got an unpleasant surprise.

"What do you want, Special Agent?" Jacob glared at someone over Kareem's shoulder. "I need to get my client processed so he can go home. We don't have time for any of your threats or intimidation tactics this morning, so you'll have to find someone else to pester."

Turning, Kareem discovered Brady standing there, right in his face. Kareem was always happy to play a little cat and mouse with the feds, especially when he'd just won a round against them, but today was different. He hadn't had a chance to recover from his stunning reversal of fortune just yet, for one, and there was a crazy new light in Brady's eyes since last night, for another.

Brady was one of those cats who were easy to read. Everything was black or white with Brady, good or evil, Luke Skywalker or Darth Vader, them or us. There was no in between. Since Brady put himself firmly in the good guy column, he did things by the book. He generally didn't break rules and he rarely colored outside the lines.

Kareem got all that about Brady.

What he didn't get was the way Brady was looking at him now, all complete stillness, narrowed eyes, and slow murder, as though he'd said to hell with the justice system and decided to go rogue and deal with Kareem himself. As though he'd break every rule in the book and happily spend the rest of his life in prison for the privilege of gutting Kareem and dancing barefoot through his steaming innards on the floor.

Staring into Brady's face, Kareem again felt the hairs on the back of his neck stand at attention. This reaction gave him the kick in the ass he needed, because being afraid of anything really pissed him off. Time to turn on the bravado.

"What's up, Brady?" He flashed an insolent smile, although it didn't come as easily as it normally did. "You miss me during the night?"

Brady didn't answer. Didn't blink. Didn't seem to breathe.

Jacob, meanwhile, was springing into action. "Jayne?" he called, pointing at Brady. "You want to come over here and call off your attack dog? We really don't need this right now."

Jayne paused while packing up her briefcase, looked over, saw Brady, and rolled her eyes. "Everything okay over there, Dexter?"

"It's okay," Kareem told her. "My friend Brady has something on his mind, don't you, Brady?"

A muscle now ticked in Brady's jaw, adding to the whole bat-shit crazy effect. He seemed incapable of answering, which was Kareem's cue to twist the knife a little deeper.

"Did you hear my good news, Brady? I'm going home. It'll be nice to sleep in my own bed again. Relax. Maybe have a little wine. Feel free to drop by and visit."

Something shifted in Brady's expression. It was too dark to be humor, but it loosened him up enough to talk. "You go on home, Kareem. I figure if we give you enough rope, you'll hang yourself one day."

"Brady," Kareem chided, "you know me better than that."

This time Brady did smile, only it wasn't a smile. It was a demon's leer, or maybe an invitation to hell. It chilled Kareem's blood. And then Brady eased closer, mouthing the words so that only Kareem could hear before he turned and left the courtroom, letting the door ease shut behind him with a gentle whoosh.

"I think I'm going to have to kill you one day, Kareem."

Chapter 8

Outside on the courthouse steps, Dexter pulled out his phone and called Kira, driven by that same primal urge that kept tightening its fingers around his neck in a choke hold.

Warn Kira, protect Kira—especially once she left the hospital.

Keep Kira safe.

She answered on the third ring. "Brady?"

"Hey. Where you at?"

"I'm just . . . ah, running some errands. When can I pick up Max?"

"Later."

"Did he do okay last night?"

What was up with her and that dog? Did they not have more pressing issues to be worried about? "Yeah. Fine. He slept on the end of my bed. Ate a bowl of Cheerios with milk for breakfast. He was sleeping like a baby when I left this morning."

"Cheerios?"

"Listen. I don't have all day for this. I just left the detention hearing. Kareem got bounced on bond."

Silence, for a long time. "I figured. So he's going home?"

"Yeah." Brady hung his head, cowed by a nasty emotion: shame. He was ashamed of himself for not killing Kareem back there in the courtroom when he had the chance. It would have been illegal, yeah, but not immoral. More along the lines of a priest exorcising a demon. He was, further, ashamed of the federal government, of which he was a representative, for letting that monster walk free. Most of all, he was ashamed for not protecting Kira when she asked for help, and anticipating more shame, because even now, he didn't know if he could keep her safe. "He got home confinement. Ankle bracelet. I'm . . . sorry."

"It's not your fault." She sounded brisk now, downright chipper. "I don't blame you."

Well, that was great because he blamed himself enough for sixty or seventy people already. "I need to get back to the office right now, but I can meet—"

"It's okay," she said. "I'll catch up with you later."

Now wait just one minute. There was a note in her voice that didn't match up with breaking events as he understood them. What the hell was going on? And why was this feeling of dread swelling like a mushroom cloud inside his chest? "Where are you?"

"I've got something to take care of," she said.

She could do this, Kira told herself.

It was dark now, and that primal fear of monsters in the shadows did nothing to boost her bravery level, which was hovering at around zero percent. Plus, the temperature had dropped, and the cold was inside her bones, systematically converting every molecule in her body into ice cubes. Headache and trauma contributed to her lingering exhaustion, and the bottom line was that she didn't want to do this.

Tomorrow was another day, right? Nothing stopped her from walking that half a mile back down the road to where she'd hidden her car on a private lane. She could pick up Max, drive back to the motel, take a hot shower, and spend the rest of the night curled under the blankets in the fetal position.

Except that that would make her a coward. She was many unpleasant things, but a coward wasn't one of them. And she wasn't going to put herself through this whole agonizing routine again tomorrow.

Taking a deep breath for courage, she walked up the long drive to the Mediterranean style villa that she'd left a little less than twenty-four hours ago. The house where she'd lived as Mrs. Kareem Gregory, drug dealer's wife. The house she'd hoped never to see again.

Wow. The massive front door had already been replaced since overzealous DEA agents splintered it with a battering ram during the raid last night. That was Kareem for you. It would take more than a little thing like being arrested and detained to stop him from keeping his precious house in tip-top shape. Luckily for her, he'd kept the same locks, though, so that made things easy.

Unlocking the door, she slipped inside the foyer of her beautiful prison. Only the bars, razor wire, and rifle towers were missing; God knew she'd had a warden. Back in the day, she'd foolishly thought of it as a house and treated it as such. There'd been decorators, trips to high-end furniture stores, and even several custom made pieces that'd cost an arm and a leg and several thousand dollars of Kareem's hard-earned blood money.

It had been her beloved sanctuary, the place where she thought nothing could touch her.

Now she knew better.

As usual, strategically placed lamps lit the way down the hall and into the great room, where she could hear the low murmur of voices . . . male voices . . . Kareem's voice.

Deep in the pit of her belly, that knot of fear twisted and pulsed.

Another couple of silent steps closer, and Kareem's cologne, the one she'd bought for him and loved, with warm, earthy notes of wood, mint, and basil, skimmed her nostrils. It was a private blend that she'd had made for him, and now it made her skin crawl with memories that he'd seared too deeply into her body for her to ever forget.

You wanted this, Kira, didn't you—

No, Kareem! Stop! Please, please—

Huh? You like it hard, don't you, baby? You've been asking for this, haven't you?

The fear spread to her knees, making them shake, and that pissed her off. He would not do this to her. She would not collapse to the floor in a heap. She would not go down like this.

Pausing only long enough to take a deep breath, roll her shoulders a couple of times, and tip her head from side to side to work out some of the kinks, she strode into the room, making sure her footsteps were loud enough to startle.

It worked. Kareem, who'd been sitting on the sofa in urgent conversation with Jacob Radcliffe, his lawyer, whipped his head around, realized it was her, and jumped to his feet as though he'd been launched from a catapult.

Home incarceration did not, she knew, involve a ball and chain shackled around his legs and bolted to the floor. He probably had some sort of monitoring device attached to his ankle, which was currently hidden behind his creased and cuffed gray wool trousers. There were also no prison stripes, no guards, and no unidentifiable chow cooling on a compartmentalized metal tray.

There was, in short, no sign that his life had changed one iota. She might have interrupted him enjoying his predinner glass of wine, and that really screwed with her head. He had raped her and she fled to a motel that probably attracted every bedbug in the area, but he got to live in his personal palace like a king? The DEA arrested and jailed him on major trafficking charges, but now he was back, wearing designer clothes and sleeping in a bed with feather pillows and sheets of the finest Egyptian cotton?

Why wasn't he chastened? What would it take for him to show humility? Why was it that nothing ever made so much as a dent in his armor of invincibility?

"Kira." The wide-eyed surprise in his expression didn't take long to melt into smug satisfaction as he crossed over to her. "I knew you'd come back, baby. But this isn't a good time for me."

"I'm sorry to hear that." It took everything she had not to turn and run when he got too close. Instead, she held up a hand to stop him when he reached for her, enjoying the way her rejection made shadows darken his face. "But this is a good time for me. And what I have to say won't take long."

He stilled. One corner of his mouth twitched, as though he was trying to work up a nonchalant smile, but it never came. "You're not coming back?"

"I told you. I'm never coming back."

That same side of his mouth moved again, this time with the hard curl of a sneer. His voice dropped, becoming rough and dangerous. "We settled that the other night. Maybe you need another lesson."

That was the thing, though. He *had* taught her a lesson. Just not the one he'd hoped. Hell, maybe she should thank him. This whole time she'd been living in fear, afraid to leave, afraid to stay, afraid of her own shadow, but now she got it:

Nothing he could possibly do to her would be worse than what he did the other night. That made her free, whether she had the divorce papers to prove it or not. He could still kill her, of course; maybe that was the fate God had in mind for her.

Fine, God.

As long as they all understood that she meant to take Kareem out with her.

So she reached into her purse and pulled out the Glock.

"Yeah," she said, "I think I'm good on the lessons, but thanks. It's your turn for a lesson."

From over on the sofa came Radcliffe's shaky voice. "Oh, shit."

Kareem, meanwhile, had a respectful new glint in his eyes, but otherwise looked unruffled, as though he wouldn't let her ruin his day any more than he'd let a few aggressive ants ruin his picnic.

"What're you doing, baby?"

Kira kept the gun at her side, pointed toward the floor,

relishing the power it gave her. Too bad she'd never gotten one before. She and Kareem could have done a much better job communicating.

"I'm having a discussion with my husband."

"With a gun? You never liked guns. You never wanted them in the house."

She shrugged. "Things change. People change."

His face hardened, except for a wry glint in his eye. "You're proof of that, aren't you? But I still don't think you want to go around threatening people with guns. You don't want to do this."

"Actually, I do." For one quick second, she let her gaze flicker to Jacob Radcliffe, who was trying to act casual while furtively thumbing numbers on his cell phone. "Tell your lawyer not to call the police, Kareem. I won't be here long."

Without looking away from Kira, Kareem waved a negligent hand. Radcliffe put the phone down, muttering a curse under his breath.

"What's on your mind, baby?" Taking all the time in the world, Kareem leaned against the sofa and crossed his ankles. "Don't keep me in suspense."

Confidence began to pump through Kira's veins. It was either that or a poisonous amount of adrenaline, or maybe she was just as twisted as Husband Dearest here. Whatever. The bottom line was that she was beginning to enjoy this little discussion.

"Here's the thing. I want a divorce. I want to move on with my life. I don't want any of my clothes or jewelry, and I'd never ask you for support. I just want a divorce." She paused. "I assume you're not going to agree to any of that."

Utterly still, Kareem studied her with narrowed eyes and said nothing.

"Right. Well, then. Here's what you need to know. I'm going to file for divorce. I'm going to live my life. I'm not going to hide. You're not going to control me any more. Not one more day."

A glimmer of amusement lit Kareem's face.

Since he didn't seem to be taking her seriously, she raised the gun, clicked off the safety, and leveled it at his face with her two-handed grip.

"Jesus," breathed Jacob Radcliffe.

Kareem's amusement vanished.

"You will not stalk me. You will not follow me or have one of your goons follow me. You will not call me and hang up. I don't even want you thinking about me. And if you reappear in my life, and try to bother me, I will kill you. I'm going to have this gun with me all the time—it'll be under my pillow at night and in the shower with me—and I'm just looking for an excuse to use it on you. Don't try to tell yourself that your sweet little wife would never hurt you. I will. I'm just waiting for my chance. Do you understand me?"

The moment lengthened. It stretched between them, encompassing everything they'd been to each other over the years. The joy. The ugliness. For half a second, Kira remembered the man she'd loved, the one she'd thought she'd married. Too bad she was too young and naive— or just plain stupid—to know that the man she'd loved so much had only ever existed in her imagination.

Apparently Kareem was experiencing some of the same ambivalence, because his face softened into something that might have been sadness, but of course there was no percentage in trying to read a sociopath's emotions.

"How did we get here, baby?" he wondered.

"You brought us here."

"I loved you."

Funny how those words meant nothing to her. It was hard to remember when they'd ever mattered. "And I loved a man who never existed."

His eyes flashed. "I'm sorry it has to be this way."

Sorry. Kira swallowed some of the bitterness collecting on the back of her tongue and snorted with something that might have been a laugh. "Not half as sorry as I am. Trust me."

And there it was—that invisible wall of malevolence radiating from him like a force field. She could almost feel the room's temperature drop. His expression flattened out, as though even the charred remnant that passed for his soul had left the building, and she knew that this was the real Kareem, the one he'd hidden so well in their early years together.

This was as much of a warning as she'd ever receive, as close to a pair of horns, forked tongue, and pointed tail that she'd ever get. Much as she wished the Glock equalized the power between them, it didn't. Nothing ever could because—bottom line—she was human and he was some unidentifiable other.

He scared her to death.

When she was ready to scream with the spiking tension, he straightened and came closer. One step . . . two steps . . . and then he was too close, right in her face, less than a breath away. Her knees, which had done a remarkable job of holding up for the last several minutes, softened into warm pudding. Even so, she would not show weakness to this man. Not again. Never again. So she stiffened her spine and stared into those eyes that were emptier than a shark's.

"You remember what I said when we got married, don't you, baby?" Kareem asked in that velvety voice that used to make her skin sizzle and now made it crawl. "My vow was to have and hold you all the days of my life, wasn't it? You remember that, don't you?"

"I remember."

That was it, then. The battle lines were drawn.

"So," she said. "Either I'm going to kill you one day, or you're going to kill me. I think that about covers it."

"Oh, no." His features eased into a chilling smile that made her wonder if he'd descended from a long line of dragons, and despite all her bravado, she wanted to run. To hide. "You can come home any time you want, baby."

There was only one response to this invitation.

"I'd rather be dead," she told him.

He tsked and reached up a hand to touch her cheek. And she surprised herself by taking her finger off the trigger and, in one swift move, whipping him across the face with the pistol.

Nose bleeding, he stared at her with wide, shocked eyes.

"I'd rather be dead," she repeated.

Kira's strength lasted just long enough to propel her through the door, across the porch, and down the steps. As soon as she reached the relative darkness and shelter of the mature oak to the right of the driveway, she leaned against it, her courage exhausted. Bracing her hands on her thighs, she doubled up as a sickening wave of dry heaves and dry sobs wracked her down to the marrow of her bones.

And then, quite suddenly, she'd had enough.

No one would reduce her to this. Not even Kareem. Fuck him.

Right. To the car, Kira.

She slipped through the gate and started walking down the middle of the street, concentrating on individual steps rather than her exhaustion or the half mile that stretched between her and her little hunk o'junk.

The street was quiet, the few houses immaculate and well lit with their tasteful little porch lights, the neighbors well behaved and genteel. What would they say if they knew of the unfolding domestic-violence drama down the way?

A semihysterical giggle burbled out of her throat and she bit it back by clamping her hand over her mouth.

One step . . . another step . . . keep going . . . you can do it.

The cold, sharp air rejuvenated her, making her feel . . . she felt . . .

Good.

Was that wild, or what?

After all those months of pretending she wanted to save their marriage, of cat-and-mousing it while she bought herself time to finish her nursing degree and gain the means to financial independence, it felt wonderfully, ecstatically, orgasmically good to tell Kareem where she stood and give him a dose of his own medicine.

Hell, she was proud of herself for confronting the bully, and wasn't that a strange feeling after spending so much time with shame as her BFF?

Laughing again while she swiped the tears and clammy sweat from her cheeks, she wheeled around to face Kareem's house again.

She needed to gloat a little.

"Fuck you, Kareem," she called, not caring if anyone or everyone heard her. "Fuck y—"

Without warning, the house exploded in a blinding flash of orange heat that sent Kira flying through the air.

Chapter 9

Kira landed flat on her back, slamming into the grass and hitting her head with a force that had stars streaking across her vision. The blast's percussion seemed to go on forever, reverberating inside her skull and shooting out her ears like splintered razor blades. Debris showered from the sky, and she stopped scuttling backward long enough to cover her face with her hands. Sharp bits of something—glass, probably—prickled and pierced her skin, and blood filled her mouth. Stunned, she spat, and then spat again. What was that? Had she swallowed glass or—? No, wait. It was her tongue. She'd bitten her tongue.

The house . . .

Shock roared out of her on a bewildered cry that turned into an endless scream. No. No, no, no. And then there was another, smaller explosion, and she dropped her head again, trying to escape the projectiles. It didn't work; she'd have had more success trying to dart between air molecules.

This could not be happening.

Houses just didn't explode, and Kareem was too evil to die.

Frozen by her disbelief, she sat on her butt and watched the inferno. That was the only word for it. One second ago, a million-dollar house had sat there, but now there was only a blackened shell and flames licking through doors and windows toward the sky, as though Hell had opened up a portal and reclaimed Kareem as its own.

"No." It took forever for her to climb to her feet, longer for her legs to solidify. "No!" She started walking toward the furnace, propelled not by courage or Good Samaritanism but by the need to confirm what her gut already knew:

This was a trick. Kareem was not dead. Kareem would never die.

Monsters needed to be exorcised, staked, or shot with silver bullets. They didn't just conveniently die and set their victims free. Life wasn't that easy and never would be. Kareem was not dead.

"Kira." Running footsteps came up on her right, but she ignored them. "Oh, my God, what happened? What happened?"

Kira kept walking.

From every direction came the sounds of more doors banging open, more shouts of alarm, more shocked cries from neighbors. None of that mattered. The only thing that mattered now was stopping this farce before it got going. Kareem would not get away with this, and she was just the woman to stop him.

"Kira." Some worried neighbor—she had no idea who—kept pace with her, trotting alongside and grabbing her arm. "What are you doing? You can't go in there. Kira!"

Kira jerked free, driven by both her righteous mission

and rising hysteria, attracted to the crackling blaze like
a suicidal moth. "Kareem." If she looked hard enough,
she knew, she would find him—probably streaking
through the flames and trying to escape out the kitchen
door in the back. "Kareem!" Maybe he'd snuck down
to the wine cellar—God knew he spent enough time
down there—or maybe he'd already climbed out through
a side window. But he was still alive. Maybe she was
insane, but the scent of him was in her nostrils, even over
the assault of scorched wood, melting plastic and rubber,
and the stark stench of her own fear. Kareem was still
alive. She could smell it. *"Kareem!"*

"Kira!" roared a new voice. "Kira!"

Breaking into a run, Kira raced for the front door
before anyone could stop her. It was, once again, dangling off the hinges he'd just had repaired, and wouldn't
that piss Kareem off when he reappeared? But there had
to be a way inside—

"Kareem!" she shrieked. "You come out here right
now, you son of a bitch— Oh, God!"

An invisible wall of heat slammed into her from head
to toe, so fierce she could feel the sizzle of her bare
hands and face and the singe of her hair and eyebrows.
Her coat, so warm during the winter months, now felt
like an aluminum-foil wrapping designed to roast her
alive.

Frustrated by this unexpected barrier and possessed
by the overwhelming need to see Kareem either dead or
alive, either a crispy critter or the smirking and arrogant man she'd always known—to know, one way or the
other—she prowled the perimeter, looking for an opening and ignoring the pain.

A little heat would not stop her from finding that bastard—oh, no, it would not. Burns could heal, and—

Wait. Maybe if she climbed through the dining room's shattered picture window. Yes. Yes, that could work if she just ran straight through the heat—

"Kira!" That new voice thundered at her again, this time accompanied by a strong arm that hooked her around the waist and swung her off her feet. "You're not going in there."

"I have to see!" she screeched, twisting and kicking because this was her one chance—her one and only chance, ever—to stop Kareem from committing more wickedness. If she didn't stop him, who would? "I can't let him get away with this!"

"You're not going in there."

The voice finally registered with her frantic brain, and with it came enough relief to make her body go limp. Brady. Oh, thank God it was Brady. He would listen to reason. He would understand that this was a trick.

"Brady." Apparently reassured that she had calmed down, he set her down and held on while she got her footing. She twisted within the circle of his arms and grabbed his jacket collar, determined to make him understand her urgency. "Kareem's in there. He's alive. I know he's still alive."

Brady shook his head, his expression grim, his lips a thin line of intransigence. Everything about him screamed *no*, and then *no* again, into infinity. Panic flared again, because this man did not look like an ally.

"Kira," he began gently, "no one could survive—"

"Kareem could."

"No. Not even Kareem."

Why did she have to explain this? Why couldn't he see? Tightening her grip on his jacket, she shook him so he would open his eyes and help her. The flames were growing brighter, and it would never get any easier to go inside that house and find Kareem.

"This is a trick, Brady—"

Another grim head shake. "No."

"Yes, it is. You don't know what he's capable of."

"No, Kira."

Increasing mania made her voice shrill. "And we both know that it'll take more than an explosion to get rid of Kareem—"

"No. Look at those flames. The whole house will be gone in a minute."

Now was not the time to be reasonable. She didn't want to look, didn't want to reconsider what she knew in her gut to be true. "We have to verify—"

"Someone does, yeah." His features became, if possible, more stubborn. More forbidding, as though the sun would fall out of the sky, hit the earth, and bounce back up again before he let her take another step closer to the house. "But it's not going to be you."

"You can't stop me."

He stared at her without a hint of compromise in his expression.

"Try me."

That did it. This additional brick wall, when she'd expected his help, snapped her shaky hold on control and sent her spinning into insanity.

"Kareem!" Breaking and running, screeching for all she was worth, she sprinted back toward the house and got exactly two steps before Brady caught her from behind and held her. This time, she knew, he wouldn't make the mistake of letting her go, and that meant one thing: Kareem had won, and no matter what Brady said—no matter what the police, fire marshal, or anyone else said—he had escaped, and, despite all the steps she'd taken to build a new life for herself, she would never know a moment's peace. "Kareem!"

"I'm not going to let you go, Kira." Brady held her tight around the waist while she stared at the fire, writhed to get free, and sobbed, rocking her and pressing his lips to her temple as he spoke. "I'm not going to let you go."

Sanity crept back to her in bits and pieces, anchoring her to reality. The relentless burning of her cheeks and forehead became uncomfortable, as though someone had slid her into the oven and set the dial to Broil. Sweat dripped down her face, mixing with her tears for a stinging combination. She became aware of the solidity of Brady's body, its strength, and the comfort of its fit against hers. Worse, she realized that she had, once again, failed to save herself. If Brady hadn't stopped her from running into that house, she'd be dead right now, and if she needed any further proof of that fact, it came with the crashing collapse of one section of the roof.

Stepping away from Brady, she watched the shower of sparks and ash for a few seconds before facing him and opening her mouth to begin her thanks. Except that when their gazes connected, there was something so intense in his eyes, so primal, that her thoughts scattered and her voice wimped out.

Swiping at her wet face, she needed a couple of attempts to manage it. "Thanks."

Brady also seemed to have trouble with the whole

speaking thing and had to clear his hoarse throat. "You okay?"

In trying to smile, she discovered that that was another thing about her that didn't work right now. "I've been better."

"You will be again." He paused. "What the hell were you doing here? Or do I even want to know?"

Unrepentant, she told him the truth. "Showing Kareem my new Glock."

"Jesus Christ." Pacing away from her, he muttered a few more colorful phrases, none of which were G-rated. When he wheeled back around, he stared at her with a clear and strange combination of pure horror and unwilling admiration. "You're a menace to yourself. You know that? Someone needs to put you in lockdown for your own safety."

"I've been in lockdown ever since I married Kareem." Sheer defiance made her hike up her chin. "I'm not going back."

Sirens and flashing lights announced the arrival of the fire department and police before he could throttle her, which, judging by the hard glint in his eyes, was what he'd planned to do. Four engines pulled up, disgorging shouting firemen suited up with helmets, masks, and jackets like warriors from an invading army of aliens. They hustled around with hoses and ladders, and Kira watched with mild but detached interest, as though she was viewing a documentary about emergency procedures on TV.

Maybe that was shock setting in to buffer her from this latest Kareem-induced nightmare.

One of the firemen—the chief, maybe—hurried over and addressed Kira. "Are you the owner, ma'am?"

"Yes."

"Who's inside?" he demanded.

"My husband. His lawyer."

"Anyone else?"

"No, not that I know— Oh, no. Oh, my God."

Brady stepped closer and rested a supportive hand on the small of her back, his face lined with concern. "What is it?"

"Wanda. My mother-in-law. She lived there too. I didn't see her in the house, but I don't know if she was there—"

They didn't have to wait long for the answer to this mystery. The high-pitched screech of tires announced the arrival of another vehicle, and they all looked around in time to see a dark Mercedes sedan bounce onto the curb and shudder to a halt. The driver's door flew open and Wanda lurched out, her mouth already open in a scream piercing enough to rupture every eardrum within a ten-mile radius.

"Oh, Lord, he sent me out to get him some salmon to cook for dinner. Lord, why did he send me? Why wasn't I here, too? Why didn't you take me, God?" Aging a thousand years right before Kira's eyes, her body shrinking and curling in on itself, Wanda staggered a few short steps toward the house and collapsed to the lawn in a rag-doll heap.

"Why, God?" Raising her hands toward heaven, Wanda begged and sobbed for answers that would never come. "Why? Tell me why. Jesus, tell me why—yyy—yyy?"

There was a right thing to do here, but Kira couldn't think what it was as she stared down at the woman who had never welcomed her to the family, never had a kind word for her, and never thought she was worthy of her precious son. Nor had Wanda ever seen Kareem for what he was, or recognized the role she had played in raising a man who built an empire by selling drugs to children. The battle lines had always been clear between them: Wanda didn't like Kira, and Kira returned the feeling with interest.

Except that . . .

Hadn't Wanda comforted Kira after Kareem's attack the other night? Hadn't she held Kira and let her cry on her shoulder? Hadn't she gone with Kira out into the cold dark night to find Max when he was lost? And wasn't Wanda now, simply, an old woman who thought she'd lost her beloved only son?

This eleventh-hour compassion for her mother-in-law was an unwelcome surprise, but there was nothing Kira could do about it. Propelled by her unexpectedly soft heart, Kira knelt by Wanda, wrapped her arms around the woman's fragile shoulders, and tried to comfort her as she rocked and shrieked.

They watched the fire together, and while Wanda wept to God, asking him to spare Kareem, Kira silently prayed for another miracle altogether.

Please let Kareem be in the house, after all. Please let him be dead.

Chapter 10

It was three in the morning before the fire was under control, and the first streaks of dawn were lighting the sky before the investigators could begin sifting through the ruins, looking for bodies. Dexter stayed on the periphery and out of the way the whole time, feeling edgy, useless, and, worst of all, foolish, because he wasn't driven by any sense of DEA duty or professionalism, or even prurient interest in an impressive fire. No. The thing that kept him rooted to the spot was his irritating and misguided need to watch over Kira and make sure she was okay.

Having been grilled by the police, she currently stood a few feet away, watching the proceedings wrapped in one of those silvery space-age blankets that the firemen had produced from somewhere. Her cheeks were shiny with ointment, her hands bandaged, her brows and hair singed. Given her concussion, it had to be a supreme act of will that kept her on her feet, and that was one of the things that fascinated him about her: that hidden strength. She wouldn't sit down until she dropped, and she'd never give up. Why was that so intriguing? If she wanted to indulge her obsessive side and freeze her ass off out here in the cold, that was her business, wasn't it? What did it have to do with him?

He couldn't figure it out, but he damn sure wasn't going home and getting in the bed where he belonged, either.

She'd bought a Glock—a nicer model than his, by the way, because he'd had her show it to him—and come here to confront Kareem with it. What kind of crazy shit was that? Was she suicidal or what? He'd bet his left testicle—and he was very fond of his testicles—that she'd never handled a gun before. She just didn't seem like the type, way too princess-y.

So what was she trying to do?

Did she not understand that a man like Kareem, a thug since birth who was a murderer on top of all his other lovely traits, was likely to have the gun out of her hands and shoot her with it before she could aim and fire? Did this trophy wife and college student really think she could walk into the lion's den, go toe to toe with that fiend, and come out alive?

Well . . . she had come out alive, hadn't she?

And what was behind her maniacal need to go back into the burning house and find her loving husband, he wondered moodily, watching her accept a steaming mug of coffee from one of the neighbors with a quiet word of thanks. Was she really hoping he was dead? Or was she still in love with him? That was a possibility, wasn't it? That was a whole syndrome, wasn't it—abusers and the women who loved them?

Why did the mere thought make his stomach clench?

Maybe she was that damaged and scarred. Maybe she and Kareem had a whole codependency thing going. Clearly her mental state was questionable at best, given the fact that she'd married Kareem in the first place. On the other hand, she was nineteen when she married him, and only twenty-three now, and God knew Dexter'd been unaccountably stupid when he was that age, so he couldn't judge.

Either way, he could understand her suspicions and hysterical need to verify Kareem's fate, whatever it was. Kareem Gregory, as they all knew from long and painful experience, was a slippery player of the shrewdest kind. That was why he was still walking free when, if there was any justice in the world, or even a marginally functional justice system, he should have been buried under the jail years ago. If you gave him an inch, he'd steal ten miles. If there was a loophole, he'd find it. If there was a one-millimeter opening, he'd flatten himself like the cockroach he was and crawl through it.

He wouldn't put it past Kareem to blow up his own house to prevent the feds from seizing it and to fake his own death to stay out of jail. If there was a Machiavellian trick to pull, Kareem was first in line.

So, yeah, this whole explosion could be a ruse, and if he hadn't been here and seen the fire with his own two eyes, he'd say it was a ruse. But the thing was, he had seen. No matter how he tried, he couldn't figure out a plausible way that Kareem—even Kareem—could pull off a stunt like this, no matter what Kira suspected.

The crazy thing was, if he had to stake say, a year's salary on it, he'd say she was as sane as he was.

She was, in short, a mystery that he couldn't figure out—

Oh, shit.

They'd found a body. Through the damaged picture window, he could see several investigators lifting a black body bag between them. Kira saw it, too. With a gasp, she dropped her blanket and ran toward the house, intercepting some workers who were unfolding a stretcher on the front porch just as Dexter got there. Her mother-in-law, who'd been sitting in the back of one of the police cruisers where it was relatively warm, was two steps behind her.

"Oh, Lord, Jesus." Wanda resumed her tortured lament, getting in the way and plucking at the body bag as they placed it on the stretcher. "Please don't tell me it's my boy. Please don't tell me. Jesus, please—"

One of the workers blocked her from throwing herself over the body and gripped her arm to keep her upright. "The coroner will be out in a minute, ma'am."

Kira, looking wild-eyed and moving like a woman possessed, met the coroner at the door as she emerged. There was one moment when the women's gazes connected and it might have gone either way, but then the coroner put her hand on Kira's arm and squeezed it.

"I'm so sorry."

Wanda's wails kicked into overdrive, but Kira stayed calm. "It's Kareem?"

"I believe so," the coroner said. "We also found the lawyer."

Kira nodded as if she'd expected this much, but continued her interrogation. "How do you know it's Kareem?"

"We won't know for sure, not until the autopsy, and I'll have to check his dental records, but there was a monitoring band on his ankle. And he was in the area of the great room, where you said they were."

Kira nodded again. "It looks like Kareem, yeah, but it could be anyone."

The coroner, who was probably used to dealing with relatives in denial, gave her a kindly look. "I think it's him."

"I don't." Murder flashed in Kira's eyes, and for a moment, Dexter was afraid she'd pull out that Glock again. "I want to see him," she said, and reached for the zipper.

The coroner covered her hand with her own, stopping her. "I'm afraid I can't let you do that. You don't want to see him like this."

Dexter had been thinking the same thing. The body bag wasn't the smooth and flat shape of, say, a man who'd died while sleeping peacefully in his bed. It was humped and misshapen, as though the body inside had either died while twisted in the throes of agony or been roasted and solidified into an unrecognizable horror of a pretzel.

Much as Dexter had wished—and wished often and hard—for Kareem to suffer a painful death for all his sins, he hadn't quite had this in mind. No one was asking him for his vote, but he agreed with the coroner: Kira never needed to see what was on the other side of that zipper.

Apparently Kira disagreed. She laughed the hard, maniacal laugh of the unhinged, jerked free, and grabbed for the zipper again. "The hell I don't."

The coroner signaled to some of the uniforms, one of whom took Kira by the arm and pulled her away, hissing and all but spitting. The unhappy sight of some punk manhandling Kira woke a dormant but vicious beast deep inside Dexter, and his fingers twitched for his own Glock. Luckily, some modicum of common sense remained and took charge.

"I've got her." He flashed the uniform a look that must

have communicated his violent intent, because the guy winced, dropped his hands immediately, and backed up a step or two. "Come on, Kira."

She tried to shake him off. "I need to see him. I have to make sure—"

Dexter kept his arm around her shoulders and held on, steering her out of the way so they could wheel the stretcher to the ambulance. Only when the stretcher was safely inside and the doors shut behind it did some of the tension leave her body. It was probably safe now for him to let her go, but the feel of her body was too good to sacrifice to any social niceties.

"He's gone, Kira," he said gently. "It's over."

"Don't you get it, Brady?" He felt the kick in his gut as she looked up at him with those big brown eyes, which were shadowed and haunted. Hunted. "It'll never be over."

Dexter took her to his house to pick up the dog, which she could not, apparently, live for another second without seeing. Pulling into his driveway, he saw the place through her eyes. This was not good for his morale. He found his brain scrolling through a catalog of ridiculous and demoralizing thoughts that went something like this:

Why had he stayed in this crappy neighborhood?

His little cottage looked like a potting shed compared to her former home, the torched McMansion.

Thank God the next-door kid had cut the grass yesterday like he was supposed to.

So he was surprised when she stared out the window and emitted one of those enthusiastic little gasps that women do.

"This is your house, Brady?"

Putting the car in park, he cut the engine.

"You were expecting—?"

She shot him an amused glance before she unbuckled and got out. "With you? Military barracks. One bed. One chair. No dust."

Irritated by this assessment of his stern personality, which was more accurate than she probably suspected, he climbed out, slamming the door.

She, meanwhile, was admiring the flower boxes on the two picture windows framing the front door. Since it was the dead of winter, they were currently empty, but— whatever. They seemed to float her boat.

"I love flower boxes. What do you keep in them?"

"Petunias," he said grudgingly.

Nodding with approval, she scanned the yard, her glance touching the landscaping rocks, the blue spruce that wasn't as blue as it should have been, and the Japanese maple. "What color petunias?"

"Ah . . . pink."

She trailed him to the front door, still assessing everything in her field of vision. "I always wanted flower boxes." She paused, her voice faltering. "Kareem always said no."

Kareem was a fucking blight on humanity.

"Well," he said quietly, "now you can do what you want, can't you?"

Instead of answering, she did another one of those stare-up-into-his-face maneuvers, and his thoughts scrambled accordingly. Much as he'd tried, there was no bracing for the impact those sparkling eyes had on him. It would be great if they could develop some sort of early warning system for when she planned to look at him like that. Something like the bell on a cat's collar. Give him a chance to prepare.

"You didn't have to chauffeur me. I could have driven myself."

There were thoughts in his head and words in his mouth, but the two systems seemed to have trouble connecting and crystallizing into something coherent. Still, he tried.

"I don't think so. When you've just gotten out of the hospital, threatened someone with a gun, watched your house burn down, and spent all night in the freezing cold without sleep, you get driven. It's a rule. Check the manual."

Those eyes crinkled at him. "I know you're not my biggest fan, Brady, but I like you. You're good people."

If there was an answer to this pronouncement, it ran and hid from him. Fumbling and silenced, he worked on unlocking the door and getting it open. Max met them in the small entry, racing around the corner from the living room, his little nails clicking on the tile. With a happy cry, Kira squatted to pick him up, which was quite a project since the little guy was wagging and squirming with clear canine joy.

Unaccountably touched by this reunion scene, Dexter stilled and watched.

Kira straightened with the dog tucked under her arm in a football hold. "Mommy missed you," she cooed, tears streaming down her cheeks. "Yes, she did. Mommy missed her sweet little puppy. Were you a good boy for Brady? Huh? Were you a good boy?"

After a minute of this enthusiastic cuddling and loving, Kira seemed to catch herself. Flushing with embarrassment, she swiped at her wet eyes and shot Dexter an apologetic smile.

"I love my dog."

"I see that."

Her face twisted with remembered pain, but she quickly mastered it. "Kareem hated Max. He turned him out into the woods the other night to punish me."

Seething with quiet fury, Dexter looked at Kira's face. Then he looked at Max, with his dangling ears and doggy smile. The little guy had been a quiet and mellow guest, much neater and more considerate than some of his college buddies. He thought about Kareem and all the sick ways he'd found to punish his wife for her crimes, whether real or imagined, and, once again, felt the urgent need to distinguish himself from that monster in every conceivable way.

"I would never hurt Max," he told her.

Another dimpling smile, one that made his chest squeeze. "I know that."

"Ah." Turning away, he tried to gather his thoughts and decided he should make like a host. It took about two steps for him to reach the tiny kitchen and another half step to get to the fridge. When had he last gone to the store? Was the milk any good, or had it turned to cottage cheese three weeks ago? What about the eggs?

"I'll make some coffee," he babbled. "And I've got oatmeal—it's only instant; you probably prefer the stuff you really have to cook—and cereal. That's my biggest food group around here, so you can have your choice, unless you want one of those healthy tree-bark cereals. I don't believe in those. And I'm not sure about the milk." Picking up the carton, he gave it a tentative sniff and didn't immediately keel over dead. "You might be taking your life into your hands with this stuff. I had some bananas, but—oh." Embarrassed, he picked up the squishy brown remnants of what may once have been a bunch of bananas and dropped them into the trash. "Okay. So we'll pass on the bananas—"

"Brady."

"Yeah?" He paused in his relentless quest to find something edible to serve this woman, feeling surly and clumsy, like a bad-tempered chimp with his knuckles scraping the floor.

She was in the kitchen now, apparently operating under the mistaken belief that the tiny galley could accommodate more than either an adult male or two children under the age of twelve at the same time. "I know this isn't Cracker Barrel. You don't have to feed me."

This graciousness did nothing to improve his sour mood. "Someone needs to." Moving to the cabinet, he surveyed the cereal options. Cap'n Crunch? What the hell was a grown man doing with Cap'n Crunch in the—

To his annoyance, she edged around him, reached into the fridge and pulled out the eggs. "You sit down. I'm happy to scramble some eggs—"

Snatching the carton out of her hands, he pointed her to a chair at the table. "Not this time." This time? What was up with the implication that they'd have breakfast together again? Where'd that come from? "You sit down. Be a guest."

"But—"

"Sit."

She sat. Grudgingly and with a frown, but she put her ass on the stool and kept it there. With a last warning glare, he ran through his inventory again. What could he—

Orange juice! There was orange juice concentrate in the freezer. Pay dirt. Now to find the pitcher . . .

The woman, it turned out, could not sit still and shut up. Fidgeting as though she didn't know what to do with herself, she smoothed her hand over the speckled countertop. "Nice. Granite?"

"Yeah. This little kitchen remodel was one of the last things my mother did."

Her face fell. "Oh, I'm sorry to hear that. I didn't know—"

"Oh, she's not dead. She's in assisted living."

"Oh. Good. What about your father?"

"He died a year ago. Just after their forty-fifth anniversary."

"Forty-five years? That's wonderful. Were they still speaking to each other?"

That gave him a grin. "Well, there was some bickering. But they were in love with each other until the day he died."

She withdrew a little. The cooling of her spirit was palpable, as though Jack Frost had poked his head in the room and blasted them with his icy breath. "My parents have been married for thirty years. They don't have a good marriage. I don't think they ever did."

The answer was as plain as the eggs in his hand, but he asked anyway. "Can they help you now?"

"No," she said flatly.

"But you need—"

"No."

That was that, then.

Only that wasn't that at all. It was another layer to this fascinating woman, another mystery he wanted to solve.

And when the hell had he turned into Columbo?

With nothing else to do, she scanned what she could see of the house, a faint and—he hoped—approving smile on her lips. A framed picture over the table seemed to hold her special interest.

"Houseboat, eh?"

Though he saw the weathered and faded family snapshot every day, he rarely looked at it. Too painful now that he was pretty much all that was left of his little family. There he was, age twelve-ish, sandwiched between his father and mother on the boat's deck on a perfect summer day, their fishing poles standing next to them, Dexter's catch, a respectable catfish, dangling from his line.

"Yeah. That boat was my father's pride and joy. He was a police officer and they saved and saved for that boat. I remember the day we went out on her the first time." He shrugged away the bitter and tried to focus on the sweet. "She's mine now."

"Oh, yeah? What's her name?"

"Breezin'."

"Breezin'. I like that."

Hurtling out of nowhere, slamming into him like a drunken hit-and-run driver, came the image of her on the boat with him . . . another perfect summer's day . . . laughter . . . sunshine . . . paradise.

The image (Want? Craving? Need?) didn't help his equilibrium.

Focus on the eggs, idiot.

She stared at the picture for another minute, and then her smile was swallowed up by a massive yawn. Exhaustion seemed to be claiming her. Resting her elbows on the counter, she ran her unbandaged fingertips over her face and then jerked her head up with surprise. "Where the hell are my eyebrows?" she demanded.

He'd been cracking the eggs into a bowl, but now he paused to shoot her a wry grin. "You singed them off during your misguided attempt to run into the burning house."

Getting the idea, she sifted her fingers through her short, curly hair, which was also looking the worse for the wear thanks to the fire, and her eyes widened with comprehension. "Oh, my God. Don't look at me. I'm horrible."

"Not quite."

"Oh, sure. You say that now, but what about when I have to pencil in some brows and wind up looking like the Joker from *Batman*?"

He snorted back a laugh, nearly sloshing the eggs onto the counter with his fork.

"Why did you let me in here, Brady? I foisted my dog on you, I have no hair and no eyebrows, and probably look like Al Jolson in *The Jazz Singer*. I'm sure I smell like smoke, and I'm probably trailing soot all over your nice house. I'm not even good for cooking breakfast. Why don't you kick me out?"

She was sixty percent joking, yeah, but there was far too much genuine curiosity in her tone. As though she couldn't conceive of a world where she mattered if she wasn't waiting on a man hand and foot, if she didn't look her best at any given time.

Something came over him. The eggs could wait.

Turning to give her his undivided attention, he caught her gaze. Held it. Waited until she'd stilled, a flush creeping over her soot-and-tear-streaked cheeks.

"Since you apparently never heard it from Kareem, let me be the first one to tell you: You don't have to do anything. You don't have to look like anything. You just have to be to Kira. That's more than enough for anybody."

She stared at him, her eyes wide and unreadable.

Now *his* cheeks were burning. Where had that little declaration come from? Who put all that emotion into his husky voice? It was time to dial back the tension level in there, so he shrugged.

"But I'm happy to give you a paper bag to put over your head, if that would make you feel better."

One arrested beat passed, and then she smiled. A real, honest to God, ear-to-ear smile that made him feel awed and wondrous, like the first man in the world to ever behold a rainbow.

Jesus, she was beautiful.

He might have stared forever, with the eggs half stirred and the pan smoking on the range behind him, but the phone—one of those old landline deals that hung on the wall—rang, snapping him free of her magic.

"Phone," she said.

Screw the phone. He wracked his brain, tried to imagine someone whose call was important enough to interrupt this moment, and came up with no one. Not even the director. Hell, not even the president.

He shrugged. "The machine'll get it."

Rarely had he regretted a decision so quickly. The machine clicked on, his message played, and a throaty female voice purred, promising sexual availability like a bitch in heat at a dog park. The sound had a precise clarity that he'd never heard outside a movie theater with Dolby surround sound, and he froze, wishing he'd switched to the phone company's automated voice mail system when he'd had the chance.

"Hey, baby—pick up the phone. Pick up the pho-ooone. Dexter? You there, baby? Hello? I missed you last night. And the night before that, and the night before that. Is there a reason you're not answering your cell phone? Hello? Hello-ooo?"

Belinda. Shit. Ignoring Kira's wickedly amused smile,

he lunged for the receiver and snatched it off the wall before Belinda really got going with the sex talk, which was a distinct possibility.

"Ah, hey, Belinda," he muttered, turning his back on Kira. "What's up?"

"Hey! You are there! Are you screening my calls?"

"No, it's just been a busy couple of days. Can I, uh, call you back?"

"Okay." He could hear the pout in her voice. "But what about tonight?"

"I'll have to, ah, get back to you on that. Okay?"

"Okay, but—"

"Great. Bye."

There may have been more, but he hung up before he could hear it. If he knew anything about Belinda—and he did—the punishment later would be dire, but that felt like a distant and unimportant consideration right now for reasons he chose not to explore.

Cheeks burning, he turned back to Kira while on his way to the stove and the cooking eggs.

"Who was that?" she asked with bright and unabashed nosiness.

Using the voice and the face that made his men shrink into chastised and fidgety preschoolers when they got out of line, he shot her a glare. "None of your damn business."

This wouldn't slow her down, not if her widening smirk was any indication. In fact, she smelled blood and zeroed in for the attack. "Sounded like a booty call, is all I'm saying."

"Okay. Why are you talking?"

"You've never been married, have you, Brady? You should get married. Don't let my poor example stop you."

"I don't think so."

"Why not? Don't tell me you're a"—she made quotation marks with her fingers—"confirmed bachelor. You're not on the down low, are you, Brady?"

This made him crack an unwilling smile. "Having fun?"

"Well, you're not getting any younger—"

Wasn't that the truth? Next to her early twenties, his thirty-nine felt like a hundred and five, easy.

"—and how're you going to have a long and happy marriage like your parents' if you don't get started soon?"

There was an easy answer to this, and he gave it to women all the time, right up front at the beginning of any sexual relationship: he was married to his career. Allied answers? He didn't have the time and inclination to devote to a serious relationship and/or he didn't want any part of a woman crazy enough to get seriously hooked up with a DEA agent.

So it was with some surprise that he opened his mouth and none of those things came out. He stared at her. "I'll know when the right woman comes along."

This seemed to unsettle her. She floundered and her smile slipped, despite her efforts to keep it in place. "Maybe that was her on the phone."

"That wasn't her."

"Oh." Ducking her head, she looked away—a little desperately, he thought—and focused on something over his shoulder. "Brady! The eggs!"

Huh? "What? *Shit*." Wheeling around, he snatched the smoking pan off the burner and dropped it, clattering, into the sink. He ran some water into it, generating a blinding cloud of steam that engulfed his head. "Shit," he said again, sucking his burning fingers into his mouth. Damn hot handle. Brilliant. There was one edible thing in the house, and he burned it. King of Hospitality—that was him. "This is why you shouldn't yack so much," he told her. "You're a distraction."

"Well, sorry."

"You should be. Luckily, I've got more eggs."

"Great. Your cooking skills are inspiring a lot of confidence. I can hardly wait to eat them."

"Keep it up and you'll get the burned ones."

They laughed together for one delicious moment, and then, with zero warning, her face contorted into a sob. Trying to choke it off, she slapped a hand over her mouth. When that didn't work, she rested her elbows on the table and buried her face in her hands, shoulders shaking.

"Kira."

Agonized, he took a step toward her. He was a strong man, yeah, but there were some things even he couldn't do, and watching Kira Gregory cry without taking her into his arms was one of them.

But when he reached out to her, she pulled back and swiped at her wet eyes, already embarrassed at this normal show of emotion on what had to be one of the worst nights of her life.

"Sorry," she said again.

He dropped his hand, uncertain now because God knew he didn't do emotions well. "Don't be."

She stared into his face, searching. "Can I tell you something, Brady?"

Okay. This was another one of those questions that should have a simple answer. No, he should say. As a man with a firm and abiding belief in rules and boundaries, he knew when he'd crossed them, and he'd been doing that with alarming frequency where Kira was concerned. He shouldn't have come home with the drug lord's wife, shouldn't have agreed to watch her damn dog. Shouldn't have offered her breakfast, shouldn't have admired her beauty and courage or anything else about her. Playing true confessions with her now and offering comfort also fell firmly into the *shouldn't* column.

When had all his boundaries become so blurred?

No, Brady. Tell her no.

He started to speak, no longer in control of anything that came out of his mouth. "You can tell me anything."

Her chin quivered and a shuddering breath rippled through her body. "I'm so tired. I'm so tired of being scared."

He couldn't answer.

"I'm scared of being Kareem's wife and scared of walking out on him. I'm scared of making my own way in the world. I'm scared of dying without ever really being free. I'm scared that a mistake I made when I was nineteen will always be the defining thing about my life. I'm scared I'll always be scared."

"Why don't you try not being so hard on yourself?"

She let this question pass. "I don't think he's dead. Nothing could ever be that easy with Kareem."

"We'll know soon enough. In the meantime, you're going to eat a plate of eggs and drink some juice to keep your strength up. And then you'll handle whatever comes your way because you've got the courage for it. Okay?"

"You think so?"

"I know so."

One side of her mouth curled as she dabbled at her eyes with one of the blue paper napkins from the holder on the table. "Okay. Maybe I should wash my face?"

"Okay. The bathroom's down there." He tipped his head toward the hall.

"Great."

And then, to his absolute horror—and, worse, to his absolute, heart-stopping, breath-freezing pleasure—she stood and did the thing she'd done once before: patted his jaw with her soft hand and kissed his cheek.

"Thank you, Brady," she said, and slipped away, taking his brain with her.

Undone, he watched her go and tried to ignore the persistent tingle where her skin had brushed his. And then he made busy work for his fumbling hands.

What had he been doing? Making eggs?

Okay. He could do this.

With remarkable efficiency now that his distraction was out of the room, he scrambled up a second set of eggs and made the juice. When he'd fixed their plates and set them on the table, it occurred to him, for the first time, that he hadn't heard the water run in the bathroom.

He set off down the hall to find her, but she wasn't in the living room, the half bath off the living room, or his cluttered office/weight room.

Where the hell—?

Two more steps, and he found her. In his bedroom. On his bed.

Jesus.

He watched her, his heart contracting. It wasn't a pretty scene, and if any photographers from *Playboy* magazine wandered through the neighborhood and peered through the window, they'd keep going without taking a single shot.

Sprawled spread-eagle on her belly, Kira lay diagonally across the king-sized bed, looking as though she'd staggered in from a trek through the heart of the Sahara and barely made it to the bed before collapsing. Her head was nowhere near a pillow; one arm, meanwhile, dangled off the side, and her soft, even breathing was the kind of thrilling music he wasn't sure he'd ever heard.

Max had assumed a post on the floor near her curled fingers and had his snout resting on his front paws. Looking up through drowsy eyes when Dexter crossed the threshold, he thumped his tail once or twice in greeting, yawned, and curled into what was evidently a more comfortable position.

This unexpected silence, after the night's chaos, gave Dexter the chance to think a few thoughts he'd been postponing. Like how he didn't know what the hell he thought he was doing with Kira Gregory, but he didn't plan to stop doing it. Like how this house felt different—better—when she was in it. Like how Kareem's death had unlocked a strange feeling of hope inside him, and it had nothing to do with his wishes for a drug-free Cincinnati and everything to do with her.

Standing in the doorway, he discovered, was way too far away. It seemed dangerous to move any closer, but his body wasn't counting his vote. He crept to the bed. At this distance, his fingers began to flex and itch, desperate for the feel of her skin. There were so many things he was hungry to know. The curled silk of her hair, for one, even if it was dirty with soot. The curve of her brow (the unsinged part, anyway), the smooth arch of her neck, the tenderness of her lips. Any of those were his for the touching right now. She wouldn't wake up; he'd stake his life on it. Now was his moment, the one he almost felt he'd willed into existence—who would know?

He would know. That was the problem.

If he touched her without her permission, he'd be no better than Kareem, the man who'd violated her. And if there was one thing that Kira absolutely, positively needed to know about him, it was this:

He wasn't Kareem. Not even close.

So he wouldn't touch her. Yet.

But shit, man. Shit. More than anything else, he wanted to touch her.

In his life he'd seen some moving sights. The Grand Canyon when he was a kid came to mind, and so did the newborn face of his nephew, and the reunion he'd once witnessed between a neighbor girl down the street and her dad when he came home from the war.

None of that had prepared him for this.

If he lived another sixty years, he doubted anything would stir him quite as much as the sight of Kira, fully clothed and asleep on his bed.

Chapter 11

After drawing the bedroom shades to block out the sun's blinding glare, covering Kira with a blanket, and leaving her a note saying that he'd gone to the office but would be back soon, Brady left.

He did not go to the office. At least not right away.

"Hey," he said when Belinda opened the door of her condominium. "Sorry to just show up like this—"

"It's okay." She broke into a delighted and dimpled smile that made him feel like a two-inch layer of green pond scum. "Come on in."

She'd be much less thrilled to see him in a minute. Maybe sooner, because when she leaned in for the usual hello kiss, he stiffened and drew back. It was one of the curses of a habitual straight shooter like himself, he supposed: if there was a way to hide the fact that he just wasn't that into a woman, he hadn't yet discovered it.

"Got a minute?"

"Yeah, but I have to get to the office in a few minutes." She stepped aside to let him pass, her gray eyes darkening. He could almost feel her steeling herself for the worst. No one would ever accuse her of being a rocket scientist, but she was no dummy, either. "What's up?"

"Ah," he began, trailing her down the hall to the immaculate vaulted living room, where they sat on the immaculate leather love seat next to the immaculately decorated coffee table. That was one of the things about real estate agents—they had good taste. And Belinda was a lovely woman despite the fact that she didn't make his heart stop or even stutter. Resting his elbows on his knees, he rubbed his hands together, stalling for time while he wracked his brain for a diplomatic sentence or two. "The thing is—"

"Oh, my God." Her gaze riveted to his face with so much dawning horror that you'd think he'd grown fangs, a snout, and whiskers, and was halfway through his transformation to a werewolf. "You're dumping me."

He could understand her consternation. For one thing, she had a body so smoking hot it was enough to make a man swallow his tongue, and she probably hadn't been on the receiving end of much rejection in her life.

For another thing, they'd been, well, for lack of a better word, dating for the last six months or so. The "dates" generally consisted of meeting up at his place or hers, often with carryout food and sometimes with a DVD, for several hours of no-holds-barred sex.

There'd been no strings and no expectations, at least not until he heard the bewildered disappointment in her answering machine message a little while ago. Then it hit him: he didn't expect anything, but Belinda was only pretending not to expect anything.

Which wasn't okay, especially now that—

Now that what, Brady?

That was the million-dollar question, wasn't it?

He didn't give his brain time to formulate an answer. Now wasn't the time.

"I'm not dumping you," he said, a lie. "It's just that you know I'm all about my career and I don't have time for any kind of—"

Belinda—sweet, sexy little Belinda, who'd brought him honest-to-God homemade chicken soup six weeks ago when he had a killer cold—turned nasty on him in the beat between one blink and the next. Her eyes narrowed down to flashing slits of gray fire and her lush lips flattened into a sneer.

"Bullshit. You met someone else, didn't you?"

"No," he said, wanting to mean it. Or maybe it was just that he wasn't ready to put all the separate puzzle pieces of his feelings together and see what kind of picture they made. "I'm not seeing anyone else."

"But you want to."

Another lie was right on the tip of his tongue, but he couldn't say it. Maybe because the question cut too close to the bone, and he couldn't deny Kira even if it would be more convenient if he did. Maybe because the want was embedded so deep inside him, flowing so freely inside his veins, that there was no possibility of pretending it didn't exist. Whatever. The bottom line was simple:

He wanted. Where Kira Gregory was concerned? He wanted in parts of himself that had nothing to do with his body's physical needs. That was scary enough. Admitting it, even in the privacy of his thoughts, was monster-in-the-closet terrifying.

So he said nothing, and that was answer enough.

"Oh, my God." Belinda put a hand to the base of her throat, covering a pulse that was ticking furiously. There was more, but she seemed to have trouble forcing the words out of her hoarse throat. "Are you fucking her?"

"Belinda—"

If she heard the warning in his tone, it didn't slow her down any.

"Are you?"

"That's enough."

Belinda flinched.

Regret was already hitting him by the time the first tear trickled down her cheek. Jesus. He hadn't meant to roar at her like some overzealous drill sergeant, but he wasn't going to submit to an emotional interrogation or any other bullshit, either. Working hard to control his temper—it wasn't Belinda's fault his growing infatuation with the drug lord's widow had him in a stranglehold, and he didn't mean to take it out on her—he spoke more gently.

"Look." He tried to take her hand, but she fisted it and snatched it away. "You're a wonderful woman. I've enjoyed my time with you. I wish you all the best."

She didn't—or couldn't—speak for a long time, but the glaring reproach in her eyes said it all.

"I'm sorry," he told her, meaning it.

She said nothing, which he took as permission to leave.

"Good-bye." Getting up, he walked down the hall with her on his heels, put his hand on the knob and was inches from a getaway that was, if not clean, at least not horrible.

Inches.

And then she lobbed the unanswerable question, the one he'd been asking himself with alarming regularity since the day—the first second—he laid eyes on Kira Gregory.

"What's she got that I haven't got?" Belinda flung the words at him, each one a malice-filled dagger that sliced just a little bit out of him. "What is it about her?"

What did Kira have?

Like he knew.

Was it mystery? Courage? Beauty? Strength? Humor? All of that? None of it? She was a mess right now; he knew that. Damaged, physically and emotionally, financially unstable, the poster child for the kind of yawning black hole of need who could suck a man dry faster than an undernourished vampire.

And yet . . .

And yet.

What did Kira have?

He didn't know. He just knew that he needed it.

Shaken, he opened the door and left, striding away from both Belinda and troublesome questions that had no answers.

"Kira? Wake up for me. Come on, now."

"No," she murmured. Why would she bother waking up when the bed was so comfortable and she was so warm and drowsy? Curling in on herself, she tried to block out the annoying distraction and the nagging feeling that she'd escaped long enough and now needed to check back into the real world. "I'm sleeping."

"I know you're sleeping." What a nice voice. Smooth, deep, and dark, the verbal equivalent of a lake's still waters at midnight. She'd happily listen to it forever if it wasn't trying to pull her out of this wonderful nothingness.

"But you're starting to scare me, so you need to wake up. I don't want you lapsing into a coma. I could do without the drama."

A coma. That sounded great, actually. "Shhh. Go away."

"Kira." The voice changed, morphing from command to pleasurable caress. Even better, gentle fingers stroked across her cheek in a feather-light touch that made her toes curl. "What am I going to do with you?"

Caught in that floating world between dreams and reality, where everything was acceptable and nothing could hurt her, she felt the smile ease across her lips. "Don't stop . . . don't stop."

The hand hesitated. Lingered. Disappeared.

The loss of that sweet warmth against her face had the effect of a dumped bucket of ice water. She woke up with a violent jerk.

Oh, God. Brady loomed near the bed, watching her in the semidarkness, an indecipherable gleam in his eyes. Wait. Brady? She looked again.

Yeah, Brady.

Where was she—?

She remembered with a sudden burst of embarrassment, scuttling to an upright position on her butt and thunking back against the headboard. Her aching head didn't appreciate the abrupt change in altitude and throbbed accordingly.

"Oh, man." She rubbed her temples, praying for the sudden appearance of an ax man who could end the pain by beheading her. "Kill me now."

"Sleeping Beauty lives." Brady's voice now held a definite note of amusement. "Praise God."

Now was not the time for jokes. Glaring up at him,

she worked on looking a little more formidable. "What time is it?"

He checked his watch. "It's about five hours after you headed down the hall to use the bathroom. The eggs are now cold, in case you were wondering."

She looked around, smoothing the soft khaki duvet and fluffy pillows on either side. "I'm not sure what happened. I think I needed a nap."

"Brilliant deductive reasoning. Good job."

That, finally, made her grin, which was something she hadn't done enough of lately. "Don't tell me you have a sense of humor, Brady. What did you do? Go out and buy one while I was asleep?"

"Nah. I pull it out from time to time."

"Good to know." She smoothed the pillows again. "You have a very comfortable bed. Thanks for sharing."

It took him several beats to answer. "No problem."

For no reason whatsoever, a hot flush crept up her neck. It was too dark for him to see it, but she still felt exposed and had to lower her gaze. "I should get going. Max and I have imposed on you long enough. Wait. Where is Max?"

"He's in the backyard, keeping us safe from squirrels and other vermin. And I need to talk to you for a minute."

"Oh." The new concern in his eyes made her belly contract and twist into a knot the size of a watermelon. She tried to brace herself, but that was difficult when marriage to Kareem had trained her to live every moment in the Red Zone. "Okay."

"Okay," he said, but then strode over to the window and back, taking so long to collect his thoughts that she began to wonder if the conversation in question would take place today. At last he sat on the corner of the bed, scrubbed a hand over the top of his head, and plunged in. "I've been to the office."

"Okay."

"The preliminary word from the fire investigators is that it was a gas leak."

"Oh." Her mind floundered around for a reaction and came up empty. Gas leak, atom bomb, IED . . . did it really matter? "I figured it was something like that."

"The lines were tampered with. It looks like arson. The ATF is getting involved."

Hold up. This was the big news flash? He woke her up for this? "Of course it was arson. Kareem did it. I've been telling you that."

"It wasn't Kareem. It's looking like it was either the Mexicans or the Russians—"

"What?"

"The Mexicans or the Russians." He said it gently and with infinite patience, as though he was prepared to repeat everything he said, until it finally sank through her thick skull. "You didn't think you and I were the only ones who wanted Kareem dead, did you?"

"But why? Why now?"

"Because we had him on major trafficking charges. They probably wanted to take him out before he started singing like a canary and pointing fingers at his suppliers so he could make himself a deal with the feds."

Made sense. Kira tried this on for size, trying to make it work: Kareem got out of jail on bond, came home to begin his house arrest, and was killed by his cronies before he could take them down with him. Kareem had lived by the sword and he'd died by the sword.

Poetic justice. Karma. End of story.

Except that her gut wouldn't stop screaming its warning:

This story is just beginning, sweetheart.

She tuned back in to Brady, who was watching her, waiting for a reaction, and shook her head. "Kareem did this."

Something about her absolute conviction irritated him out of his patient routine. "Jesus. Stubborn much? I keep telling you—Kareem didn't do this."

"You don't know that—"

"I do know that, Kira."

"Do you know how many times he swore he'd take a bulldozer and tear down that house—his beloved house, with his Egyptian furniture, and his high-def TVs, and his precious wine cellar—before he'd let the feds seize it? And now you think it's just some huge coincidence that someone else destroyed the house? You're not serious, are you?"

"I am serious." His chest heaved with a harsh sigh. "We also got the preliminary ID from the coroner. With the dental records. It's a match."

"Oh, please."

"A match, Kira. A match."

The third time she heard it, the M word began to sink in.

A . . . match.

The dental records matched the body.

Kareem was . . . dead.

No, screamed her gut. *Listen to me. Trust me.*

Staring into Brady's face, she waited for the other shoe to drop. The big *but.* The punch line. Something. Anything. But all she saw was that freaking patient expression again, the one that said he would wait and wait and wait and wait until that glorious day when she finally came up to speed with everyone else and accepted the obvious and inevitable:

Kareem was dead.

For the first time since the explosion, her absolute conviction wavered.

This information mattered, didn't it? The coroner's identification counted for something, right? If the coroner said that that blackened, twisted, and unidentifiable body belonged to Kareem, then Kareem was dead.

Wasn't he?

Mute with shocked disbelief, there was nothing she could say.

Could she be this wrong about something she felt so strongly about?

"Say something," Brady told her. "You're scaring me again."

"I don't know what my life looks like without Kareem in it." She hated to lay her twisted soul out there for Brady to see and judge, especially when he was such a Boy Scout with his right vs. wrong and rules vs. chaos view of life, but she couldn't keep her sickness inside, either. It was eating her alive. "I've spent so much time trying to survive Kareem and escape Kareem that I can't even understand what you're saying. I don't know what to do with myself now. I don't know what my life looks like if it's not a reaction to him."

Brady shrugged this dark confession away, as though she'd described nothing trickier than a bad case of poison ivy and he had complete faith in her self-healing abilities. "That's what you need to figure out, isn't it?"

"Is it that easy?"

"It won't be easy. But you can do it." He said it with unwavering conviction. "I know you can."

Wow. How had someone with judgment this misguided ever become a DEA agent? Had they relaxed their admission standards and let him slip through the cracks, or what? "Why do you have that kind of faith in me, Brady?" she wondered. "I barely have any in myself."

"If I can see the woman you're becoming, so should you."

"The woman I'm becoming?" Why did he say it with that kind of quiet admiration, as though he thought she'd turn into Oprah if she continued on her current trajectory? "You're sure about that, huh?"

"I'm sure."

"How can you be?"

That unblinking gaze of his caught her in an unshakable grip. When he watched her that way, with that bright and indecipherable gleam in his eyes, she found it a little bit harder to get air into her lungs, a little bit trickier to regulate her heartbeat.

"How can I be so sure about you?" Another shrug. "No idea. I just am."

They stared at each other, the pregnant silence enveloping them in an unexpected web of intimacy. She meant to look away from his shadowed face, but her body was, suddenly, no longer accepting commands from her brain.

Something happened to her then, a powerful zing of awareness that sizzled up and down her spine and reminded her that she was still a woman, no matter how damaged. And Brady was unmistakably a man, and this was his bedroom and she was sitting on his bed.

A wave of panic chose that moment to hit, unsettling her even more. Not that she thought Brady would ever hurt her in any way—not emotionally and certainly not physically, not in a million lifetimes plus one—but there were many kinds of threats to a woman, including those to her equilibrium, and she was maxed out on those just now, thanks.

So she sucked in a deep breath and focused on the immediate crisis, which was all she could handle.

"What about Kareem's lieutenants?"

"They're in custody. We've got plenty on them and it doesn't matter whether Kareem is dead or alive."

This just got more and more incredible. "So his organization—?"

"Is in tatters."

Kareem's mighty drug empire in ruins. Unbelievable.

"Oh," she said, staring at a frayed seam on her jeans. "Oh."

Brady's gentle voice snapped her out of her spinning thoughts. "What will you do now?"

Do now? Like she knew. Running a hand through what was left of her hair, she forced a smile. "I think I'll go back to the hotel with my dog and take a shower. Leave you in peace. That seems like a good place to start, don't you think?"

Brady didn't whoop with cheer at this news that he'd soon be rid of his houseguests, but that was probably just his good manners kicking in.

"Okay." He cleared his voice, which sounded a little rough. "Yeah. Great."

She swung her legs off the side of the bed and started to get up, which prompted him to take a giant step out of her way, as though she'd threatened him with some invisible weapon that had a ten-foot radius.

"I don't bite, Brady," she said irritably.

It took him a couple of long beats to answer. "Good to know."

Feeling huffy now, she stuck her feet into her shoes and headed off toward the hall, but then a thought hit her. She paused, turning.

"The coroner will release his body after the autopsy, right?"

"Yeah. Probably by the end of the week. Why? Are you anxious to plan his funeral?"

"No." Bitterness made her voice sharp and her words clipped. "I want to see it with my own eyes when they put that bastard in the ground."

Chapter 12

Assistant US attorney Jayne Morrison appeared at Dexter's shoulder and spoke in an undertone that produced a white puff of steam in the frigid early afternoon air. "These drug dealers' families sure know how to throw a funeral, don't they? Someone should have put them in charge of the services when Princess Diana died. They could have shown the British how it's done."

Brady snorted with no real humor because: 1) they were in the middle of graveside prayers, and it wouldn't do for the assorted feds watching the proceedings to express too much glee in front of the bereaved family; and 2) he was freezing his ass off.

The sky was a mournful slate gray, perfect for the occasion, and the rain was holding off, at least for now, but the wind was sharp and relentless, weaving through the monuments here in the high-rent section of the cemetery with the ferocity of those nor'easters folks in Maine were always talking about. It'd be a miracle if he didn't have a severe case of frostbitten fingers and/or toes by the time he left the cemetery.

Jayne was right, though. In just three short days, using

money that had, no doubt, come straight from the pockets of teens on the playground as they used their hard-earned allowance money to buy a little Mary Jane or blow to get them through those party-filled weekends, Wanda, Kareem's mother, had thrown together a truly impressive memorial for her lamented son. The only things missing had been a caisson with riderless horse and bagpipers in full regalia, but, hell, it was early yet. Maybe they were on their way.

There'd been shiny black limos, several hundred mourners in the church, flower arrangements the size of Volkswagen Beetles, and the best luxury coffin drug money could buy, bronze—yes, bronze—with, reputedly, a black silk lining. They'd all have to take the lining on faith, because the thing had been closed. But Wanda had thought of everything, providing a dignified but oversized portrait of a smirking Kareem, in one of his thousand-dollar suits, looking down at them from an easel at the foot of the coffin, just so the heartbroken could remember Kareem at his vital best.

The entire entourage had filed over to the cemetery in a traffic-stopping caravan complete with motorcycle cops and flashing lights, and they all huddled together for warmth, grouped loosely according to allegiance: family and friends in the inner circle, observing feds at a respectful distance in the outer circle.

He and Jayne, along with a pair from the FBI and an ATF agent, were on the lookout for . . . stuff: other suspected members of Kareem's organization or rival organizations, potential suspects in the explosion, or any other suspicious activity they could sniff out. It was always fun to take down license plate numbers and see who they were dealing with and who they should look into, but so far the funeral had been just that. An impressive funeral, to be sure, but still just a funeral and not a hotbed of criminal activity.

Dexter had never seen this kind of crowd at a graveside commitment ceremony, which usually only consisted of the family, but, hey. It wasn't every day that the Midwest lost the rough equivalent of John Gotti or Tony Montana, and no one wanted to miss a second of the fun. The sight of all the mourners in black clustered together reminded Dexter of emperor penguins, a thousand deep, incubating their eggs at the South Pole.

The coffin was now perched over the open but covered grave, waiting to be lowered, and there, off to the side, was the monument—a phallic black marble obelisk ten feet tall—that had presumably been a rush job so it'd be ready for today.

KAREEM JASON GREGORY, said the inscription.

LOVING SON AND HUSBAND (it hadn't escaped Dexter's notice that Wanda gave herself top billing over Kira)— *SLEEPING WITH THE ANGELS*.

That's right, sports fans. Kareem Gregory, murderer, rapist, and drug kingpin, was now, according to his tombstone, sleeping with the angels.

Ah, yes. It had all been the picture of class. Dexter got emotional just thinking about it. And he'd make damn sure the IRS traced the funds that had paid for this little display. If they were dirty, maybe there was a way the government could seize that ugly-ass coffin right out from under Kareem's charred body. The mere idea almost gave Dexter a hard-on with giddy excitement because, as far as he was concerned, no punishment was too great for that demon seed, and a little thing like death didn't cancel the debt.

"And did you see the latest addition to the grieving hordes?" Jayne continued, tipping her head toward a bare birch tree several hundred feet away, where a lone woman stood, watching. "What's up with her? Why doesn't the bereaved widow take her rightful place in front with the mother?"

"Let's ponder that for a moment," Dexter murmured. "How bereaved would you be?"

"Not very."

"That's what I thought."

The minister's solemn and commanding baritone rose over the wind, which whipped around his robes, making for an impressive sight.

"In hope of the resurrection into eternal life, through our Lord and Savior Jesus Christ, we commend to almighty God our brother Kareem, and we commit his body to the ground, earth to earth, ashes to ashes, dust to dust. . . ."

Right on cue, Wanda began to sob and wail, turning her face up to God and calling to him, which was a tricky maneuver because the brim of her feathered and ribboned black hat was roughly the size of a trash can lid. Unmoved by this display of raw maternal grief over the criminal she'd raised, Dexter checked his watch and wondered idly whether she'd do the whole throwing herself on the coffin thing. The people on either side of her seemed to be thinking along the same lines and took her by the arms, holding her upright.

Over at the tree, Kira stood, still and rigid as Kareem's obelisk, watching.

"I've always wondered what kind of marriage they had." Jayne rubbed her hands over her arms for warmth and frowned in Kira's direction. "What kind of woman—"

"Who knows?"

Dexter shrugged, the topic making him wary and irritable. God knew he'd spent more than his allotted time thinking about Kira and her varied and mysterious motivations, but he couldn't risk any of his colleagues suspecting that his feeling for or interactions with Kira had been anything other than professional and unremarkable. Developing a relationship with the kingpin's widow certainly wouldn't help him to a letter of commendation for his personnel file or a promotion.

"Is this in your job description now?" he continued. "Government shrink?"

Jayne paused in her contemplation of Kira to flash him a narrow-eyed look. "What's got your panties in a bunch, Special Agent?"

Kira Gregory, that's what.

"Nothing. Except that I'd like to eat sometime before I'm forced to gnaw off my own arm. And I've got frostbite in three toes. And I'd like to close the file on Kareem Gregory and his organization for good. You feel me?"

"I feel you, my brother," Jayne said. "Amen."

"Amen," Dexter echoed, his gaze and thoughts inexorably drawn back to Kira.

He's here.

Where is he?

Here . . . where . . . here . . . where . . .

The words swirled around Kira and through her, surging in her blood, beating in her heart, and luring her brain farther away from its fragile hold on reality and beckoning it toward insanity.

Coming to Kareem's funeral wasn't the brightest idea she'd ever had, clearly. She wasn't a grieving widow nor was she inclined to pretend otherwise, which was why she'd avoided Wanda and other family members who really were heartbroken. That being the case, she should have stayed her butt back at the hotel with Max, where they could've toasted the monster's so-called death with champagne and carryout pizza.

Except that she'd needed to be here. To see. To verify.

But it had all gone wrong, and every second of this travesty of a funeral that passed without Kareem's reappearance took five years off her life. Why? Because she was sure he was still alive and equally certain she was losing her mind.

Nice psychological cocktail, eh?

Her current mental condition could best be described as unstable, and even that term was unduly optimistic.

It was as though she'd been snatched from her old world, the one ruled by all things Kareem, and placed into a new world that made no sense. Here, everyone said, there was no Kareem. He was dead and gone. Forever. Buh-bye.

Yeah. Sure.

Why was she the only one who was out of step with the rest of the world? Why couldn't anyone else see what she saw?

Because Kareem was here. Despite what Brady had told her about the coroner's findings (which she'd wanted to believe, tried to believe), she just couldn't accept that Kareem wasn't here, somewhere, watching the proceedings and making notes about who'd been appropriately heartbroken and who'd been insincere and therefore needed to be punished later.

Wasn't it everyone's fantasy to attend their own funeral and see what was what and who was loyal and who wasn't? Kareem wouldn't miss this kind of opportunity. He was here. Hiding among the mourners. Waiting. Planning. Seething.

She knew because his malevolent presence electrified the air, and the scent of his cologne—wood and basil, earthy warmth—drifted closer on the wind, filling her nostrils.

Was this proof scientific enough to stand up in a court of law?

Absolutely not.

Would she stake her life on it anyway? You betcha.

This absolute conviction of hers was irrational bordering on paranoid. Kira knew that. She understood, in her brain, that Kareem couldn't pull off a phony death and make it look this good, the coroner wouldn't fake her findings, and Kira had absolutely no logical reason to suspect, much less believe, that Kareem was still alive.

Her soul, on the other hand, understood that if Kareem really were dead, she'd feel light and free rather than persecuted and exposed.

And she felt exposed standing here under this tree and watching the services. As though she'd pulled back her collar to expose her jugular to a starving vampire.

If she could just find him. That was the thing. If she could just rope off the cemetery and search every male face before he left, she would find him. Oh, yes, she would. If she could—

"I am the resurrection, and the life," the minister was saying, his voice booming now to be heard over Wanda's ongoing histrionics.

Wait. Was that it, then? Was the service almost over, and with it her chance to find and expose Kareem? She hadn't had the chance to look that closely into the faces, and once everyone left here, there'd be nothing she could do—

"He that believeth in me, though he were dead, yet shall he live—"

Kira's frustration level rose with each word. Maybe she should just go up the hill and join the others. Then she could see the faces more clearly, and she'd have the chance to—

"And whosoever liveth and believeth in me shall never die. . . ."

Wait! Was that Kareem? There in the brown wool coat, with the fedora pulled so low over his eyes? Kareem had a coat like that, and the guy was certainly the right height and build! His skin was about the same shade of brown as Kareem's, and he stood with that same sure footing that was almost a swagger, as though he owned the world and always would.

Could that be him?

Powered by desperation and growing hysteria, Kira charged through the frozen grass and up the hill, beyond caring who saw her or what they thought about it. Screw it. They wouldn't think she was insane once she exposed Kareem for the lying bastard he was, putting them all through this charade—

"Amen."

The minister raised his head, finished at last. Everyone else followed his lead and began to murmur their good-byes and disperse to their cars.

Kira watched the crowd spread and thin, taking her chances along with it, and she tried to keep that man in sight. Where was that brown coat now? How had he disappeared that quickly?

"Sister Wanda." The minister's tone now was hushed and tragic, perfect for this oh-so-solemn occasion. "Would you like some flowers from the bouquet to press in your Bible?"

"Thank you, Pastor." Sniffling, Wanda took a brave step forward, reached for the huge spray of lilies, and withdrew several stems, which she passed to some of the nearby women.

At the top of the hill now, Kira wheeled around, panting and searching. Was he still here? Was he over there? She plowed through the crowd, shoving a man—Kareem's Uncle Claude, wasn't it?—between the shoulder blades when he didn't get out of her way fast enough and nearly toppling another man with a cane.

"Kira?" someone said. "Is that you, honey?"

A murmur of interest rippled through the crowd, but she ignored everyone except that man, who was the key to everything.

"Stop!" she yelled. "You're not going to do this to me, Kareem! I know it's you! You're not going to get away with this!"

With a final triumphant lunge, she grabbed the man's sleeve and jerked it, stopping him, but the man was already turning, lured by all her frantic commotion, and he looked her in the face.

It wasn't Kareem.

The skin tone was right, but the face was too broad, the nose too long, the brows too shaggy. And these eyes were kindly and understanding of the poor widow, who was so clearly unhinged by her grief, and Kareem didn't have a kindly bone in his body.

She blinked several times, bewildered and not daring to trust her lying eyes.

But—?

Wasn't that him? Hadn't she seen him?

Her head chose that moment to renew its ongoing throbbing, and she floundered, taking a second to rub her temple and regroup. It was so hard to think since the concussion, so hard to keep her thoughts straight, but she could do it.

Okay. Okay. So that hadn't been Kareem, obviously, but that didn't mean that Kareem wasn't here, somewhere. And all these stupid people, meanwhile, were standing in her way, blocking her from seeing where he might have—

"Kira?" A woman touched her shoulder, trying to calm her down. "Why don't you come—"

"No."

Shaking her off, Kira pivoted in another circle, searching all the avid faces now turned in her direction . . . looking . . . looking . . . there! There he was! Just past the clump of scandalized church ladies with their fancy hats was a broad-shouldered man in a wheelchair, his back to her. He wore a black knit cap pulled low, so it was hard to tell by his face, but his puffy blue ski jacket looked exactly like Kareem's, and she wouldn't put it past that bastard to impersonate a disabled person if he thought he could get away with it.

"Mrs. Gregory."

That warning voice calling her name again belonged to a man this time—she knew that voice, didn't she?— but no one would interfere with her mission. If she didn't expose Kareem, who would? If she let him slip away from the cemetery and escape, hiding among the general populace, how could she ever live her life without looking over her shoulder every second of every single day?

It was as if she knew there was a cobra loose in her bedroom but she couldn't find it. How on earth was she supposed to lay down her head at night and go to sleep?

"Kareem." Screeching now, she darted through the crowd and around the wheelchair to confront that lying bastard. "Kareem, you cannot get away with—"

Christ Jesus. That wasn't Kareem either. It was a teenager, no more than fifteen, looking up at her with startled eyes the color of warm syrup.

Not Kareem's eyes, then. Not Kareem's eyes at all.

"Oh, God."

Staggering back a step and closing her eyes so she wouldn't have to see all these people staring at her like the three-armed woman at the freak show, she pressed that hand to her head again, trying to squeeze away the ache. Had she truly lost her mind? Couldn't someone leave her a trail of breadcrumbs or something so she could find her way out of this nightmare and back into a world that made sense?

"God. Please help me." If only the throbbing would let up, just for one freaking second, so she could think about what she needed to do, where she needed to look next—

"Mrs. Gregory."

That male voice spoke again, inexorable now. Opening her eyes, she realized that it was Brady, looking very forbidding today with his lowered brows, flashing eyes, and dark topcoat, and yet his calm presence was exactly what she needed. If Brady was here, then things were under control. If Brady was here, then she wasn't the only one on the lookout for fiends in the shadows.

"I know this is a very difficult day for you, but your husband is dead. You should let someone take you home so you can rest."

"But—"

"He's gone." Brady's gaze held hers, and it didn't waver with uncertainty. Though he had on his gruff special agent persona for all the onlookers, she knew him well enough now to see beneath the surface to what he was really trying to tell her.

It's okay, Kira. Trust me.

And, just like that, she trusted him.

Kareem was dead and locked safely inside that coffin. In a few minutes, they'd lower that coffin into the ground, and that would be that.

He was dead. His reign of terror was over. She was free.

Staring into Brady's eyes, she felt, for the first time, those feelings she'd needed, the ones she'd been waiting for:

Lightness. Hope. Quiet joy.

It was over and her life was now hers to live as she saw fit.

"I understand, Special Agent," she said, trying to match his aloof formality with her own. "Thank you."

Brady gave a sharp nod and melted away into the crowd, his expression shadowed.

Wanda appeared in his place, and the women's gazes locked. Poor thing, Kira thought, studying the puffy eyes, deep grooves that seemed to have appeared overnight in her forehead and bracketing her mouth, and stooped shoulders. Wanda was, suddenly, an ancient woman whose sole reason for living was now gone. If she lasted five years without Kareem, Kira would be surprised.

"Will you be coming to the church for dinner?" Wanda asked, her voice raw from sobbing.

Wow. There, finally, was an invitation into the inner sanctum, the one that had been barred against Kira all these years. Kareem's death had apparently moved her beyond all that pettiness, but it was way past too late as far as Kira was concerned. Wanda had been kind to her the other night after the rape, true, but the women had never been friends and now never would be. Anyway, these were Wanda and Kareem's people, not Kira's. Kira didn't have people.

"I can't."

"Do you need a ride to your hotel?"

"I have my car. I'm fine." Kira squeezed Wanda's arm, offering what little comfort she could. "You take care of yourself, okay?"

"You too."

An awkward beat or two passed, and then Kira dropped her arm and started to turn. To her astonishment, Wanda caught her up in a baby-powder-scented hug so fierce it knocked Wanda's hat to the ground, where it was soon tumbled away by the wind.

Instinct took over because there was only one thing to do when an old woman who'd lost her only child cried on your shoulder: you hugged her back.

"I'm so scared," Wanda whispered against Kira's neck. "I don't know what to do without him. I don't know how to live."

Yeah. There was a lot of that going around, wasn't there? Kira gripped Wanda's frail shoulders and rubbed her curved spine.

"You'll be okay. We both will."

With a great, shuddering breath, Wanda got a grip

on herself and let Kira go, but not before a final pat on Kira's face with her soft hand and a kiss on Kira's cheek that nearly reduced Kira to tears. Then she was gone, escorted into one of the waiting limousines by a gaggle of her solicitous friends, and Kira was left alone at the cemetery, except for the groundskeeper.

She took a minute to breathe, turning her face up to the sky and catching a weak ray or two of sunlight. The throbbing in her head eased back, just enough, and she went back down the hill to a bench, where she planned to sit and watch while they lowered that coffin six feet into the ground and buried it forever, taking her old life with it.

Chapter 13

The best word for the whole casket burial process was *startling*. The groundskeeper, or whoever he was, drove up in the backhoe that had, until now, been kept at a discreet distance, probably so that the mourners could imagine it would later be used to replant a large tree or something.

The casket was lowered and the groundskeeper, working with the kind of quick efficiency that made Kira wonder if he'd get a bonus for filling in ten or more graves before dark, shoveled the dirt in with great heaping clods.

The clouds drifted away and the sun came out. Kira stayed where she was, cold, but warm enough with her gloves, scarf, and hat to see this through to the bitter end, probably because she couldn't shake the fear that if she turned her back, even for a second, Kareem would pull an undead routine and climb out of the coffin to resume his dastardly deeds.

That didn't happen, though.

After the filling of the dirt, there was the tamping of the dirt with the backhoe's bucket and, finally, the smoothing of the dirt. After a quick break for a cigarette and what looked like a Snickers bar, the groundskeeper used a small crane to lift the headstone into place, and that was that.

That was that.

Stunned, Kira waited for the euphoria to hit, and it crept up on her in stages as she thought about all the choices opening up before her, all the opportunities that she'd never had.

The first part of her new life involved, obviously, finding somewhere other than that bedbug-proving-ground motel shit hole to live. Well, no, not quite. The very first part involved taking her boards and getting her license. Then she could start working in obstetrics (thank God she'd kept her grades up and graduated with a 3.9 GPA; there was nothing like offers coming to you before you graduated rather than you having to pound the pavement and hope to find something, especially in this economy), and then, once she'd worked for about a month or so, maybe six weeks, she'd have enough for a deposit on an apartment.

So she'd have a little while longer at the motel, but that was fine. She could certainly use the time to look for an apartment, right? When she left here, she planned to swing by the grocery store and get a couple of things, so she could look for one of those free apartment guides that they always kept in the newsstands near the carts.

Other things to do? Well, she'd need a credit card. Oh, and she wanted to start therapy ASAP because she knew she had issues with a capital I and didn't want to spend the rest of her life as screwed up as she currently was. So she'd better get a recommendation for a psychologist.

Maybe she should make a list of all the things she needed to do.

Yeah. Good idea. Rummaging in her purse, she found a notepad—

Behind her, a twig snapped.

Kira jumped to her feet in a wild explosion of movement that sent her purse flying, its contents scattering in every possible direction. Wheeling around, her limbs already spiking on adrenaline and shaking with fear, she tried to sound like she was tough and commanding rather than scared enough to send her heart leaping into cardiac arrest.

"Who's there?"

No one was there. A frantic glance in every direction revealed no one there (the groundskeeper had driven off in the backhoe a while ago) other than an industrious squirrel using his little two-handed grip to work on an acorn twenty feet away.

No one was there, she reassured herself.

No one is there, girl. Chill out.

But, she realized for the first time, the short winter days meant that dark would be here soon and was already well on its way. The shifting light had thrown everything into shadow, and what had been a bucolic setting was now, simply, a sinister graveyard with hulking objects and potential hiding places in every direction. As one of the nicer sections, this area had mature trees, shrubs, and huge monuments, any one of which could hide . . .

Who? Who was she hiding from with Kareem dead and in the ground? One of his minions? But why? None of them should have a beef against her. The boogeyman?

Garden-variety attackers and robbers? Did it really matter?

No. All she knew was that the hairs on her scalp felt like they were standing straight up and she needed to dodge a mine field of potential ambush spots before she made it to the relative safety of her car.

Go, Kira. Move.

Hands still shaking, she crouched down to gather up the contents of her purse. Lipstick, keys, phone, wallet . . . wallet . . . where was the— Oh, there. She snatched it up and shoved it in the bag. And her pistol. Nice, huh? Her first chance to protect herself from attackers and rabid squirrels, and she thought of her pistol last. She had a real eye-of-the-tiger thing going there, didn't she? But where the hell did it— Oh, there it was, in the higher grass under the bench. It felt nice and heavy in her hands, safer already, and she checked the safety, just in case.

Okay. Walk to the car. Hurry.

She hurried, trying to navigate between the headstones while staying far enough away from each one that someone—if anyone was there—would have a hard time reaching out and grabbing her.

Almost there, now, and she wished that her little bucket o'bolts had a key fob so she could click it and hear the reassuring chirp-chirp of the doors unlocking and see the lights blink on to guide her, but this wasn't the time—

"Kira."

With no further warning, a dark figure stepped out from behind a monument just to her right, blocking her, and she raised her gun and screamed, ready to die, yeah, but not before blasting Kareem to kingdom come as she went.

* * *

Jesus. He hadn't meant to scare her like that.

There was a flash of black, and the next thing Kerry knew, he was staring down the barrel of a nice-looking piece that would blow a hole the size of a grapefruit in his head. Reacting on instinct, he stepped back and held his hands up, praying he hadn't escaped Kareem only to be accidentally taken out by Kareem's wife.

"Don't shoot, Kira! It's me! Kerry!"

Kira had a hard look in her eyes, flashing, intent, and murderous, and he imagined she'd look just like this if she were fighting on some battlefield in Afghanistan. He froze, hoping for the best but waiting for that bullet to the forehead, because a person who looked like that was in killing mode, but then she blinked and her alert level eased back from red to orange.

Lowering the gun one inch, she blinked again and took a closer look at his face. *"Kerry?"*

"Yeah." He tried to breathe again, but his lungs couldn't seem to master the procedure. "And I don't want to die today, so please don't shoot me. Okay?"

She looked from him to the gun with dawning horror. "Oh, my God. I'm so sorry."

They stared at each other, both panting and spiked out on nerves.

"When the hell did you get a gun?"

"The other day."

"Do you know how to use it?"

One corner of her mouth curled. "I guess we were about to find out, weren't we?"

That was reassuring. And she had the pistol lowered now, pointing in the general direction of his dick, which was not, in his opinion, much of an improvement over pointing it at his head.

"Can you put that thing away, please?"

"Sorry!" Clicking the safety back on again, she shoved the thing in her purse and watched him for another beat or two. He could almost see the wheels turning in her mind, feel her vibrating curiosity. "Was it you? Did you tell the DEA about the real warehouse? Were you the informant?"

"You mean *snitch,* don't you?"

"No. Because whoever turned Kareem in is a hero in my book. Was it you?"

He hesitated, thinking about the marshals and the secrecy, and the measures that'd been taken to ensure his safety. He thought about the horror he'd see in the eyes of both Dexter Brady and Jayne Morrison if they knew he was having even a hypothetical discussion about this with Kira. Then he looked into those dark eyes and thought about how nice it would be if they saw him with admiration.

"Yeah. It was me."

She did a choked laugh-sob thing, quickly stifled, and before he knew it, she was launching herself at him, all open arms and thrilled female. And then she was pressed up against him, melting into him, and, Jesus, she felt better than he'd remembered. Better than he'd dreamed during all those dark and endless nights since he'd held her last.

Buried emotions bubbled inside him, shifting and churning the way the earth's layers do right before a tsunami or a volcanic eruption, and he couldn't hold her tight enough. Couldn't believe he'd lived long enough and been lucky enough to hold her again.

They swayed together for a few seconds and then, too soon, she pulled back to arm's length. His consolation was that her sparkling gaze held his and he could see— he could finally, finally see—that he meant something to her no matter how ruthlessly she'd pushed him away.

"Thank you," she said.

"You're welcome." Full disclosure seemed like a good idea, especially since he'd lived too much of his life in the tricky shadow world of lies. "But I didn't do it for you. I did it for me."

"Does it matter why you do the right thing, as long as you do it?"

"I did it so I could look myself in the mirror again. So don't go thinking I'm a hero, okay? That's one thing. And the other thing is, I was scared shitless."

"That just makes you human."

She said it with such infinite understanding that his chest contracted, reminding him in painful detail why this woman was thrumming in his blood and he couldn't get her out. It also reminded him of why he didn't deserve her and never would.

Not that his foolish heart would let him stop hoping.

Tugging her hand, he pulled her back to the bench, where they sat. There was so much unfinished between them and so much still to be said that he had to tackle it like a man eating an elephant—one small piece at a time.

"How are you?" he asked urgently.

"Fine," she said, too quickly.

"Don't lie to me. Do you think I don't know when you're lying?"

She ducked her head and refused to meet his gaze, shame making her cheeks bright. "If you don't want me to lie to you, then don't ask me questions like that. I can't talk about it with you."

This one boundary was perfectly understandable and it shouldn't hurt so much, but being sliced in two with a circular saw had to cut less than this.

"Why not?" he demanded. "I was there that night—"

"*Don't,* Kerry."

"—And I should have protected you from Kareem."

"Really?" There was less anguish in her voice now and much more bitterness. "I'm not your responsibility. And when has any of us been able to protect anyone from Kareem?"

Not his responsibility. Yeah. Thanks for the reminder. "I should have killed him for you. That night. When I had the chance."

Her head and eyes were lowered, but the minute thinning of her lips and flare of her nostrils said it all, as did the measured pause before she spoke, as though she needed the time for a careful edit of her words.

And then, to make things worse, she glanced up at him, a flash of accusation that acted like that circular saw again, slicing another chunk of his flesh from his body. In the end, though, she mastered all that dark emotion.

He wished he could.

"I'm not your responsibility. I never expected you to avenge me or rescue me."

"I expected it," he said flatly.

That brought her head up, and their gazes connected with a startling jolt of electricity. He stared at her, refusing to look away, and willed her to see all the things she'd never let him say.

That their few short nights together two years ago hadn't been enough. That the inherent and suicidal danger of having an affair with the wife of his boss, the drug kingpin, had been a price he'd been willing and happy to pay for the pleasure of her body against his and her whispers in the night. That new hope had sprung to life inside him and was leeching through the pores of his skin now that Kareem was dead and things were possible again.

"Kira," he began, agonized.

The play of emotions across her face said it all. The dawning understanding. The gratitude, quickly replaced by embarrassment, and then, horribly, the pity.

That pity killed him every time, but this time was so much worse because it'd been preceded by thirty seconds of the sweet joy of possibilities.

"I can't, Kerry," she said.

She couldn't. Not exactly a news flash there, and yet his stupid mouth kept blathering.

"Kareem's dead now, baby. We could try again—"

More pity. More intense pity. So much pity that he had to look away before it shamed him.

"I don't want to hurt you, Kerry. Don't make me say it."

The unspoken *it* had always been there, much as he'd tried to wish it away: she didn't love him—never had and never would.

Except this was somehow worse because there was nothing for him to hide behind and mitigate the rejection. Before, there'd been Kareem. She'd loved Kareem and been hung up on him, and he got that. Then she'd been afraid of Kareem and afraid for him if Kareem ever found out about them, and he got that, too. But now Kareem was gone and the naked truth was that, with her field wide open and her future bright, she still didn't want Kerry.

Which made sense because, having gotten rid of one thug in her life, why would she sign on with another one? And that was all he was, wasn't it? A man who'd had choices and always made the wrong ones. A kindler, gentler, better-quality criminal than Kareem had been, and a criminal with a medical degree, but a criminal nonetheless.

Still, it hurt. In his heart and the remnants of what passed for his soul, in the cells of his organs, the marrow of his bones, and the drops of his blood, it hurt.

The bitterness collected on his tongue, and he swallowed it back, twisting his mouth in the process until he felt like a gargoyle grimacing on the side of some building.

God, it hurt.

She knew it, too, because, looking off down the path to give him the space to get his act together, she reached out and took his hand. His pride, which had clocked out and gone home for the day, didn't stop him from hanging on to that hand for as long as she'd let him.

His nostrils flared; his chin trembled; his throat and eyes burned. And then he got it together. With a final squeeze, he let that hand go.

"What will you do now?" she wondered.

"I don't know. I'm not sure the feds won't still prosecute me. But they don't seem that interested. I was a smaller fish. They wanted Kareem. But I'll keep a low profile for now. I'm probably not real popular with the other guys."

Concern crinkled her forehead. "Do they know you're the one who flipped?"

He shrugged. "I don't know. But they know it wasn't them."

"So maybe they'll point the finger at each other."

"That's what I'm hoping."

They sat in silence for a while before Kira mentioned the obvious. "You're not going to take over, are you? Now that there's a job vacancy at the top—"

"Nice." He knew what made her ask, but he still resented her for it. "Is that what you think of me?"

She shot him an apologetic smile. "It would be the easy way."

He stared, hating her for this shrewd assessment of his morally challenged life.

"You can be the first to know: I'm finished taking the easy way."

"Good," she said flatly. "So what will you do? Open a practice somewhere?"

"We'll see."

She grinned. "You can do it."

He wanted to smile back, but suddenly his mind was full of all the bad choices he'd made, all the times that he'd had the option between right and wrong and he'd sprinted toward wrong.

What kind of fool, after all, crawls out of the wrong side of town, works and scrapes together the money to earn a medical degree, and yet lets himself be lured into his buddy's criminal underworld?

Yeah. That would be him.

He could be a partner in some practice group by now, with a wife, kids, and a dog.

Instead, he was now the lieutenant in a failed drug empire, still under threat of both indictment and, probably, vendetta killing by his cronies, with only the dwindling supply of tainted money hidden beneath a

carpet-covered loose floorboard in his apartment to
keep a roof over his head.

Brilliant, you stupid punk.

He stood, wishing he could leave the old, self-
destructive Kerry here and take home a shiny new model.
"I should get going. And I don't want you staying here
by yourself."

"Don't worry," she said, also getting up. "Will you
stay in touch with me? Let me know you're okay?"

God, he wanted to. Except that he still had a tiny
flicker of a protective instinct left—hard to believe,
wasn't it?—and he was smart enough to know he couldn't
handle being halfway in Kira's life.

"I'm not sure that's a good idea."

Naturally, Kira wouldn't make things easy for him.
She turned those sweet brown eyes on him, pleading
now, and he could no more turn her down than he could
run for president.

"Just send me a text every now and then, so I won't
worry, okay? Please? You can do that for me, can't you?"

I would do anything for you.

"Yeah," he told her. "I can do that for you."

Chapter 14

Back at the motel, Kira took Max out for a quick walk (the manager had taken to pretending he didn't see her or the dog when she came and went) and then defrosted her limbs with what was meant to be a long shower but in reality only lasted until the hot water gave out, a period of roughly thirty-eight seconds. Then she snuggled down for the night in a long-sleeved T-shirt, a pair of plaid flannel pajama bottoms, and her lined pink moccasins.

After ordering a pizza, she clicked the TV onto the Discovery Channel, where they were showing a bunch of *Shark Week* reruns, and collapsed onto the oversized chair to work on the list that had gotten sidelined when Kerry appeared out of the blue. Max made this task more difficult, if not impossible, by curling up in her lap the second she sat cross-legged, but she compensated by twisting at the waist and resting her pad on the chair's arm.

Okay. Where was she?

Apartment.

Credit card.

Therapist recommendations.

Oh, and she couldn't live without a laptop, so she'd better start saving for one of those.

Thank goodness she'd wear scrubs at the hospital, because she sure didn't want to have to buy a whole new wardrobe for work—

Max's head came up. He stared at the door, tilting his head and cocking his ears. As warnings went, this one was pretty clear, but she still jumped straight up in the air when someone knocked on her door.

On cue, all her hard-won relaxation went straight out the window, and her pulse rate rocketed up into the triple digits. Paralyzed with a fear that was faceless now that she knew Kareem was dead, she stayed where she was and ran through her options while Max trotted to the door and glanced back at her like she'd lost her mind.

She was seriously considering either grabbing her gun, which she'd stored under her pillow for just such an emergency, or hiding in the bathroom and locking the door—see? This was why she needed therapy—when a voice came through loud and clear.

"Kira? You in there?"

Brady.

Oh, thank God.

Her body going jelly-boned with relief, she got up, checked the peephole, and opened the door. Having changed since the funeral, he had one sardonic eyebrow raised, wore a leather jacket, hoodie, and track pants, and held two stacked pizza boxes in his hand.

"Everything okay in here?"

"No, it's not okay. You scared me to death, but since you brought food, I'll forgive you."

"Must be my lucky day."

Relieving him of those precious and savory boxes,

she set them on the small table between the chairs and grabbed a couple of washcloths to use as napkins.

"What are you doing here, Brady? Don't you have a life?"

"None to speak of."

"What about your little booty-call friend? Won't she be looking for you?"

Taking his jacket off, he tossed it onto the bed, chose a chair, sat, and glared. "There you go being nosy again."

She laughed. "It'll take more than that to get me off your tail. So what about her?"

"She's not really a consideration. And have I complimented you on your attire?"

Another laugh rose up her throat and out, more laughter than she'd generated in the last two years. "I'm not trying to win a fashion show. I'm allowed to choose my own clothes and be comfortable now rather than look like I just slithered out of a La Perla lingerie catalogue, aren't I?"

She said it all without mentioning Kareem's name—at some unidentified point today, she'd decided never to speak his name again if she could help it—but he understood anyway.

His eyes crinkled at the edges, warming her far better with his approval than the shower had. "Damn straight you are."

Ridiculously pleased with herself, she set to work on the pizza boxes and opened the first one, which was a thin crust with spinach, tomatoes, and hunks of sausage the size of grapes.

"Wait a minute—this is the pizza I ordered."

Brady frowned at her selection. "Yeah. I intercepted

your delivery guy in the lobby. It's a good thing I did, too, isn't it? What kind of crap is that?"

"It's my favorite pizza. And you got—?"

He opened his lid with a flourish to reveal . . . extra cheese.

"That's it?" She looked back and forth between man and pizza, just to verify, but there was, in fact, nothing else on that pizza or in that box, not even a little packet of red pepper flakes for flavor. "Brady, you're *boring*. How is it possible for a DEA agent to be this dull?"

This didn't abash him in the least. Taking a huge slice, he folded it in half, chomped off about four inches' worth from the point, and spoke out of the side of his mouth before chewing approximately once and swallowing.

"Guess what my favorite ice cream flavor is?"

"Please don't tell me it's vanilla."

"Bingo."

More laugher came and she leaned back her head to let it flow until she was giddy with it. Was this what freedom felt like? Was happiness something like this? A slice of pizza with a friend without having to fret about what her husband would say or do next? Could life really be this simple?

"You have to try my pizza. You might like it."

He shuddered, gulping down another big bite. "I want no part of that pizza."

Helping herself to a piece of hers, she sank her teeth deep and nearly moaned with ecstasy. "This is sooo good."

Brady wiped his mouth, reached for his jacket, and pulled a Pepsi out of each pocket. Passing one to her, he gave her a considering look. "You have eaten since this morning, right?"

Uh-oh. "Define *eaten*."

"Consumed something with protein in it."

"Not exactly," she admitted, thinking fondly of the Egg McMuffin she'd had on her way to the funeral. His brows lowered, and she held up a hand to forestall a lecture. "I'm going to do better."

"See that you do."

His voice had that quiet authority you wouldn't think of questioning, but his heavy-handedness didn't bother her. Much. Someone out there in the world cared whether she ate or not, which was a first in a really long time. Yeah. She could get used to that, but that didn't mean she had to make like a doormat.

"Aye, Captain."

Apparently he didn't apprcciate the humor, because he shot her another of those flinty looks. "How's your head?"

"Still attached."

Another frown, but this time, instead of the stern talk-ing-to she expected, he did something exponentially worse. He reached out and took her wrist in his firm grip while his thumb caressed the back of her hand.

"Stop the bullshit, Kira," he said urgently. "Tell me how you are."

With that, she unraveled. Emotions she'd managed to suppress, more or less, for most of the day, squeezed her chest and throat and burned her cheeks into cinders. What was it about Brady? Why couldn't she put up brick walls with him the way she could with Kerry? Why didn't she want to? Was it because it was such an un-speakable relief to shift some of her burden to his broad shoulders for a little while? Was it that she needed a brief reprieve from keeping all her balls in the air while tap dancing and trying her best to be strong?

"I'm okay." Embarrassed, she swiped at her sudden tears and worked at giving him a reassuring smile. "I'm trying to be okay."

"How's your head?"

"It hurts. Not so bad, though."

"Did you take your meds?"

"Yeah."

"What happened to you at the funeral? I was worried."

"I can't explain it. I thought I saw him everywhere. I felt him there, like he was watching."

"What about now?"

"Now I know he's gone."

"And how does that feel?"

"It feels like I'm free," she said simply.

"And how does *that* feel?"

It sounded so cheesy to say it, but if there was another possible description, her floundering brain couldn't find it.

"It feels like I've been born again."

"Good." Brady dimpled with obvious satisfaction, smoothed his thumb over her hand one more time, and pointed to her pizza. "Now eat."

They ate.

Dexter had the strong urge to count every bite of food that went into her mouth and watch her swallow it but, thanks to his long years of law enforcement training and resulting self-control, was able to resist the temptation.

But she ate two and a half pieces, and that was pretty good for someone her size, even if her pizza was nasty. He only wished he'd brought her some milk or fruit to go with it. Whatever it took for her to get strong and healthy again.

Still, she was looking better by the time he returned from dumping the boxes in the trash down the hall by the vending machines. Her cheeks had a little more color and her expression wasn't quite so feral. Maybe one day soon she'd realize that she was no longer being hunted, and wouldn't that be a beautiful thing?

Letting himself back into her room, he checked his watch: eight-twenty. Time to go. He'd come, delivered the sustenance, watched her eat it, and the official portion of his mission was at an end. Anything beyond this would be purely personal and, therefore, indefensible, and he wanted that to matter. He reminded himself about their relative positions. She: drug kingpin's widow. He: DEA agent. He reminded himself that she was emotionally raw right now and therefore vulnerable. Duly noted. He reminded himself of his father's stricture to always do the right thing—the honorable thing—even when it was hard and no one was watching. Check.

And then he looked over at Kira, sitting on the sofa with Max's furry head resting on her thigh. He saw the curve where neck met shoulder, and the velvety warmth of her skin in the lamplight. Beneath his fingertips he felt the phantom memory of her wrist in his hand and wondered what she'd do if he ever kissed her there. He caught the elusive and delicious scent of her flesh— water lilies, he thought—and imagined that the smell would be stronger if he pressed his mouth to the valley between her breasts.

Then he put all those considerations on an invisible scale and tried to balance them out, which was about like putting a mastodon on one side and a dragonfly on the other:

The thrill of being with Kira vs. the trouble he could buy for himself if he developed a personal—well, more personal—relationship with Kira.

It wasn't even close.

So he told his yammering conscience to shut the hell up, walked back to the sofa, and sat.

Max, the manipulator, rolled over and squirmed around until his head was on his thigh, and Dexter concentrated on stroking the dog's sleek fur to keep his twitchy hands from reaching for Kira.

While it was great to be occupied, the silly dog only deepened his sense of comfortable belonging, and he thought, with increasing dread, about going home to his empty house, which he was beginning to think of as the Fortress of Loneliness, once he left here.

Yeah. Not fun.

But he was here now, and that was enough. For now.

He stared at the TV, which was on some animal show—sharks, apparently—and tried not to notice that Kira's eyes were growing drowsy with sleep and her yawns were growing much more frequent.

"Sharks, eh?"

"I love animal shows."

"Yet you call me boring."

"You are boring. So did you see my list?" She handed him a pad from the table and waited while he read it. "All the things I need to do to get my life together. Well"—she shot him a wry grin—"it's a good start, anyway. This should keep me busy for a while."

"Impressive," he said, meaning it. "And what will that look like—when you get your life together?"

"That's easy. It'll look like me being a self-sufficient and productive member of society for the first time in my life."

"Yeah?"

"And I want to feel content, for once." Curling her legs under her, she shifted and came closer—dangerously closer. Close enough for him to see how bright her enthusiastic eyes were. "And I want to be proud of myself. You probably always feel proud of yourself, don't you?"

He stared at her, thinking of all the times in the past year when she'd come to him for help and he'd questioned her motives and then sent her away, back to the monster who'd made her life a living hell before raping her and giving her a concussion.

Swallowing hard, he prayed he had enough voice left for a coherent sentence and produced only a rough croak. "Not always, no."

"That's hard to believe, Brady. What did you do—jaywalk once ten years ago?"

"I'm not real proud of the way I've treated you, now that you mention it."

This was the wrong thing to say because it made her question his motives. "Is that why you're here, then? Pity for a crime victim?"

"No," he said softly, holding her gaze and willing her to see. "That's not why I'm here."

He'd wounded her pride, so it took a couple of long beats for her to switch gears and come up to speed on this subject he hadn't meant to broach just yet. But now it was here and he wasn't going to turn away just because the path was twisty and he couldn't see the end.

He couldn't turn away.

"Brady," she gasped, her eyes widening with slow comprehension. "Are you telling me you *like* me?"

The utter astonishment in her voice was understandable. Hadn't he bent over backward, twisting himself into advanced yoga poses to keep his fierce attraction to her under wraps the whole time he was trying to bring down her husband? Hadn't this made him surly and gruff around her? Hadn't he forbidden himself from ever giving her so much as an appreciative glance? And, worst of all, hadn't he tried to hate her for being married to someone else—the worst possible someone else—when he wanted her so much it threatened to choke the life right out of him?

"*Like* you?" he echoed, trying it on for size. "Yeah. Let's go with that. For now."

Taking advantage of her drop-jawed silence, he got up, found his coat, and went to the door. This wasn't the time, and it wouldn't be the time for a while yet, if ever. And she needed to decide because she'd had way too many decisions snatched away from her capable hands.

"I've gotta go. You take care of yourself, okay? I won't be seeing you for a while."

This snapped her out of her temporary paralysis. "What? Why?"

He tipped his head toward her notebook. "Because you need time to get yourself together, like you said. And I'm trying not to pressure you, but I'm not the Boy Scout you seem to think I am, so I'd better make myself scarce so you can have space."

"But—"

"And because . . ." He paused, taking his time to get to the heart of the matter so she'd have the chance to see it coming. "I really hope that, when and if you ever get ready, you'll come to me and we can find out whether we have anything to talk about other than your first husband."

Their gazes locked across that space of ten feet or so, and he was pretty sure, honest to God, that he heard her shallow breathing stop. He was gratified to see that she didn't recoil in horror, thrilled to see the deep flush of awareness that crept up her neck to her face and made her wide eyes sparkle.

"Brady," she began.

"And when you come," he continued, because he could feel the growing and absolute certainty as a part of himself, the same as his pulse or his heartbeat, and there was no longer any question in his mind of *if* now, only *when*, "I want you to work on calling me Dexter."

He left, taking care not to let the door bang behind him.

Chapter 15

Six Months Later

Dexter strode through the sliding glass doors of the Pine Lake retirement community, his brain already scrolling through his checklist like a clipboard-carrying state inspector. The receptionist was sitting her post behind the marble counter, her smile cheery, welcoming, and wide, so that was good; but the place still—always—had that unfortunate scent of determined freshness layered over the stronger scents of bodily functions and illness, so that was bad.

All the employees he passed in the hallways sported pristine uniforms and attitudes of open friendliness, so that was good; but that one poor woman, the ancient one who moaned and babbled in an endless and excruciating loop, had been left to her own devices in the corner chair over by the wall aquarium, and that was bad.

Mom, a former nurse named Lorraine, was looking lovely, with her salt and pepper hair curled and her makeup on, which was great, but she was dozing in her wheelchair over by the huge cage occupied by chattering yellow finches, and that was terrible because her disorientation was always a thousand times worse after she woke.

He hovered near the doorway, undecided.

Option 1: sneak out like a cat burglar and come back tomorrow morning, when she was more likely to be awake and reasonably lucid.

He hadn't seen her in a couple days, though, and he preferred to keep a close eye on her.

Option 2: wake her up and risk either not being recognized at all, which had happened twice in the last month or so, much to his dismay, or being called by his father's name, her brother's name, a random cousin's name, or the name of the orderly who most recently brought her a meal.

Nice choices, eh?

Brady, would you like your shit sandwich on whole wheat or white bread?

Maybe the best thing to do was just sit and hang out for a few minutes and see if she woke up on her own. It was Friday night, true, but his social calendar had a lot of blank spaces on it these days, and God knew no one was waiting for him to show up and get their party started. In fact, once he left Pine Lake, that swinging hub of social activity and entertainment, the chances of him speaking more than two words to another human being between now and Monday morning when he went back to work were somewhere between 0 and 1 percent.

So yeah. Why not sit his ass down in a chair and stay with his mother for a while? Maybe if he looked pitiful enough, they'd scrounge up an extra plate of turkey tetrazzini and orange Jell-O for him come dinnertime.

That was something to look forward to, oh, yes, indeedy.

He loosened his tie and sat, wishing he had a beer or

thirty to drown his sorrows in. Well, *sorrow,* anyway.
Singular. Because other than Mom here losing her memory
inch by inch and there being way too many dealers still
on the streets despite all his best efforts (and he was,
sadly, used to both of those situations by now), he had
only one source of sadness in his life:

Kira.

Even the name . . . the image . . . the mere hint of her
weighed him down, an anchor of loss and longing
around his soul, pulling him under just a little bit more
with every day that passed. Exhausted with the wanting,
he rested his elbows on his knees and his head in his
hands, letting the woe-is-me wash over him until it was
up to his chin.

Come to me when you're ready, he'd said, like some
goddamn freaking new age guru. What kind of thing to
say was that? Come to me when you're ready? Please.
The thing he hadn't considered, when he was spouting
shit from the mouth the way fountains spout water, was
this: what if she didn't come? Huh? What now, genius?
If you set a butterfly free and it didn't come back to you,
were you allowed to go after the little fucker with your
giant net?

Why had he said that? Come to me when you're ready.
Brilliant. Why hadn't he put a shelf life on it? Come to
me when you're ready, but don't take longer than sixty
days, because I'll become unhinged if you do. Wouldn't
that have made more sense? Why hadn't he said *that*?

Well, he knew why. He'd been trying to do the right
thing and not pressure her, for one. For two, he'd
wanted to give her the space she needed to get her
ducks in a row, just like he'd said. Third—and this was
the thing that really stuck in his craw—he'd been so

sure, so absolutely, eerily, inexplicably sure that she was into him, too, and the chemistry between them wasn't all coming from him. There'd been something in the way she looked at him during that last conversation, something in the brightness of her eyes, or maybe it was that she'd blushed. . . .

Wow. Did he have superlative analytical skills, or what? Something in her eyes. What a stunning mind he had. All those years of training hadn't been wasted on him, buddy, no siree.

He squeezed his skull between his palms, wishing he could pop it like a melon or at least make his eyes shoot out and bounce against the far wall. Then he'd be excused from further obsessing about Kira, and wouldn't that be nice?

So, okay, he'd made this bed of nails for himself, and now he was lying in it. The question was—what now? Did Kira's extended silence mean that she wasn't ready yet? Or did it mean that, God forbid, she wasn't into him after all? And what should he do to verify her position one way or the other? What if he kept giving her more time and discovered in, say, a year or so, that she'd remarried? Wouldn't that be a nice kick in the teeth for his trouble?

Sitting on his hands and waiting just wasn't in his nature; he'd been stupid to think he could manage it even for a month. Hell, he hadn't managed it—who did he think he was fooling? Thus far, he'd illegally used his law enforcement resources to find out where she was working (in the OB/GYN department at one of the university hospitals) and where she was living (in a rented house on a nice street with mature trees and a fenced yard for

Max), and he'd done five or six drive-bys of her home, just to make sure she was still alive (she was).

Yeah, he'd sunk to new and humiliating lows.

But he hadn't approached her, and of that he was proud. He might be a stalker, but he was a stalker with principles, dammit, and he could walk tall with his head held high.

Now what? The question reverberated inside his skull, clattering like a dozen skillets dropped ten feet onto a tile floor. Now what . . . now what . . .

"Now what?" he asked of no one, rubbing his hands over his scalp and raising his head at last, too tired to deal with his exhaustion for another second. "Now what?"

"What's wrong, D?"

Rattled, he looked over to Mom. She was awake now, sitting straight in that damn chair with her eyes open wide and as clear and focused as they'd been that long ago time she and dad caught him sneaking back into the house via the basement window after a night of partying. His heart contracted because these moments were far too rare and would soon go the way of the dodo and the passenger pigeon.

But she was here now, and for that he was grateful.

He tried to smile. "Hey, beautiful. How are you?"

Tutting, she shook her head. "Don't try to sweet talk me, boy. What's wrong? And don't tell me *nothing*."

Okay. Now he was freaked out. Because their conversations these days, such as they were, consisted mainly of him asking how she felt, if she was hungry, and if she needed another pair of pajamas or a velour warm-up suit to wear while sitting there and waiting for the rest of her mind to go.

He was wondering how to begin when her mother's instinct kicked in to higher gear and saved him the trouble.

"It's a woman, isn't it? Have you finally found someone?"

Found someone sounded more momentous that he wanted to make it, but, on the other hand, his interest in this one particular woman now spanned a couple of years and had reached a fever pitch in the last several months, so why split hairs?

"Yeah," he admitted.

She beamed, no doubt envisioning all kinds of grandchildren bouncing on her knee in the near future. If he'd thought there was a snowball's chance in a Sahara summer that she'd remember the conversation later, he'd really be worried.

"So why the long face?"

"I'm not sure she's ready, Ma."

"Ready for what?"

He shrugged, trying to put it into words. To get it right. "Ready for me."

Mom studied him with those wise old eyes and then cut right to the heart of the matter, whether he was prepared to hear it or not. Which, as a matter of fact, he wasn't. "If she doesn't know a good man when she sees one, son, then she's not the one for you."

Yeah. That was what worried him.

What if Kira was one of those adrenaline-addicted women who always went for a bad boy? Hell, maybe she had her eye on another felon right now. Maybe she'd already struck up a pen pal relationship with some dude at Lucasville, or maybe she'd hooked up with some local professional athlete. A Bengal, maybe. That was a nice image to take to bed with him tonight, one guaranteed to cause him screaming nightmares: Kira wrapped around some oversized linebacker who drove a flashy car worth more than Dexter made in two years.

After all, if she'd fallen for a bad boy like Kareem, wasn't it a safe bet that Dexter wasn't her type? Could never be her type? And, if so, then Mom was right, wasn't she? And moms were almost always right; everyone over the age of twenty-one knew that.

Except this time.

The tiny little voice, rock hard with certainty, crept through his doubts, drowning them out. *She'll come to you,* the voice continued. *Have a little faith. Wait a little while longer. What have you got to lose?*

That's when it got weird.

"Just wait," Mom said, right on cue, like she'd done in the old days, when she'd peeked inside his head and read his thoughts before he had them. "Give her a little time. Why don't you do that?"

"Maybe I will," he said. "Thanks, Ma. That really helps."

"Good."

With a final and decisive pat on his knee, her eyes sliding back out of focus, she put her hands on the arms of the chair and tried to press herself up even though it'd been months since her body forgot how to follow the commands to walk.

His heart, knowing what was coming, broke again. It never stopped hoping and therefore never stopped breaking.

"Now help me get going," she said. "I don't want to be late for my shift at the hospital."

* * *

Kira knocked on the door, hoping several things in no particular order.

She hoped Dexter was home because she'd taken weeks to gather the courage to show up at his house, and she didn't think she could do it again anytime soon. On the other hand, she hoped he wasn't home because what the hell did she think she'd say to him? Wouldn't it be better to slink off into the night without him ever knowing she'd come?

Maybe.

Still, she hoped that, if he was home, he was alone. If he was home and alone, she hoped that he also wasn't in the middle of getting ready for some hot date, but what were the chances of that for a handsome man on a Friday night after work? Why didn't she also hope she'd find a stray bar of gold bouillon on the sidewalk while she was at it?

And what if he was in some committed relationship now? Or engaged? God, she hoped he wasn't engaged but, let's face it, men didn't like to be alone and they all got married eventually. What if he barely remembered her? Surely he hadn't thought she'd take six freaking months to get her act togeth—

Without warning, the door swung open.

Brady stood there in his white shirtsleeves, dark slacks, and a loosened red tie around his neck. She'd apparently caught him in the middle of a postwork drink, because his head was leaned back for a long pull on a bottle of beer, and his brows were lowered with apparent annoyance at the interruption.

But then he realized it was Kira, and two things happened: his eyes widened with surprise.

And he choked.

Oh, man. See? She shouldn't have come.

As he hacked and sputtered, trying to clear his airway and holding up his index finger in a *give-me-a-minute* gesture, she chattered with the uncontrollable and non-sensical enthusiasm of a cage full of parakeets.

"Hi! I didn't mean to startle you like this. I should have called first. I knew I should have called. But I just thought that, you know, I'd be spontaneous and see if you wanted to, I don't know, maybe have a drink with me or something because it's, ah, Friday night, and that's a fun time for drinks because it's the end of the week and I thought maybe you wouldn't be busy. But I can see that you're busy—you probably just got home from work, right?—and you already have a drink, so I'll just"—she gestured vaguely over her shoulder, in the general direction of her car parked at the curb—"go and leave you in peace. Okay? Great. Bye!"

She took a quick step away, reminding herself not to break and run, because that would just be pathetic, but he'd recovered after her ridiculous monologue and put a hand on her arm to stop her.

"Wait." His voice was strained and hoarse, about like Louis Armstrong moments after a tonsillectomy, and he had to pause and clear his throat. Enduring his piercing gaze was like submitting to nude X-rays in front of a studio audience. "It's been six months."

"I know. But I had to get my life together, like I said, and I have. I passed my boards, and I'm working at the hospital now, and I'm renting a really nice little house and saving the money to buy it at the end of the year."

For crying out loud. Why couldn't she shut up and stop yammering out her résumé? He was only a man. That fact alone, by definition, meant that he wasn't perfect, right?

So why did she feel this relentless drive to prove to him that she was worthy of his interest? Was this what her shrink meant when he kept wondering where she'd gotten her feelings of inadequacy?

Just shut up, Kira. SHUT. UP.

"And of course I've been in therapy." Lovely. The blathering continued, with no signs of stopping. Really, he should just slam the door in her face right now and put them both out of their misery. "Because I know I have some stuff to work on—"

"*Six months,* Kira."

"I know, and I—"

"I haven't slept. What are you trying to do to me?"

Opening her mouth again, she started to say something about it having been too long, of course, and she realized that whatever offer he'd made had long since expired—duh!—and she was sorry for disturbing him.

Except that his words sank in, their gazes connected, and she couldn't look away from the quiet intensity in his eyes or the sudden, vibrating urgency in his body. Instead of apologizing and scurrying off with her tail between her legs, she found herself saying something altogether different—the thing she wanted to say and he, clearly, needed to hear:

"I didn't mean to take so long."

"You look like a new person."

What did he mean? He was talking about more than her hair, which she'd let grow to her shoulders, evidently. Could he see her new peace and serenity? Did it show on her face along with her shimmery new lip gloss? Or did he intuitively know that she could eat like a longshoreman and sleep like a comatose baby now that her husband had done her the courtesy of getting himself blown to kingdom come?

Could he see how happy she was these days, and how she'd done everything she could think of to get herself ready for this next phase of her life? And, incidentally, to make herself worthy of an honorable man rather than a drug dealer?

"I feel like a new person," she told him.

Without looking away, his slid his hand down her arm and took her hand between both of his, encompassing her in so much strength and warmth that she wondered if she could let him go when the time came.

"Good." His eyes crinkled at the edges, and there was more warmth. A bigger welcome. "Are you ready now?"

There was no doubt, no hesitation, even though it might have made sense to pause for a moment and clarify: ready for what? A drink? Dinner? More? What did *more* look like?

And while she was at it, she probably should have taken the time to wonder why her being here now felt inevitable. The whole time she'd known Brady (up until that last day six months ago, when he'd made his declaration), she'd thought that he either didn't like her or, at best, barely liked her. She, meanwhile, had been so busy trying to survive and disentangle herself from Kareem's toxic web that she hadn't had the chance to think about the exact nature of her feelings for Brady.

All she'd known was that the air prickled with electricity when he was around, and she'd always felt the dizzying intensity of his personality. Now, finally, she knew what that meant, and she was ready to explore it. More than that, she had the unshakable certainty that she was supposed to be here, now, with him.

Crazy, huh?

So why did this feel so good? Why was she filled to bursting with a deep, quiet peace she was sure she'd never experienced before, not even once—as though she was, finally, arriving at the place where she was supposed to be in her life?

Why did her hand feel so great wrapped inside his?

Maybe it was too soon, and maybe they'd crash and burn before their drinks arrived at the table tonight, and maybe Brady would have to be insane to think about spending time with a woman with her track record, which could best be characterized as abysmal.

But she didn't think so. She really didn't think so.

"Yes," she said. "I'm ready now."

"Good." He paused, drifting closer now, close enough that she smelled the starch of his shirt and the soapy clean of his deodorant. "And you should know—I was planning to give you another thirty-six hours or so, and then I was going to show up on your doorstep."

Chapter 16

They went inside, where Brady ditched his tie, ducked into the bathroom, and then grabbed his car keys, all before she could blink or digest what was happening, and how quickly.

"How have you been?" she asked, not sure what to do with herself now that she wasn't holding his hand. Plus, they had so much catching up to do, it was tough picking a topic to get them started. "How's work—"

"Shh." Taking her hand again—yeah, she could seriously get used to this—he tugged her back out of the house and to the driveway. "Wait."

"Wait?"

"Yeah, wait. I don't want to miss anything while I'm driving."

With that, he deposited her on the passenger side of his car, which, she noticed for the first time, was a truck, and opened the door for her. Whereupon she grinned at him with the uncontrollable delight of a cat that'd been presented with an extra large bowl of buttery rich cream.

He paused, arrested. *"What?"*

"I'm really glad I'm here."

"Jesus," he murmured. A quick beat passed, and then, without warning, he caught her smiling face between his hands and lowered his head even as she tipped her chin up to meet him.

They came together so naturally it might have been their thousandth kiss rather than their first, except that the gentle brush of his lips against hers melted her up against a thrilling body that was as foreign to her as the dark side of the moon. His forearms were hard beneath her fingers, bunched with muscles thrumming with tension, and his lips were firm and demanding, and yet, somehow, tender. Beseeching.

He touched his tongue to her lips, seeking permission, but she was already opening for him, already surging, and if she'd been able to speak she'd have told him he didn't need to ask. His hands slid into her hair as the kiss deepened, caressing her scalp, and she tasted his hunger for her as strongly as she tasted the mint of the toothpaste he'd used. She found herself shifting closer, fully into the rock solid strength of his arms, and that, finally, was too much, just as it wasn't nearly enough.

They broke apart, both trying to catch their breath.

"Sorry." He hesitated but then gave in to the temptation to touch her again, smoothing the hair at her temple. "I'm trying not to go too fast for you. I meant to ask first."

She grinned, unable to stop herself. Did he expect her to slap his face? "I would have said yes. In case you're wondering."

He stared at her mouth, which felt dewy and deliciously swollen, and then flicked his hot gaze up to her eyes.

"You're beautiful. You know that, right?"

She didn't know that. Not at all. And he wouldn't be

so mesmerized by her face if he could see all the inner demons she'd been trying so hard to conquer these last several months. If she was any kind of a woman at all, she should warn him.

"Brady," she began.

His brows contracted. "What's my name?"

Wow. This one didn't forget a thing, did he? Wouldn't let her get away with anything and probably was straightforward with his thoughts and where she stood with him at any given moment, and wasn't that a refreshing change?

"Dexter. I'm nothing but trouble. Why don't you find a nice girl to be with?"

"I already have," he said flatly. "Now let's go eat."

"Five Guys Burgers and Fries, eh?" Dexter watched Kira unwrap her loaded burger from its foil with great relish, pausing to lick some of the oozing condiments—yes, she'd ordered, if he recalled correctly, mayo, ketchup, mustard, barbeque sauce, *and* hot sauce—off her thumb. *"Really?"*

"Really. I've had enough dinners at overpriced restaurants where they serve you half a baby carrot with the stem still attached and one scallop and call it a meal to last the rest of my life. No thanks. Besides. Where else are you going to get burgers like this?"

Opening his mouth to answer, he found his thoughts derailed by the way she bit into the thing with orgasmic delight, complete with closed eyes and satisfied moan. Until this moment, he'd rarely noticed a woman eat or found anything particularly sexy about anyone inhaling food as though it was his or her first meal after a three-week forced fast, but he couldn't look away. Nor could he do anything about the sweet ache growing between his thighs.

"Eat much?" he wondered, fascinated, as always, by everything about her.

"Yeah." Grinning around her mouthful, she kept right on going. "And if you don't get started, I'll eat yours, too."

Since he was pretty hungry and she looked fully capable of eating his burger and then climbing over the counter and grabbing them straight from the grill, he pulled his tray closer in a protective gesture.

"I was planning to take you someplace fancier. Somewhere with, you know, more than burgers and fries on the menu."

"Well, first of all, they also have hot dogs here. Don't forget. Second, you're not taking me. I'm taking you—"

"I beg to differ. Who drove?"

"—And third, I love burgers. As you may recall."

This pointed reference to that day, six months and several lifetimes ago, when she'd snuck out to meet him at a T.G.I. Friday's and beg for his help in escaping Kareem (she'd been willing to risk her neck by trying to find evidence of Kareem's criminal activities) reminded him that they had several housekeeping matters to attend to before they could focus, as he fully intended to do, on steering their fledgling relationship out of the past and into the future.

He hadn't meant to have this discussion here, among the chattering patrons, red-shirted employees, and cheery red and white tiled walls of Five Guys while Duran Duran blared over the speakers, but what the hell. No time like the present.

"I remember." *I remember everything about you.* "And I owe you an apology, don't I?"

"Hmm." Looking thoughtful if not particularly forgiving, she grabbed a napkin and wiped the corner of her mouth. "For what? Not trusting my motives? Making me jump through a few hoops? Reminding me that my hands weren't entirely clean? And anyway, you already apologized."

"No," he said, shining his megawatt examination light inward for once, on his unforgiving nature. It wasn't pretty. "For being a judgmental SOB. How about that?"

"You *were* very hard on me that day."

"I'm sorry."

"I deserved it."

Those three quiet words tied him up in knots because if she thought she deserved his harsh pronouncements about her motives and choices, did she also think she deserved the rape?

"No, you didn't. And you need to understand something."

Hesitating—man, he really hadn't meant to get into this right here and now, over burgers on their first date without even a drink or two to soften the mood—he tried to say it right without putting all his emotions on the line, but screw it. By this point she had to know he was wild about her.

"That day was about me doing a terrible job of keeping my feelings for you in check—"

"I was so sure you hated me."

"Well, don't get me wrong. I tried to hate you. Wanted to hate you. Needed to hate you. I just never managed it. And I didn't understand you."

"You think you understand me now?"

He couldn't tell if the idea amused or horrified her more, but either way she didn't seem to know what to make of him. "I understand now that you were young when you married . . . him." An inverse relationship was growing between his feelings for Kira and his hatred of Kareem; the more he cared about her, the less he could tolerate anything about the bastard, including his memory and his name. "Too young to know what you were doing."

Demons and shadows moved in, crowding out the light in her face, and her lips twisted with self-derision. "You shouldn't make excuses for me."

"And you shouldn't be so hard on yourself. You want to know my theory?"

"Probably not."

"My theory," he continued, ignoring the way her eyes narrowed into chips of brown flint, "is that you married him because it was a better option than staying at home."

She stilled.

"I'm hoping that one day—if you're still speaking to me after this—when you're ready, and you feel comfortable about it, you'll tell me what happened to you."

"Why would you want to turn over those rocks and look underneath?"

"You know why. But I can say it if you want me to."

An impromptu staring contest broke out at that point, with her searching, he supposed, for his motives and him wanting her to see how he felt, and that if she thought he'd turn away from her just because she'd had a few rough spots in her life, she'd better think again.

She looked away first, which made him the winner.

"Wonderful," she muttered. "Dinner with you is like being analyzed by a psychic."

Her little defensive maneuvers weren't going to keep

him away, either. "Not at all," he said. "I'm just making sure we understand each other up front."

Since this portion of the conversation seemed to be making her nervous—she fiddled with a fry, swirling it in ketchup, but didn't eat it—she reverted to something safer. "So that day in the law library, when I hugged you to thank you for helping me, and you pushed me away . . . ?"

"I wanted to swallow you whole," he said simply.

All around them, things began to disappear: the crowd . . . the music . . . the mom and pop ambiance in all its unrelentingly friendly glory. Only Kira was left, with her dark eyes, beautiful soul, and mysterious woman's smile curling the edge of her lips. Christ. If given half the chance, he'd swear he could stare at her until the day he died, never looking away, never getting bored, and never wanting to see anything else.

"You've got a way with words, Dexter."

"I've got a lot of things to say to you."

A pause, and then, softly, "I've got a lot of things to tell you."

At that point in the proceedings, his need to touch her overcame everything else, including things like, say, his general sense of decorum and his sharp dislike of public displays of affection. Maybe he should alter his perspective a little: witnessing PDAs was to be avoided, but participating in them, with Kira, was perfectly acceptable, and if other people had an issue with that, then they were heartless morons with decimal points in front of their IQs.

That decided, he rose up in his chair just enough to lean across the table and plant a lingering kiss on her sweetly smiling lips.

Yeah, he thought, sitting down again and finally

giving a name to the feelings that had tiptoed up on him and then plagued him since the moment he first saw this woman.

He could really get to love this one.

"So," she said, her cheeks flushed and pretty.

"So." Man, he felt like an idiot. He felt like a teenager who'd just squeezed his first pair of breasts. He felt happier than he'd ever felt in his life. "Tell me what you've been doing this whole time."

"Oh, no." She went to work on her fries, smothering them in so much ketchup she'd need a spoon in a minute. "That's more than enough about me. What have you been up to? How's your mom?"

That made him grin, and he wished, suddenly and vehemently, that the two women in his life could meet each other. He'd have to arrange that. "She's great. I saw her a little while ago. She was excited because they were having sundaes and a movie tonight."

Lorraine Brady fidgeted in her wheelchair, fighting a yawn and wishing she had her blanket.

They were in that one big room (the fun room, they called it—or was it the activities room?), all their wheelchairs lined up at the long table for now, but soon, she knew, they'd turn them all around to face the big screen, and they'd watch a movie. A good movie, too, an old black and white with the actor she loved so much. What was his name? Not Spencer Tracy. Not Clark Gable. Well, it would come to her later. This was the movie with the plane at the end, and the Swedish girl with the accent. Oh, what was her name? She couldn't remember much of anything these days, which was why she was here, living with a bunch of old farts who drooled and said the same damn thing over and over again because they'd all lost their minds.

"Excuse me," she said to the nearest woman in uniform. She smiled, too, because it was important to be polite, even when you were an old fart saddled with a wheelchair and a fading mind. The employees worked hard around here, and they deserved nice manners even if they keep it too cold. "Can I have my blanket, please?"

The woman turned. She'd been wiping the gaping mouth of the woman in the wheelchair next to Lorraine's— yeah, they always drooled around here—but now she paused and smiled. Oh, dear. Her face was so familiar. Had they met before? Should she know her name? Why couldn't she remember any names these days?

"Cold again, Lorraine?" Oh, no. They *had* met before, and Lorraine would be embarrassed in a minute when it became obvious she had no earthly clue who this woman was.

"Honey, I haven't been warm since the sixties. Now how about that blanket?"

The woman laughed. "Give me a minute, Lorraine. I need to get Ethel here cleaned up first."

Lorraine frowned and shifted in her chair, wishing the damn thing was more comfortable, but of course when you sat on your bee-hind all day, any chair was bound to make you stiff.

She looked around the crowded room, bored. Now what? And when would they start the . . . the . . . what was the activity tonight? There was an activity tonight, wasn't there? She hoped it wasn't show tunes with Betty again because Betty, frankly, couldn't play the piano to save her life. Bingo would be better, and she wouldn't mind watching a movie, either—

"Is that you, Cousin Lorraine?"

Startled, she glanced up, adjusted her bifocals, and discovered a man standing there. A good-looking young fellow he was, too, with smooth brown skin (she did like nice skin), sleek black hair, and a goatee that gave him a devilish glint. Oh, this one was a rascal, all right. And look at that smile! Dimpled and charming, as though he knew she didn't get many visitors and certainly never had any handsome young men looking for her. Except for Dexter, of course, but he didn't count because he was her son.

She didn't remember him, though. That was always the problem thesc days. Still, she could fake it, because she'd gotten quite good at faking it.

"Hello, honey." Beaming, she extended her hand and discovered he had a nice, firm grip, which was a good sign. You could always tell whatever you needed to know about a person by his grip. "It's so good to see you."

He leaned down to kiss her, his mustache tickling her cheek. Oh, my. He smelled so good. Fresh and clean with a hint of the kind of expensive cologne she'd never been able to get her husband to wear. "It's good to see you, too. And these are for you."

"Oh," she breathed, accepting a beautiful bouquet of pink flowers from him, the ones that had that wonderful scent. What were they called? Daffodils? The name wouldn't come to her, but they were gorgeous. "Thank you. They're my favorite."

"You like roses?" Roses! That was the name! He pulled a chair out from the table, a regular chair, not a wheelchair, and sat next to her, taking her hand between both of his. Oh, he had nice fingers. Strong and clean, with trimmed nails. They were long fingers, too, and she wasn't too old and forgetful to remember what *that* meant, she thought, blushing. "I was hoping they'd brighten your day."

"They have," she assured him. "And how have you been?"

His smile flickered but didn't go out completely. "I've been out of circulation for a while, but now I'm back."

"Oh?"

"I have a few things I need to straighten out."

"Well, I hope you won't be too busy to come back and see me."

Dimpling again, he squeezed her hand. The flirt! She squeezed back because what was the harm and when had she last held hands with a handsome man?

"I'll be back real soon," he assured her. "Don't you worry."

"Have you called Dexter yet?"

"Not yet. I want to surprise him."

Lorraine blinked. Why had he said it like that, with that new edge in his voice? Oh, no—had she done something wrong? Did he realize that she'd forgotten both his name and the fact that she knew him at all? That must be it, because now he was getting up, and his visit was over already, reminding her of the worst thing about having a stroke and losing your mind: no matter how much of your memory might be gone, there was always enough left to know that you'd once been much less alone than you were now.

"You're not leaving?" she asked, tightening her grip on his hand.

"Like I said, I'll be back, Cousin Lorraine. I'll take you for a nice walk in your wheelchair, okay?" He smiled again, and he didn't seem angry after all.

Hope filled her up, pushing some of the dark confusion away, at least for now. They could still be friends and, more importantly, he'd come see her again and break up the monotony of her empty days.

"But I need to go now," he added. "I've got a busy night ahead."

Chapter 17

After dinner, they went to Graeter's for ice cream, where Dexter, true to his word, ordered vanilla, although, to be fair, it did seem to have specks of bean in it, and he did try, a little reluctantly, a spoonful of her chocolate coconut almond chip. They managed to stretch the dessert portion of the evening into two hours, which, combined with the three-hour burger/fry dinner and chat fest they'd already had, made for a grand total of five hours for a first date.

Pretty good for an evening that didn't include sex, she thought, possibly a world record, and that seemed significant.

And then, too soon, they were back in his truck, holding hands but otherwise silent. Maybe his throat was sore from so much talking, but she was silent because she was thinking that even if she saw him again tomorrow morning at seven, that would be a long time to wait. A really long time.

Too soon after that, they were back at his house, standing in between his truck and her car, staring at each other by the light of a reluctant moon hiding behind a gray fluff of clouds, their fingers laced together and down by their sides.

"So," she began, and got no farther.

Her thoughts didn't want to be gathered, probably because her body was so excruciatingly aware of everything about him. His height. The palpable heat radiating from him on this balmy summer night, enough to keep her warm for hours to come, possibly days. The harsh planes of his cheeks . . . the lush softness of his lips . . . the strength of his fingers.

The restrained power of his thighs so close to hers aroused her unbearably, and she wanted to look down, between his legs, to see if she affected him anything like the way he affected her. Did he know that? Did he have the slightest idea that she was hot and slick for him, her dormant body alive again when she'd spent so much time wondering if it would ever recover from Kareem's assault?

"I should get home and check on Max."

"Hmm." His distracted gaze strayed to her lips and stayed there. "I was wondering where he was."

"He's got a little in-out door flap thing, and a fenced yard with a doghouse."

"Oh."

More staring ensued. While she was pondering the compelling mystery of whether his brows had always been so full and expressive, they drifted closer, and the next thing she knew, his arms were around her, bringing her up against the hard wall of his chest and the harder bulge of his groin, and all four of their hands were clasped together behind her back. She sighed helplessly, drifting deeper into the hazy area where she knew it wouldn't be smart to sleep with him tonight but she just couldn't make herself give a damn.

A shudder of restrained need rippled through him, and his voice, when he spoke, was mellow. Husky. "Do you have any idea how good you feel to me right now?"

"I've got some idea, yeah."

"I'm not going to let you go until you promise that I can see you tomorrow. You can't disappear on me for another six months. Okay?"

"You're the genius who told me to take some time."

"I wouldn't have said it if I'd known how I'd feel when you were gone."

"And how is that?"

"Lost," he said, lowering his head.

It was a slow and thorough kiss, unbearably gentle, their lips fitting together and sliding against each other in every wondrous combination possible. He kissed her senseless, until her bones melted into the purest spun gold and her skin shivered with readiness, and then there was more.

Freeing one of his hands and using the other to keep hers in that gentle hold behind her back, he angled her head and kissed her deeper, tasting little nips of her until she mewled like a helpless kitten and her hips began moving of their own accord, thrusting with embarrassing insistence against his.

"Dexter," she whispered, urgent now, desperate, but he let her go and gently set her aside, apparently having more faith in her ability to stand upright that she did. Hazy and bewildered with desire, she put a steadying hand on the hood of her car and hoped she didn't look as wobbly as she felt. "But—"

"Good night, baby. Send me a text to let me know you got home safe, okay?"

"Oh."

She blinked up at him, thoroughly turned out and trying to hide it. Maybe it was the moonlight, or maybe it was her long sexual drought. Most likely it was the man. Whatever it was, she was ready to swear on a stack of Bibles that, if she'd ever been kissed before (and she couldn't remember any previous kisses, so there was some question in her mind), she'd certainly never been kissed like *that*.

"Good night," she managed.

"Good night."

Okay. Now walk, Kira. She headed off around the hood of her car to the driver's side, taking one grudging step away from him, and then two. On the third step, she remembered something important she hadn't told him and glanced over her shoulder to discover him watching her with absolute stillness.

"I had a really good time tonight. In case you didn't notice."

His eyes gleamed warm in the moonlight, intense with emotions she wouldn't dare try to identify. "Oh, yeah?"

There went that crazy flush again, creeping over her cheeks and culminating in a slow burn of a smile that made her feel like a seventh-grader with her first crush. "Oh, yeah."

"Well, that's good. Because this thing we're working on here—it's about more than us hooking up for a little while. You get that, don't you?"

How could she not, when being with him was so easy

and yet so thrilling, like falling off a cliff and landing safely in the place she was always meant to be?

"Yeah." The moment was so delicious she could barely look at him and had to force herself to hold his bright gaze. "I get that."

"And that's okay?"

She paused, giving herself time to consider the various caveats and wherefores she ought to be spewing right now. It was a little soon, after all, and having gone straight from her childhood home into marriage with Kareem, she probably should be taking a good long time to be alone and discover herself, or some such.

Plus, she didn't need to be rescued or protected, and maybe she needed to point that out, because Dexter definitely had a white charger thing going on. Oh, and what did she, an obstetrical nurse, have in common with a DEA agent? Anything? Really? And he was a fine man, strong and honorable, and he deserved a woman who was nothing less.

She, of course, was less.

But she was working on it with the focused ferocity of a woman trying to earn her PhD by the end of the year, and she was determined to get there. And deep inside her was the quiet certainty that, with a little patience and nurturing, this thing between them, whatever it was, could be spectacularly beautiful.

"Yeah," she murmured. "That's okay."

She heard the relieved whoosh of his breath.

"Thank God. Now go home. It's late."

Oh, she had no intention of going anywhere. Not just yet.

"How come you didn't try to get me into the house with you just now?" she wondered. "It probably wouldn't have been that hard. Did you earn a Boy Scout badge in gentlemanly behavior or something?"

"Not at all. And I'm going to be wet-dreaming about you all night, so it's not that I don't want you enough, if that's what you're thinking."

That little nagging doubt had been there, worming its way into the back of her mind. "Then why?"

"I've waited this long for you," he said simply, shrugging. "It won't kill me to wait a little longer. The important thing is to get this right."

There it was: the exact reassurance she'd needed to hear. Now she could go home. Not to sleep; her body was far too tight and agitated for that. But she would rest easy, and maybe he would, too.

"Good night, Dexter."

"Good night, baby."

Where was her phone?

Sending Dexter a text to let him know she'd arrived home safe and sound (and how sweet was it that he wanted confirmation?) was going to be pretty tricky if she couldn't find the darn phone, she thought, letting herself into her small foyer, punching in the code to silence the alarm, and locking the front door behind her. Guided by the lamp on the console, which she always kept lit when she was gone because she hated even the possibility of coming home to a dark house, she tossed her keys into the braided wicker basket and checked the charging valet right next to it.

No phone.

Hmm. That was weird, but something weirder was nagging at the edges of her consciousness.

The house, which was a pretty little three-bedroom bungalow with dormer windows and those atmospheric slanted ceilings on the second floor, was way too quiet, with no welcoming barks, jingling collar tags, or clicking toenails to greet her. If Max was in the yard when she got home, his normal procedure was to run back inside because his super-duper canine senses of smell and hearing always announced her arrival way ahead of time, and usually before she could climb out of the car.

All of which begged the question: where the hell was Max?

Maybe he'd run off, taking the phone with him in case of emergency.

Nonplussed, she walked through the living and dining rooms, checking all his usual napping spots on her way into the kitchen.

"Maxie? Don't hide from Mommy."

The place, which she'd painstakingly decorated and quite loved, was decorated in a style that could best be described as early international bazaar. Neutral sofa and leather chairs, yeah, but she had colorful scarves draped here and there, and an eclectic mix of Asian, African, and American pottery and sculptures. The dining room table was Shaker, but the bowls and candleholders atop it were Native American, in deep browns and reds, with splashes of blue here and there.

Every single thing in the house was bought and paid for with money earned from the sweat of her hardworking brow. No drugs had been sold to buy this furniture, no children corrupted, jailed, or killed. Every single rug, curtain, and, hell, fork, knife, and spoon, was chosen because it caught her eye and she loved it. Some things were expensive, but some were from the sale end caps at Target, and all were equally precious to her.

Sometimes, in unguarded moments, a flash of her past came back to haunt her. Kareem telling her he didn't like the handwoven Peruvian blanket she'd found, for example, and she'd therefore have to return it because it didn't match his vision for Casa Gregory, his shrine to all things Kareem. Ditto with the Oriental ginger-jar lamps, Turkish rugs, and coffee mugs made by local potters. He, meanwhile, had populated the house with whatever overpriced black leather or lacquer monstrosities caught his eye, most of them Egyptian.

There was nothing Egyptian in this house, nor would there ever be.

There was also no Max.

"Maxie? Come here, puppy."

A quick circuit through the kitchen turned up nothing, not even a few telltale short brown hairs on the counter near the bread box, which he liked to raid when her back was turned. She'd looped back around and was about to go upstairs to see if he'd climbed into the dirty clothes hamper in the closet and fallen asleep up there again, when she caught a flash of red out of the corner of her eye.

Her phone. On the counter, next to the bowl of fruit.

Again: weird.

She was very meticulous about her things, probably just a couple of notches short of some variety of OCD. She didn't like dust, clutter, or dog hair, and as a busy career woman now, she didn't have time to spend hunting down her keys or her phone. Hence, the setup on the console in the hall. Things went in their place, period, and the place for her phone was either on the charger, in her pocket, or in her purse.

Yet here it was, on the counter, and the explanation was obvious: she'd been so ridiculously wired and distracted about the possibility of seeing Dexter that she'd gotten sloppy. She supposed she was lucky that the poor phone wasn't in the freezer, frozen into a block of ice by her negligent and thoughtless hands.

Well, that was one mystery solved, but where was— Oh, God.

The second her reaching fingers touched the phone, she felt the crawling prickle up her spine of a ghost walking over her grave. And it wasn't a harmless ghost in passing like, say, Casper, not at all. It was the yawning and malevolent chill of . . .

Of what, *Kira?*

Nothing, that's what.

She was being stupid, obviously, afraid of the boogeyman now in her own house. *Idiot.* Could she be any stupider?

And yet she snatched her hand away from that phone because she didn't want to touch it. Couldn't make herself touch it.

The silence closed in on her, ringing discordantly in her ears. Had she heard something? Was that it? Backing into the corner where the counter stretched out into the island, she faced the room, straining her ears for a sound that never came. She didn't hear the rubberized squeak of a stealthy footstep, the protest of an elderly floorboard, or even the benign hiccup of the central air unit as it switched on.

Which was all well and good—great, yeah, sure—but

now she faced out into the dining room and living room beyond, and all she could see in every direction were shadowy spaces where someone—*who, Kira?*—could hide.

Behind the silk drapes . . . crouched on the other side of the ottoman . . . next to the sofa.

Hiding place. Hiding place. Hiding place.

Her cozy little house was, suddenly, full of them, and terror had reached out to wrap its hard fingers around her neck. Was someone here? In her house? Watching her? The flesh of her bare arms rose up in bumps, as though she could feel the slow crawl of someone's gaze over her body, and that kicked off a tremble in her knees that quickly turned into a shake.

The shaking pissed her off.

What the hell was she doing? Cowering in her own kitchen? For what? Because the phone was—*what*? Too red? Too shiny? What would she do next? Hide in the closet with her blanket over her head?

They had talked about this, she and her therapist. They'd talked about the ways that Kareem still dominated her life, and how she'd surrendered too much of her power to him. Wasn't this a shining example of that? Scared shitless for no reason, even though there were no strange sounds in her house and the alarm was on, as normal, when she came in. For months she'd thought she'd crept farther away from her old life, leaving the darkness behind her, where it belonged, but here, staring her in the face, was the truth in all its brutal glory:

She was still the same scared and broken girl she'd been the night Kareem raped her. Still the same scared and broken girl she'd been when her father—

No. She wouldn't go there, and she wouldn't give any man that kind of power over her (and she had to *give* it, didn't she, because wasn't Oprah always mentioning that Eleanor Roosevelt quote: "No one can make you feel inferior without your consent"?) ever again.

Starting now.

Furious with herself—how many times would the past ambush her and try to drag her back, kicking and screaming?—she snatched the freaking phone, the cause of her mini-breakdown, off the counter and shoved it into her pocket, where it belonged.

And guess what, dummy? It was just a phone. Not a vortex into impenetrable darkness or any other terrible thing. Duh.

But Max was still missing, and she should probably give the house a thorough look-see before heading into the yard, because he did like that hamper and—

From outside the kitchen door came the muffled but unmistakable sound of a bark. Max's bark.

"Oh, you silly dog."

Muttering to herself, her tortured knees now weak with relief rather than shaking with that formless fear, she unlocked the back door, which was one of those deals with curtained windowpanes at the top, and swung it open, flipping the switch for the floodlight as she went so she could see the furry little fool and get him into the house.

To her consternation, the yard stayed dark.

A re-flip of the switch did nothing.

Max, meanwhile, barked again, from the general direction of an enormous pine in the far corner of the yard. The thing had low-hanging branches that stretched out from the tree in a ten-foot radius, and it wasn't too hard to imagine Max getting his collar snared on one of them and being stuck.

Still muttering, she swung back around, to the kitchen's junk drawer, and found the mega lantern she kept there for power outages. No little flashlight for her, thank you; this baby had enough wattage to steer storm-tossed ships to shore if need be.

Clicking it on, she shone it in the direction of the barks, and, sure enough, there was Max, his brown eyes reflecting eerily back at her from among the needle-brush branches of the tree, waiting to be rescued.

Only he was on the other side of the split-rail fence, where the yard gave way to woods and then, on down the hill, to a creek that she knew was there but had never explored.

The other side of the fence.

How the hell did he get out?

There were three gates, all of them, she saw at a quick glance, closed and secure. There were no signs of a freshly dug hole under the chicken wire filler, and Max had never been much of a digger, anyway.

The fence was tall, coming up to her shoulder, and Max had the strong but short legs of a beagle. It was possible that he'd chased a squirrel and, in his excitement, vaulted the fence, much to his own surprise, but she'd never seen him do any such amazing feats.

Unless someone had come and taken him out, he should be here, on the side of the fence where he belonged, sleeping like the dead in his doghouse the way he always did when she was gone for a few hours. But her nearest neighbors were elderly, with no interest in a dog other than to make sure he didn't escape his leash and run through their flower beds, and the nearest kids on the street were five or six, way too young for any pranks like dog-napping.

And yet, there he inexplicably was, and that fear was creeping up on her again, ready to paralyze.

Shake it off, girl, she told herself. *Shake it off.*

Propelled by her jangled nerves, she hustled down the steps to the gate nearest Max, opened it for him, and stooped to catch him when he scurried straight at her.

"You crazy dog." Her words muffled against his sleek little forehead as she smothered the undeserving canine with kisses, she kept him tight in the crook of her arm when she swung back around to go inside. "Thanks for scaring me half to death—"

She pivoted to go back inside, and the lantern, moving with her but otherwise forgotten in her hand, swung its beam around to a cluster of mature trees at the property line on the side of her yard. From the corner of her eye, just at the edge of both her vision and the lantern's wedge of illumination, she thought she saw a large shadow detach itself from the base of a tree and slip deeper into the darkness.

Chapter 18

Like a snake's tail glimpsed just as it slithers into the cover of a pile of decomposing fall leaves, the sight came and went so quickly she could almost convince herself that she'd imagined it. There was no warning of any kind, no telltale crash of, say, hooves through the undergrowth or the flash of a fat white tail to suggest a deer.

Only the unnatural stillness of foliage that didn't rustle and a dog that didn't bark, and Max always barked at deer.

Oh, God. Oh, God, please. What was that?

Kira didn't give the creeping horror the chance to glue her feet to the ground; she ran. Screw it. This was no time for brave acts like demanding to know who (or what) was there, or shining the light directly at the spot to see what she could see, or (how stupid would that be?) plunging into the woods to give chase like some tragically misguided horror movie teen who wasn't long for the world.

Oh, hell no.

She wanted to live, and there was no room for anything else, including embarrassment. If that indistinguishable shape later turned out to be some taller-than-usual feral dog, then she'd deal with the sheepishness.

Between now and then, though, she was outta there.

Sprinting with the bursts of speed she'd shown as one of the stars on the high school track team, her heart pumping enough blood to fuel her for a marathon, she streaked across the yard, vaulted up the stairs, and banged back into the kitchen, kicking the door shut behind her and unceremoniously dropping Max and the lantern to free up her hands. When the door was locked, bolted, and triple-checked, she collapsed against it, a stitch searing up her side, and tried to master the monstrous fear, which still had her shaking even inside the relative safety of her house.

Max settled at her feet, whining up into her face with avid concern, which didn't particularly comfort her. What did it say about your mental health when even your dog thought you were crazy?

"What was that, Maxie?" she panted.

Max cocked his head. If he had any answers, he chose not to share them, the little bastard.

Was that a person she'd seen? Had she seen anything at all? If there was something, why hadn't Max barked? Should she call the police? What would she say if she did? *Hello, nine-one-one emergency? Yes, hello. I thought I just saw a shadow in the shadowy trees. Can you send a SWAT team right away?*

No, she thought, massaging her chest to get her heart to settle back down. She couldn't do that.

Maybe, much as she hated to admit it, this was the perfect time to use one of those deep-breathing exercises the shrink had taught her. Before she went into full cardiac arrest. Straightening, she put a hand to her belly and tried to remember the procedure because, yeah, she was so wired over the something she thought she'd seen that she couldn't get her freaking lungs to work.

In, Kira. Now slowly out. Again, deeper. Breeeathe.

Again. And again.

See? This wasn't so—

From the depths of her pocket, her phone vibrated, and the unexpected movement sent jolts of hysteria spiraling in every direction.

Kira went off like a rocket, screaming before she could stop herself.

By the second ring, Kira had peeled herself off the ceiling, and by the third she'd almost settled back into her skin. There was nothing she could do about the jittery adrenaline surge that made her hands fumble as she liberated the phone from the depths of her pocket, though, and she seemed unlikely ever to relax or sleep again.

"Hello?"

There was a long, irritating pause, and then a slurred voice, heavy with both alcohol and amusement, came on the line. "*Someone's* having a rough night."

Kerry. Perfect. Just the thing she needed to kill the last of the rosy glow remaining from her date with Dexter. Had she really had such a lovely evening tonight? Her hours with him now felt like they belonged on the other side of an ice age.

"Hi," she said, trying to inject enough enthusiasm into her voice to stop her from sounding like she'd just had her dinner interrupted by a telemarketer. "Are you okay?"

"'Course I'm okay. I'm great. Why do you ask?"

"Because you sound like you've been drinking." Sliding the filmy curtains aside, she peered through the window over the sink, trying to detect movement out in the yard. Seeing none, she checked the door again. Still locked. "And you know you shouldn't dial while drunk. You'll probably say something we'll both regret later."

"Oh, I plan to," he assured her.

"Kerry, please." Looping back around to the front door for a final check, she found it locked to her satisfaction and headed upstairs, Max trotting along at her heels. "It's been a long day for both of us. Can't we talk in the morning instead?"

"Don't you want to hear from me, baby?" he wondered, and she had to choke back the *don't call me "baby"* that wanted to shoot out of her mouth. "You told me to stay in touch, didn't you? Well, now I'm in touch."

He'd been a little too much in touch, if you asked her, and she regretted not checking the phone's display before answering his call. This was the sixth or seventh time he'd reached out since Kareem's death, and she was starting to be sorry Alexander Graham Bell had ever invented the telephone. He called her landline; he called her cell; he called at three A.M. or whenever the urge hit him; he texted. Each time he sounded a little bit worse, a little bit more unraveled. If he kept up at this rate, she wasn't sure what would be left of him by the end of the summer.

"You promised you wouldn't drink so much. How's, ah, how's the job search coming? Any luck?"

Another harsh sound, this one more of a snort than a laugh. Same bitterness. "Finding a job is kind of tricky, precious, when you've got a sketchy résumé and you're still under threat of indictment."

Yeah. She'd figured, but hope sprang eternal, didn't it? Upstairs now, she did a quick check of her closet and under her bed—no boogeymen—and then repeated it in the second and third bedrooms (the office and home gym, respectively). No ghosts, demons, or poltergeists, thank God, not even an aggressive dust bunny skittering across the polished hardwood floors. The house thus secured, she went back to her bedroom to get ready for bed.

"How are you spending your days?"

"Thinking of you," he said softly.

That's what she got for asking. No good deed went unpunished, did it?

"Kerry," she began helplessly, the husky yearning in his voice doing a number on her, the way it always did. "Please don't—"

"Don't you ever think about me?" When her answer took too long in coming—because, hey, what could she say? *I never think about you romantically, but I sure hope you have a nice life and never hit and kill someone while drinking and driving*—he heaved the kind of sigh that sounded like the last breath he'd ever take. "Don't you ever *remember*, Kira? Because the memories are eating me alive."

"I remember," she said reluctantly, because she did, even if she didn't care to trot the memories out and admire them like a collection of old photos.

Oh, she remembered.

She remembered the abject bewilderment quickly followed by bottomless despair upon discovering the man she'd married, the one she'd loved and thought of as her knight in polished armor, was not a businessman—or not just a businessman, she should say—but a suspected drug kingpin who sold drugs to children and ruined lives like a ground zero of contamination with a fifty-mile radius. She remembered Kareem's first trial and subsequent conviction on money-laundering charges, and the nights she'd spent missing him from their home and her bed while simultaneously hating herself for that unforgivable weakness.

There'd been the uncertainty, because what could she do then, a college student who'd earned half her degree? Where could she go? Home to the parents who'd warned her not to marry Kareem in the first place and would be only too happy to sing the we-told-you-so chorus to her for the rest of her life? To the father who'd—

No. There were some things she wouldn't remember. Period.

During this period, one of the worst in her life, Kerry had been there. He'd checked in on Kira. Asked about her life. Reached out to her. Helped her with her trickier classes, including anatomy and physiology. Comforted her when she'd been ripe for the comfort.

She remembered that first touch of his that crossed a line, that skimming stroke of her cheeks while he stared at her in a way no employee should ever look at the boss's wife, with heat and raw longing. The reverence with which he'd said her name. The glide of his lips against hers and the taste of him in her mouth.

She remembered.

Since neither of them fancied the repercussions if Kareem found out—and even from federal prison, there wasn't much that Kareem didn't find out—they resisted the lure of each other. For a while. And then, on the night of her twenty-first birthday, when she should have been celebrating with friends her own age and was instead rattling around alone in a mansion, widowed by her husband's prison sentence—not that she wanted that husband back anyway—Kerry showed up, and they didn't bother resisting.

During two stolen hours while Wanda was out playing bridge with her foursome, Kira and Kerry made love, hot and hard against the wall in the kitchen and then, later, slow and sweet in Kira's bedroom. When he left that night, there was a new hardness in her heart to go along with her sated body—a *take that, Kareem, you bastard,* that did her a world of good, but she already knew she'd made a terrible mistake, and not because Kareem would kill them both if he ever found out. It was because she could see, even then, the helpless, hopeless love shining in Kerry's eyes, and she'd seen it there ever since.

That hadn't stopped her from letting the affair continue for another month, mind you, but the guilt for what she was doing to Kerry had ridden her pretty hard.

"I remember," she told him. "But I've moved past it. You should, too."

"Don't you think I would if I knew how?"

There was no answer for that, no comfort she could give him.

"Kira," he said, and she didn't know if it was his voice breaking up, or the connection.

"We both have a new start, Kerry," she interjected before he could finish his thought and tear another little piece off her heart. "It's a miracle that he never found out. It's a miracle that he died and set us free. We can't waste this chance—"

"Why?" Kira jumped at this outburst, almost as though the sudden unraveling snap of his emotions and temper had reached through the phone to lash her across the face. "Why can't you love me, Kira? Why don't you say it?"

"I don't want to go there, Kerry. Why do you keep pushing me—"

"Do you think you're doing me any favors?" he cried. "Why don't you be a woman and tell me what I need to hear?"

That was it, then, she thought, swiping away a stray tear. She was all out of excuses and diversions. Nothing to do now but be honest.

"Because," she told him gently, "I could never love a man who chose to be a criminal. And if I could have, it would have been Kareem, not you."

There it was: the truth, as raw as she could make it.

Several seconds of excruciating silence followed, and then he sighed, harsh and resigned and almost . . . relieved?

"Thank you for telling me," he said.

"Kerry—" she began, as though there was any possible way to mitigate the damage she'd just done.

"I'm hoping that one day, before I die," he said, his words tired and slurred, every one a monumental effort for him to say and a bigger effort for her to hear, "I can do something honorable. Maybe then you'll have a higher opinion of me."

"Kerry."

He'd already hung up.

Chapter 19

Kira, awash with guilt, as though she'd swan-dived into a deep and shimmering pool of *This Is Your Fault,* tossed the silent phone onto the bed. The despair she'd heard in Kerry's voice was her fault, and her fault went back a good long way. She never should have turned to him for comfort, never should have slept with him, never should have let the affair continue. The biggest *never*? She never should have told him the truth just now, even though he was begging for it.

Drained, she collapsed onto her big queen-sized sleigh bed, propping herself up against the pillows, her butt connecting with dog tail in the process. Max, who'd been sprawled in an unauthorized spot, his belly exposed and paws in the air, yelped and gave her that reproachful *watch what you're doing!* look.

She was so not moved. "Get off the bed."

Max flipped over, whining his tale of woe. It was his ongoing lament about how comfortable he'd been, how there was room enough for both of them on the bed, and how she was an unmitigated tyrant to exile him to the floor.

Having heard the whole routine before, many times, she didn't dignify it now with a comment. Instead, she snapped her fingers and pointed to the floor, and he went. Grudgingly and with many muttered hard feelings, but he went.

Flopping back to a spread-eagle position, she stared up at the ceiling fan's slow revolutions and thought about Kerry. Maybe telling him the truth hadn't been such a bad thing after all; maybe she'd set him free, although that seemed like an awfully soap-opera-ish way to put it. Maybe she'd told him what he needed to hear to get over her. And he needed to get over her as much as he needed to stop drinking.

Would he, though? There'd been an awful hopelessness in him tonight, so strong she could almost feel the lead weight of it through the phone. She wanted to reach out to him, help somehow, but that was a major mixed signal incompatible with helping him get over her, wasn't it? Besides—what did she think she could do? Force some hospital to hire him?

What was her responsibility here? What could she reasonably do?

Give him several days to digest their conversation, that's what.

Then she'd call him next week, maybe encourage him to move out West somewhere and start a practice in a small town that needed a doctor. She couldn't make him do anything, of course, but at least she'd sleep better at night, knowing she'd tried.

Great. She had a plan. Time for bed.

She reluctantly got up off the downy comfort of her duvet and pillows and headed to her reading chair in the corner for her jammies, a cute little pink shorts set from Target—

Uh-oh.

Her jammies, which she'd left neatly folded on the chair's ivory cushion this morning, were now on the floor in a heap. She stared down at them, that unwelcome prickle of nerves crawling up the back of her neck and into her scalp for about the millionth time since she got home.

She had folded her jammies and left them on the chair, hadn't she? Then how—?

In answer, Max trotted over, snuffled at the jammies with his impressive black nose, and then sprawled across them and closed his eyes, as though she'd laid them on the floor for his special sleeping pleasure.

Huh.

Max had done this, then. Of course he had. Sometimes he got into clothes and other things he shouldn't, and he'd probably made this little nest for himself while she was out. See? Mystery solved.

Except that she couldn't shake that feeling of simmering dread, which was silly—she knew it was silly. But Kareem had always had a fascination with her nightclothes. He'd bought her these ridiculously expensive silk nightgowns, and she'd worn them because they were beautiful and decadent. She wouldn't lie. And her clothes in a heap on the floor reminded her that Kareem used to pick up her nightgowns. Smell them. Rub his face against them.

Right this second, she could conjure up the image of him by the old chair, his hands full of silk, his eyes full of heat, and the image, like all images of Kareem, was clear as day.

But Kareem was dead, and no part of him, not even his memory, was allowed in her new bedroom.

Right. Shower, Kira—

The phone vibrated on the bed. She didn't jump, shriek, or even wince, and she considered this normal reaction to a ringing phone a personal triumph worthy of a merit badge or some such honor. A quick glance at the display showed that it was someone whose voice she'd actually be glad to hear:

Dexter.

"Hi." Shower forgotten, she dropped onto the edge of the bed.

He skipped the official greeting. "So you are not, in fact, lying dead in a ditch by the side of the road. Good to know. Have a great night."

"The text!" She slapped a hand to her oh-so-forgetful forehead. "I'm sorry."

"Ah," he said, and she could hear the dry amusement in his voice, "how worried should I be that you've forgotten me already? Mildly, moderately, or greatly?"

"I haven't forgotten you. Max got out of the fence somehow—"

"Somehow?" His law enforcement instincts, apparently, made him suspicious. "Did he dig a hole or did someone let him out?"

"I wish I knew," she admitted. "He didn't go far, though. He was just at the tree line, so he's back."

"You have a woods?"

Boy, did she. A remnant of the fear she'd felt earlier when she saw . . . whatever it was that she saw moving among the trees crawled over her flesh with prickly legs. "Yeah."

She'd meant to keep her *yeah* a little more upbeat than

that, but it was too late now because he'd already heard the strain in her voice.

"What?" he demanded.

"I thought I saw—" it seemed so ridiculous to say it aloud in the soothing comfort of her well-lit bedroom— "something move."

"What, a person?"

"I didn't get a good look."

"I'm on my way." She heard the jingle of keys and pictured him snatching them off the counter on his way to the truck. "Make sure the doors are locked and I'll be there in a—"

That was crazy. Not that it didn't do her heart a world of good to know he was there and available if she needed him, but, really, there was no way she'd drag the poor man out of his house at this hour for what was surely a wild goose chase.

"Don't even think about it," she told him. "I'm fine."

"But—"

"The alarm is on, the doors are locked, and the windows are closed. I've already checked. And it was probably my imagination anyway. So you stay where you are."

"I can be there in five minutes. I'll just do a walk-around and check—"

"You will not. I'm fine. I can take care of myself. I don't need you to rescue me. What do you think I've been doing for the last six months?"

"How about we both take care of you together?"

Her pulse gave one of those delightful little surges. Wow. Could she be any crazier about this man? "How about you go to sleep and have a good night?"

He grumbled something just intelligible enough for

her to know it wasn't G rated, which made her laugh. "What was that? I didn't quite catch it."

"I don't want anything to happen to you," he told her. "Not now."

Warm and wriggly delight filled her up, making her grin so wide she was grateful he wasn't there to see, and then came the confession she'd never have the courage to make with him standing in the same room.

"You have a real way of making me melt into a puddle of chocolate, you know that, Dexter?"

"You have a real way of driving me out of my mind."

"In a good way, or a bad way?"

"In every way," he told her.

She sighed, drowsy now, and, better than that, happy. The last several months alone had led her to contentment and peace, which were wonderful. This, with him, whatever it was, was more. Better. Amazing.

"So I'm going to see you tomorrow, right?" she reminded him. "What're we doing?"

"It's a surprise. Wear your workout clothes—something skimpy if you have it—"

She laughed.

"And your gym shoes. I'll pick you up at eleven."

"Sounds mysterious. Where are you taking me?"

"On an adventure," he told her.

"You cannot be serious," Kira said.

"We've been through this already," Dexter replied. "I am serious."

Kira stared up at the rock-climbing wall, a monstrous gray slab roughly the size and shape of one side of a small office building, which meant that it was, yes, forty freaking feet high. Footholds of various colors and sizes jutted out from it, making it look, from a distance, as though it had been slashed and assaulted with several gallons of particularly violent paint.

Several people, all of whom had to be either idiots or insane, she couldn't tell which, were already attached to ropes and harnesses and climbing on this wall and others, some of which leaned at odd angles, as if climbing a straight wall wasn't tricky enough. They were secured at the bottom by other people—belayers, Dexter had said—who held the ropes and presumably made sure no one plummeted to his or her death with a nasty splat.

This, it turned out, was Dexter's idea of an adventure.

She'd been thinking more along the lines of a long ride on a bike trail culminating in a picnic by the river.

"Black folks don't climb walls for no reason," she pointed out.

"Sure we do. And there are lots of reasons."

"Name one."

"I'll name several. It's great exercise. It's a fun way for us to work together and get to know each other—"

"I thought we'd already been through a fire or two together."

He dimpled but otherwise ignored this salient point. "Depending on who goes first, we can admire each other's asses."

That made her grin. He'd worn a boring but somehow thrilling combo of gray T-shirt and black shorts, both of which showcased his mouth-watering body to perfection. Sinewy and lean, he had the sculpted arms and legs of someone who took his work at the gym seriously. His shirt was just thin enough for her to appreciate his taut belly and the broad strength of his shoulders. As for his butt and thighs, well—

"You do have a particularly fine ass," she told him.

"I know. And climbing this wall is a great challenge. That's the main thing."

"So is helicopter skiing, but you won't catch me doing that, either."

They faced off, shoulders squared, and she tipped her chin up to a belligerent angle so he'd be perfectly clear on her position: she wasn't gonna, and he couldn't make her. But then he played dirty, raising a brow and letting his lips curl into an unmistakable smirk.

"You're not scared, are you?"

Those were fighting words to which there was only ever one appropriate answer: "Of course I'm not scared."

"Great. Let's go then," he said, gesturing toward the Wall of Death.

She glared at him and then glared at the wall, trying to decide which she hated worse at that moment. It was a tie. "Why do we have to do this?"

Those were the magic words. He softened, stroking her under the chin with those gentle fingers. "You don't have to do anything you don't want to, ever again. But I hope you decide you want to because this wall is a metaphor for everything you've been doing. If you can climb this wall even if you don't like heights—"

"I hate heights."

"And you can choose and build the life you want for yourself, then I hope you know—there's nothing you can't do."

Was that true? It sure felt true, with his encouraging presence here beside her and that complete faith shining so warmly in his eyes, as though she actually deserved it. And of course Oprah, if she were here, would tell her to face the challenge.

"Let's get this over with," she said grimly.

That killer grin of his dawned across his face, all dimples and boyish enthusiasm. "That's my girl."

That smile touched her heart. Squeezed it in a way she didn't think anything else ever had. Unexpected emotions rose up and she had to look away from this growing thing between them. She didn't think she was ready and yet she couldn't sprint toward it fast enough.

As always, his raptor-sharp eyes saw everything, and his smile dimmed a watt or two. "What?"

She stepped closer and lowered her voice, teasing him because it felt so right and because he'd earned a little needling. "You know," she murmured, "if I fall four stories to my death, we'll never get to make love one day, will we?"

His face sobered into grim determination. "Don't worry. I plan to throw my body between yours and the ground if I need to."

Chapter 20

Dexter stood at the top of the wall, where he'd been for the last fifteen minutes, peering over at Kira with his breath held and his muscles and nerves stretched to the snapping point. Was waiting for your child to be born, watching your wife do all the work, anything like this? Because, if so, he wasn't sure he was man enough for the job.

Hot and scared, crabby and determined, she had about four feet to go, and she wouldn't give up. There'd been several intermediate spots where she could have made a graceful exit from the playing field without going for the summit, but she'd clung to the rocks like a determined and particularly beautiful mountain goat, her fingertips white with strain and her strong legs shaking with the effort.

He'd never admired her more.

"Come on, baby," he told her, trying to sound encouraging rather than worried or overprotective. "You can do it."

Leaning her sweaty face back, she shot him a look of deepest loathing that would have made him smile if he hadn't been so sure she'd vault to the top and rip his face off if he did.

"Shut. Up. I don't want to hear your voice right now. Or ever."

"Be nice."

"You do understand," she panted, choosing another toehold and settling her weight on it with painstaking care, "that when I get up there, I'm going to push you off the edge. So you should start your prayers now."

He laughed and took another sip from his water bottle. Her belayer, meanwhile, called up from the ground. "How're you doing, Kira?"

"Screw you," she called.

That was it. Planting her palms on the top, she gave herself enough of a boost to swing one leg, and then the other, over. Whooping with delight, Dexter grabbed her under her arms and hefted her to her wobbly feet, both of their safety harnesses jangling.

"You did it!"

"I did it?" There was one arrested moment where she couldn't seem to believe it herself, and then she lit up as though the sun, moon, and stars had all been condensed and concentrated in her face. "I did it!"

A little victory shimmy followed, and then she fell, laughing and triumphant, into his arms, and he held her tight and safe while more of himself than he'd ever shared with another person poured out of his mouth.

"I'm so proud of you, Kira. I knew you could do it. Do you know how amazing you are? Huh? You're amazing. Did you know that?"

"I'm not amazing. I'm just too stubborn to give up." Pulling back, she glowed up at him. "Thank you for bringing me."

"Anytime."

"Are you going to feed me lunch now? It's the least you can do."

"Absolutely."

"After we shower first. One of us smells like a farm animal."

"Whatever you say."

After the laborious process of extracting themselves from all the safety equipment, they went downstairs and disappeared into their respective locker rooms, meeting up half an hour later in the lobby. Fresh and clean now, her hair shower-wet, fragrant, and curly, she wore a pretty little tank top and a flowered skirt that was quite nice but unfortunately covered more of her spectacular long legs than he'd hoped. He supposed he'd been spoiled by a morning spent surreptitiously ogling her gleaming skin, shapely thighs, and tight ass in her shorts, so he'd have to get over it.

"Hey." Holding out a hand because he couldn't seem to stop touching her and didn't see any point to trying, he reeled her in for a kiss on her smiling cheek as they approached the double glass doors to the parking lot. "What do you have a taste for—"

"Jesus Christ, Brady. What the hell are you doing?"

Shit. It was Jayne Morrison, exuding so much horror you'd think she'd caught him trying to have sex with an inflatable doll in public. Drop-jawed, with her gym bag slung over her shoulder, she stared at the two of them. Beside him, he could feel Kira shrinking into her skin, trying to become invisible. That pissed him off.

"What's up, Jayne?" he said, lacing his voice with a liberal amount of frost. They were cool, he and Jayne. Professional friends who went back many cases and many years, and it was she who'd introduced him to rock climbing after several of the attorneys in her office came to the facility for a team-building exercise or some such. He and Jayne had never had a problem, but that might change real quick here because he had a zero tolerance policy for anyone who made Kira feel bad. "You forget your manners?"

Jayne's mouth snapped shut and her brows flattened. "Mrs. Gregory," she began.

"Her name's *Kira*," he snapped.

Jayne ignored him. "Would you mind if I had a word with Brady?"

"Of course not." Kira kept her tone upbeat and her smile firmly in place, but he could tell by the new droop in her shoulders and the flush creeping over her cheeks that she was rattled by the appearance of the woman who'd prosecuted her husband. Ashamed.

Fuck that.

"I'll just wait over here."

Kira went back into the lobby, selected a bench and picked out a magazine. He and Jayne went outside, already snarling at each other.

"What the hell are you doing?" she demanded.

"None of your fucking business."

"Taking up with the drug kingpin's wife? Are you serious right now?"

Choking on his anger, Dexter put his fists on his hips, stared out at the cars and tried to think about something other than his black rage at this woman who was, after all, a friend.

"What's your issue, Jayne?"

"My issue?" Aghast, she had to work on getting the

words past her lips. "My issue is that you've got a serious conflict going here—"

"Her piece of shit husband is dead. Conflict solved."

"—and don't you deserve better than that?"

His temper slipped another fifty notches. "Better than what?"

"Better than a woman who married a drug dealer and happily lived off the very nice proceeds for years. She was complicit, Brady—"

"There was never any evidence that she did anything illegal, and you don't know a goddamn thing about her."

"And you do?"

He would not explain his certainty about Kira, or his relationship with her, to anyone, nor would he be shamed or allow Kira to be shamed for mistakes she'd made and was trying to overcome.

"What do you want, Jayne?"

"I want you to *think,* Brady. What if she's still got ties to Kareem's crowd? You think they'll be happy about this? You think they won't use that against you any way they can? Maybe come after you? You're crossing a line—you've got to get that."

Oh, he got it. He just didn't care.

"I don't give a damn." He was already pivoting to go back for Kira, Jayne and her dire concerns dismissed from his consciousness because he didn't have room for negativity in his life. Not now, not with Kira in it. "And you need to stay out of my way."

Kerry rolled over and groaned, in no particular hurry to begin this—or any—day. His head was a pounding shriek of pain. For extra fun, his mouth was dead-skunk dry and nasty, and the goddamn sun sliced through his eyeballs the way those fancy TV infomercial knives cut through ripe tomatoes. He might have spent the rest of the day in bed and ridden it out, but his need to pee had, finally, overcome all other considerations, and if he didn't act now, he'd soon be lying in a wet bed.

And he wondered why Kira didn't want anything to do with him. Big mystery there.

He staggered into the bathroom, dick in hand before he had the seat up. Letting loose with his stream—ah, shit, that was better—he dropped his head back with relief and made a terrible mistake: he opened his eyes just enough to catch a glimpse of himself in the mirror.

The sight threatened to freeze his piss midsplash, but then he didn't need the red-eyed, haggard-fleshed confirmation to know the ugly truth: he was skirting the thin line between a guy who shouldn't drink and a drunk.

And, hell, maybe he was only fooling himself about which side of the line he was on.

Kira didn't love him. Had never loved him. Couldn't love him.

You'd think that a fifth of Jack chased with five or six Ambien would wash away that memory, but no such luck. He was beginning to think that Kareem was the fortunate one. Kira didn't love him, either, but at least the MF'er was dead and didn't have to worry about what he was missing.

Five minutes after he started peeing, he finally ran out of urine. Great. That hurdle cleared, he was free to start thinking about what he wanted to do today.

Option 1: He could start drinking now.

Option 2: He could start drinking later. In, say, an hour or so.

Option 3: He could clean himself up and think about being a doctor again because, hey, maybe the market had changed since he passed out last night and there was a shortage of former criminals who now wanted to walk the straight and narrow.

Man, he just cracked himself up.

Anyway, it was Saturday, right? Yeah, Saturday. No career building for him today.

No more dialing while drunk, either. Kira had finally told him the truth, he'd accepted it, and it was time to move on. End of story.

So. That just left the drinking options, and there was no time like the present to start, was there? Except that he'd drunk everything last night.

Which meant a field trip to the liquor store was in order.

Five minutes later, he was dressed and ready, headed down the hall to the entry with his keys in hand, and he—what the hell was that?

Lying on the carpet near the front door was an envelope, which was weird because he didn't get much mail, and it was made of some heavy, expensive ivory linen paper, which was weirder, because God knew no one he knew had any class.

He picked it up, his skin already doing a slow crawl.

Inside was a single-sided card typed in one of those fonts that made it look like calligraphy, elegant and beautiful except for what it said:

Did you think you'd get away with it?

Kira studied her wine list for as long as possible, and then, when Dexter still showed no inclination to talk, turned her gaze to the Ohio River, sparkly blue today rather than its other usual colors, surly gray or muddy brown. They sat on the terrace of a pretty little café on the Kentucky side, with market umbrellas protecting their faces from the sun and the Cincinnati skyline laid out for them to enjoy. Not that anyone had enjoyed much of anything at this lunch.

Dexter glared down at his menu. If she squinted just right, she was almost positive she could see slow swirls of steam coming out of his ears.

"You're going to have to help me out here," she told him.

Looking up, he made a valiant effort to rouse himself out of his dark thoughts, blinking and working at a smile. "How's that?"

"When you're in a mood, should I: a) be my usual charming and witty self and cheer you up; b) maintain a silent vigil until you're ready to talk; or c) pick a fight to help you blow off steam?"

This time his grin was the genuine and thrilling article. "Does that C option ever lead to mind-blowing makeup sex?"

Flushing until the roots of her hair burned, she tried to think of a witty reply, something to make him smile again and keep the banter going. But she was, suddenly, overcome with a flash of being naked in his arms, hot urgency, and him moving between her legs and murmuring her name between desperate panting breaths.

"Of course," she said softly, holding his gaze.

This raw honesty was more than she'd intended, but it did the trick. His expression intensified, doing a slow smolder, and, when he slid his hand across the table, palm up, she didn't hesitate to stroke her fingertips across the sensitive skin of his inner wrist and then take it.

"The thing is," he murmured, "Jayne is an old friend and she made some good points."

That's what she'd been afraid of. "Let me guess: 'Kira's no good for you. Run far, far away.' Something like that?"

"Exactly like that."

"So . . . you're upset because you think she's right?"

"No. I'm upset because I'm positive she's wrong, and I don't know where that certainty is coming from. And even if she was right, and this leads to some dire consequences with my career, I'm past caring."

What did that mean? Excited as she was to be with him, and to see how determined he was to be with her, she'd never want to cause him problems with his job.

"I'm not sure I get that. I thought you loved your job."

"I do. Nothing makes me happier than squashing drug dealers like roaches. But it's a job, not a life. It doesn't fill me up."

Oh, God. The potential answer scared her—thrilled her—but she couldn't leave an implication like that dangling without asking the obvious follow-up question.

"What fills you up, Dexter?"

"You do."

Another of those delicious moments swelled between them, filling her up, too, and she had the urge to put the breaks on, to inject a note of caution into the proceedings, because certainly nothing in her life so far had gone well, and why should this be any different?

"You say that now," she told him, "but the first time I get PMS, you'll be running for the hills, begging to be put on twenty-four-hour surveillance in some terrible neighborhood just to get away from me."

He snorted out a laugh. "Maybe—"

"Probably."

"—But I'd be back."

Between them on the table, their fingers were twining and untwining, stroking and exploring easily, as though this, and nothing else, was what their hands had been created to do.

"I could get used to being with you, Dexter."

"I hope you will."

Sudden and unhappy memories of her parents burst on the scene like a stampeding herd of Wyoming bison, and she couldn't slam the gate fast enough to keep them out. She thought of their glorious twentieth anniversary shindig at the club, and then, later that same night, the drunken and screaming accusations behind closed doors.

Then her mind shifted to her wedding day, when she was so sure she'd married the man who would take her away from ugliness forever, and the night when the DEA task force came crashing through their door, proving to her blind eyes that the man she thought she'd married didn't exist.

Then she looked to Dexter, so different from either her father or her husband, open and honest, with no hidden agendas or secret personalities, and she wondered if her life could, this once, be simple. Happy. Peaceful.

"Is it supposed to be this easy?"

Her fretful question didn't seem to bother him at all, and there was no hesitation before his answer, only a wry half smile and shrug, as if he wasn't primed for the worst, like she was, and didn't suspect doom, or even significant problems, hiding around every corner, just waiting to ambush them.

Was this the normal way between men and women, then?

Smooth sailing ahead?

"Yeah," he assured her. "It's supposed to be exactly this easy."

By the time he pulled the truck back into Kira's driveway, his head was full to overflowing with thoughts struggling against each other, as though he'd shoveled five loads of jeans and oversized bath towels into the dryer and hit Start. First of all, when would he see her again? It was only midafternoon; what about tonight? What about tomorrow? They'd had a great time together so far, which didn't surprise him one bit, but he didn't want to press her too much and send her flying back into another six months of alone time. The thought practically gave him hives.

So, yeah, he needed to cool it a little.

And speaking of cooling it, when would his diarrhea of the mouth subside? What was with all his touchy-feely confessions about the way he felt about her, and when would he shut the hell up? Where had they even come from? With other women, the most demonstrative he'd been was an extra squeeze after sex and possibly the promise to call in a day or two. With Kira, the only things that had yet to come out of his mouth were *I love you* and *marry me,* but it was still early in the day. At the rate he was going, both would be shooting out of his mouth before sunset.

Which scared him.

And yet, didn't scare him at all.

The thing was, she made him laugh. Loosened him up. Brightened the sunshine and purified the air, crazy as that sounded, and maybe his ego was way out of whack, but in the last two days she'd looked and seemed happier than he'd ever known her.

Certainly he'd never seen her smile like this when Kareem was alive.

He put the truck in park and killed the engine, thoughts still spinning. There was paperwork waiting for him on his desk at home, but maybe they could—

"What's this?" Shooting him a delighted smile, she pointed out at a pink florist's van pulling up to the curb in front of her house. "How did you know it's my birthday tomorrow?"

What? Birthday? Why didn't she say anything before now?

"I didn't," he told her.

"Right."

With an *I-don't-believe-you* narrowed-eye glance over her shoulder as she went, she bounded out of the truck and met the delivery guy at the back of the van, where the doors were open as he extracted the biggest, longest, and, from the looks of it, heaviest white box of flowers Dexter had ever seen. His limited experience ran to ordering Mom a bouquet for Mother's Day, but even his untrained eye knew that a box like that, with the giant silk bow and all, didn't carry a little ten-dollar bouquet of *Have a Great Birthday!* daisies from a work friend.

He climbed out and slammed the door, his blood doing a slow and primitive burn that he didn't much like but had a tough time reigning in.

Kira, meanwhile, seemed to have lost some of her enthusiasm. She accepted the box from the guy with a

muted, "Thanks," headed over to the porch and propped
one end of the box on the rail. Moving slower, almost
reluctantly, she untied the ribbon and slid the lid clear
with a shaking hand. With a stricken face she studied
the contents.

And suddenly whatever vague jealousy he'd been
feeling toward a faceless competitor for her favors took
a backseat to the stronger need to hunt down and, in all
likelihood, kill whoever was responsible for making her
hurt like that.

Coming to stand at her shoulder, he looked down into
the box.

They were beautiful; even he could see that. Roses, of
course, in fifty different shades of pink that he didn't
know the names for, and big, snowball ones—hydrangeas,
right?—and smaller ones, like roses, that his mother
loved so well. Ranunculus, wasn't it? Yeah, that was it.

A stunning bouquet. A fortune in a box. A knife to
Kira's heart.

"What is it?" He kept his voice quiet, not wanting to
startle her.

Her skin chalky now, her lips tinged with a worrying
shade of blue, she spared him one wide-eyed and wild
glance before letting both the box and her purse crash to
the ground.

"Kira—"

He watched with growing alarm as she dropped to her
knees besides the mess of flowers and rummaged through
them, searching with open desperation for something she
couldn't seem to find. She yelped, snatched her hand
back, and sucked her bleeding thumb into her mouth—
thorn, he thought—and then she reached in again to pull
out a card and hold it up, looking triumphant.

"Kira," he tried again.

She seemed beyond hearing. Ripping into the envelope, she extracted the card—it was typewritten, he saw—and read it aloud in a guttural voice he didn't recognize as hers.

"To my forever and a day wife, with love on her birthday, Kareem."

Chapter 21

Whatever advanced analytical skills he'd developed during his years with the DEA deserted Dexter in that moment, chased away by the ghost walking over his grave and the dread crawling up his spine. So he could only imagine how Kira felt. He floundered, his brain working furiously on explanations—it's a mistake, it's a typo, something along those lines—but she was already way ahead of him, fishing her phone out of her pocket and dialing the number printed on the card.

Call the florist, he thought, trying to come up to speed. *Great idea.*

"Hi," she said when someone answered. "This is Kira Gregory. I have a question about a delivery just now." She listened. Waited. "Yes, my husband is—was—Kareem Gregory, and he died six months ago and I don't understand how—"

The voice on the line interrupted, chattering in one of those cheery voices, unnecessarily loud, that Dexter could hear but not quite make out.

"Yes," Kira responded, "but my address has changed—" She listened again. "Oh, that's right. I forgot."

The conversation ended too soon, with Kira saying thanks and hanging up way before Dexter would have been satisfied that all stones had been overturned.

Their gazes connected at the same instant that the synapses in his brain started firing again and putting two and two together.

"It was a—"

"Standing order," he finished for her. "Same thing every year, right? Prepaid."

She nodded. "They didn't know he'd died. And I used the same florist last month, when one of my colleagues had a baby. So they had my updated address."

Mystery solved, he reached for her because she was still way too pale and her eyes were distant now, cooler, as though a sheet of glass, or maybe ice, had slipped between them when he wasn't looking.

But she backed up a step, hands up, and refused his comfort when he most needed to give it. Which hurt.

Her words were hollow. Bewildered.

"Do you think," she wondered, "that I'll ever stop freaking out whenever a reminder of him comes up?"

"Absolutely."

She managed a hint of a smile as she stooped to pick up the flowers, thankfully not hearing the uncertainty in his voice.

"You sure you're okay?" Dexter asked for the one-thousandth time, which was a thousand times too many and, in Kira's opinion, enough to justify a violent act against him.

They were in the kitchen, where he was completing his systematic check of every window, door, and potential hidey-hole in her house, including, yes, Max's doghouse, and also driving her absolutely crazy.

That scene from one of her favorite movies, *The Fugitive,* flashed through her mind again, and it wasn't that much of a stretch to picture Dexter in the Tommy Lee Jones overzealous deputy marshal role as he tried to track down Dr. Richard Kimble.

"What I want from each and every one of you is a hard target search of every gas station, residence, warehouse, farmhouse, hen house, outhouse, and doghouse in that area. . . ."

What the hell was Dexter looking for?

What or who did he think he'd find? Elvis?

Exasperation and affection went a couple rounds of a supremacy death match within her, and it didn't take exasperation long to win in a spectacular KO, prompting her to put her hands on her hips and glare. "If you ask me that one more time, I am going to hurt you. Bad. So please knock it off, because I really don't want to do time for assaulting a federal officer."

"I'm aquiver with fear," he said darkly, not bothering to look at her or otherwise pause in his systematic inspection of the window over the kitchen sink. Was he this meticulous with everything he did? God help them all if he ever decided to, say, attempt the crossword in the Sunday edition of the *New York Times*. "If you didn't still look green, I wouldn't keep asking you."

Yeah. She still felt a little shaky—nothing like an unexpected reminder of Kareem to shake her up like a child's snow globe—but that didn't mean she'd admit it. "If I look green, it's because of my near-death experience with rock climbing. Thanks to you, I might add."

"You were never near death."

Max, who was trotting back inside after a quick pee and romp around the yard to celebrate being liberated from his crate, where he'd spent the morning, hopped through the door flap. To Kira's grudging admiration (wasn't *she* the one who paid for the kibble around here, Furry Face?), he went straight to Dexter's feet, where he collapsed and exposed his belly for the obligatory rub. Dexter obliged, squatting to administer a rough scratch that had the dog groaning in ecstasy.

"You're good with him," Kira told him.

Dexter's intent gaze, unsmiling and deliciously wicked, flicked up to her as he stood and edged closer. "I'm good with you, too."

If the hot flush creeping over her cheeks didn't give her away, then the unstoppable curl of her lips surely did. "Is that so?"

"Come here. I'll show you."

The murmured command acted on her like a drug, and she was moving before she knew it, already halfway into his outstretched arms before her synapses had finished firing the command to walk.

Tipping her chin up, she parted her lips to—

The doorbell rang, a long, insistent chime.

Dexter frowned, his attention centered on her mouth and his hands settling on the curve of her hips. "Now *that's* bad timing."

"No kidding."

"Do you have other plans? I didn't mean to monopolize your day."

"You're not. I have no idea who it could be."

"One way to find out."

Yeah. Like she cared who was at the freaking door when he had his hands on her. Right. Still, she did the expected thing and headed for the front door just as another of those jarring five-second rings came over the chimes.

"I'm coming. There's no need to carry on like there's a fire—"

A quick glance through the window seized up both her voice and her feet, and she froze with her hand on the knob and no earthly idea what to do now. Stricken, she turned to Dexter, who'd followed her, and helplessly said the only thing she could think of to say because she knew that a ton of shit was about to hit an industrialized fan when Dexter saw who was on her doorstep.

"I didn't invite him."

Dexter's shrewd eyes narrowed, as though he was already up to speed and understood that a huge problem for them and their blossoming relationship stood on the other side of that door.

"I didn't invite him," she said again, well aware that she sounded defensive even though she'd done nothing wrong. There were no lies between her and Dexter, and if she had her way, there never would be. She'd have told him about this if it ever came up.

She just hadn't planned to tell him now, like this.

Out of patience and taking matters into his own hands, Dexter peered out the window and stiffened into marble when he saw who it was, his shoulders going as rigid and straight as a yardstick.

"Fuck," he said.

Yeah. That about covered it.

When he looked back at her, his expression had cooled down into the subzero range, and there was accusation there even if he wasn't ready to unleash it just yet. With a sweeping hand gesture, he invited her to open the door.

She did.

Kerry, bleary-eyed and smelling yeasty, as if his over-worked pores couldn't stop the scent of liquor from bleeding out of him, stepped inside and started to say something.

He saw Dexter, who was now leaning against the nearest wall, arms and legs crossed in a gesture of purest intransigence, and snapped his jaw shut before going utterly still.

The men stared at each other, and Kira stared at their body language, no translations necessary for her female sensibilities.

Kerry, wide-eyed and disbelieving: *Ain't this a bitch?*

Dexter, unmoving, unyielding, and unblinking: *I'm not going anywhere, and all I need is for you to give me a reason, MF'er.*

Kerry came out of it first. Propelled by outrage, he swung back around and turned on Kira, so wounded and raw that his emotions reverberated through her like a sonic boom.

"So it's like that, huh?" he demanded.

Dexter took one step forward, standing between her and Kerry's fury, and answered for her in a voice that was low and unmistakably threatening, federal officer or no.

"Yeah," he told Kerry. "It's like that."

One of the men made a low rumble in his throat—she thought it was Kerry, but she couldn't be sure and, anyway, when you were trapped between two circling and snarling tigers, did it matter which one had the shorter temper? She decided that the best thing to do was separate them before anyone's blood was shed. Dexter could wait in the living room while she spoke to Kerry in the foyer.

Great. She had a plan. Crisis averted.

"Dexter," she began, stepping forward.

Kerry didn't seem to know, or maybe care, how close he was to having his throat ripped out, and turned his humiliated fury on Kira. "So this clown's speaking for you now?"

From the corner of her eye she saw Dexter make an aggressive movement, a chilling combination of puffing his chest and a measured step forward, and she held up a hand to forestall him. He paused, but she knew it was only temporary and felt like she was racing against the clock to save Kerry from his own suicidal stupidity. The only bright spot in the situation was that she didn't think he was currently drunk, even if his thinking was seriously impaired.

That was her fault, of course.

So much of the ugliness in her life was.

"I speak for myself, Kerry, and Dexter is no clown, so you need to—"

But Kerry couldn't sprint fast enough toward his own doom, cutting right to the heart of the matter. "Are you fucking him?"

Dexter exploded in a red-faced snarl of bared teeth, flared nostrils, and throbbing forehead veins. "You'd better step the fuck off before I haul your ass downtown—"

"For what?" Kerry taunted. "Taking an unlawful aspirin?"

"I'll make something up, motherfucker, so unless you want to—"

"Dexter." Kira faced him, stepping into his personal space and demanding his undivided attention. Then, further risking life and limb, she put her hands on his taut arms and held tight, which was like hugging up to a power line vibrating with ten thousand volts. His furious gaze wavered between the two of them, finally settling on her. "I need a minute with Kerry, okay?"

Dexter shook his head with open disbelief at this outrageous suggestion. "Like I'd leave you alone with this drunk-ass punk. I'm practically getting a contact high from the fumes."

Oh, no. That wouldn't work on her, and if she and Dexter only understood one thing between them, it had to be this: she was forever done with allowing a man—any man—to make her decisions for her.

"Kerry's not drunk." She kept her voice calm and uncompromising despite her spiking heart rate. "And if you don't feel like leaving us alone, you can just leave. Your choice."

With a furious and unintelligible mutter, Dexter threw her hands off, wheeled around, and stalked off down the hall and into the kitchen, where he'd no doubt be able to hear every word of their conversation.

Fighting sudden exhaustion, she turned to Kerry and strained hard for patience. "Please stop drinking. I'm begging you."

His face twisted with bitter derision. "What? You care about me now?"

"Yes," she said, knowing she was skirting that tricky line between being a friend and giving him mixed messages about their relationship potential. "I'm sorry I don't care the way you want me to—"

He produced a biting bark of laughter. "The way you care about him, you mean," he said, jerking his head in Dexter's direction.

They would not go down that road. Her relationship with Dexter had nothing to do with him, and it wasn't open for discussion. "You mean a lot to me, Kerry. I want you to be happy."

"Happy?" he spat. "Have we met?"

Sudden sadness weighed her down, all but knocking her to her butt. It did sound delusional when she said it. *Yes, Kerry, I know you're a reforming criminal, and, yeah, I don't love you and never will, but I want you to do your best to be a happy camper, y'hear?* But she still meant it.

"What can I do for you?" she asked tiredly. Helplessly. "Is there anything I can—"

He stared at her, reproach pouring out of every line of his body and hitting her like water from a fire hose, so powerful she had to look away.

There was a long, heavy silence.

"Why are you here?" she asked finally.

"To let you know I'm leaving town."

"What?"

"I should have been long gone by now. But I was hoping you—" He trailed off, shrugging.

"Why now?"

Another shrug. "I got a warning—"

"A threat, you mean?" Rising panic cut off her breath. "From who?"

His face was stark, empty except for a twitch of ugly

amusement at his lips. "Does it matter? Pick one: One of Kareem's other associates who's afraid of what I might tell the feds. One of Kareem's enemies who's afraid of what I might tell the feds. The Mexicans. The Russians. Who the fuck knows? I'm just lucky they gave me a warning. And I don't need to be told twice."

This had to happen, of course. She knew that. When you made your living on the streets, you retired to either prison or a body bag, and the only question was how long you'd be able to forestall your fate. But this simple fact of life hadn't stopped her from hoping for Kerry.

Was this the last time she'd ever see him, then? Why did that make her feel so scared and empty? "Where will you go?"

Another shrug. "I need to figure that out."

"But you'll call me? Let me know you're okay?"

He almost managed a smile—affection tinged with exasperation. "You're a piece of work. You know that?"

Maybe she was, but she didn't care. The only thing that mattered was Kerry staying alive. The list of Kareem's casualties was already way too long. She reached out, hesitated, and then, screw it, took his hard face between her palms and stared up into the dark eyes that had meant so much to her.

"Take care of yourself, okay?" There was no way to keep the urgency out of her voice. "And don't take another drink. Promise me you won't. You need to keep your head clear."

A change rippled through him at her touch, a softening that made her sorry—again; always—that she'd hurt this man so badly when all he'd done was care about her.

"Kira."

He studied her face, touching her brows and her

cheeks, imprinting her features. And then, somehow, she was in his arms and he was clinging to her for dear life, his hold so strong she expected to feel her ribs splinter with a sharp crack. Even so, his grip didn't hurt nearly as much as the hot tears clogging her throat. He felt sweetly familiar, as though she'd opened up a box of treasures from her childhood and experienced that squeeze of nostalgia around her heart when she handled them.

And then, without warning, he gently pushed her aside and headed for the door.

"Kerry," she began, but stopped when she couldn't think of anything to say that he'd want to hear.

Pausing, he held her gaze for several long beats, and she thought, *I'll never see him again, and he'll never forgive me for not loving him,* and the despair filled her up from bottom to top.

Then his face eased. Not into a smile, but his eyes crinkled at the corners, revealing something bittersweet but not angry.

Not angry, thank God.

That was enough to relieve the strangling tension in her chest, and if it wasn't quite peace, it was acceptance. That was enough. So when he slipped through the door without a backward glance, she let him go with only a silent prayer.

Please, God. Keep him safe. He can be a good man if he has the chance.

Chapter 22

Dexter's brain knew it was a good idea to hang out in the kitchen and decompress for a few minutes. His feet, unfortunately, were already in motion, propelling him into the foyer almost before the front door was finished closing, and he didn't see any need to pretend he hadn't heard everything that had passed between the little love-birds. Fuck that.

Flattened beneath the two-ton anvil that had fallen squarely on his head, he was still able to focus on the crucial issues, and they had nothing to do with the criminal who'd just walked out of here and was probably now packing his bags so he could flee the jurisdiction.

"Are you in love with him?" he asked Kira.

He'd startled her. Quickly turning her head, she swiped at her eyes, as though that clever evasive maneuver would convince him that she hadn't just been crying over some other man.

"No."

That was a good start, but his wounded heart needed much more handholding than that. "Were you ever in love with him?"

"No."

Now some of the pressure was beginning to ease from his chest, allowing him to breathe again, but his heart was still thumping like the bass line at a rap concert. "Do you have unfinished business with him?"

"No."

Good. Great. Three perfect answers, and everything in his world should be coming up roses, except that she still hadn't looked him in the eye, and he was still agitated enough to do a Spider-Man and climb the walls by his fingertips.

"If it's so cut and dried," he wondered, "why aren't you looking at me?"

That did it. She turned, spearing him through the heart with those wounded brown eyes. Sparks of indignation all but sizzled on her skin. "I've already told you the truth. What more do you want from me? A picture? Dates and times? A pound of my flesh?"

Yes, yes, and yes. He wasn't proud of it. In fact, he was damn near split down the middle with shame. He worked hard to be a good man, and the kind of man he wanted to be wouldn't be knotted up inside with this kind of searing jealousy. He'd be circumspect and understanding, not teetering on the edge of smashing everything in sight.

So he tried to dial it back. Rubbing away at the tension in his nape, he worked on leashing his emotions, but that was like trying to stop a rampaging elephant by grabbing its tail.

"I'm just . . . going to need a minute with this, Kira."

"You're judging me," she said flatly.

"Kira—"

"I can see it in your eyes because you're looking at

me like you've never seen me before. You're wondering what kind of woman would marry a drug kingpin and then have an affair with his lieutenant. Isn't that right? And you're wondering if you should jump ship right now, before this goes any further. Let's be honest."

He didn't want to be honest. Honesty would lead to the admission that he didn't think there was a bombshell she could drop on him that would make him stop wanting her. Honesty would make him confess that he was in way over his head with this woman, and he couldn't seem to drown himself in her fast enough.

Honesty, in short, was not his friend.

Evasion was better.

"Don't try to get inside my head."

"If you don't want me inside your head," she told him, "then you need to work on your poker face."

This sort of observation did nothing for his mood, which was getting surlier by the second. What did she want? His belated blessing on her relationship with the punk—*another* punk, actually—who embodied everything he'd spent his career trying to eradicate? Why didn't she ask for his testicles while she was at it?

Frustration built inside him, making his skin tight and his voice clipped. "Look, Kira. You're a complicated woman. I get that. You had a life before you laid eyes on me. I get that, too. It's just that I'm trying to understand—"

"What?" Her lips thinned with bitterness. "How I could be such a slut?"

The word jolted him out of his jealousy and back into his right mind, where he wondered, for the first time, whether Kira was her own harshest critic and whether she was the one who couldn't get past the choices she'd made.

"Jesus," he muttered. "Of course not. Don't even think something like that."

"Don't you think it?"

"No."

"Maybe you should."

Okay. Okay. Something had changed here—something crucial—and he no longer had any idea what they were talking about. All he knew was that he needed to get up to speed, and fast.

Tenderness made his voice gentle as he reached for her. "Kira. Baby. It doesn't matter what happened before. I thought we were looking forward. Why don't we work on that?"

"'Why don't we work on that?'" Throwing him off, she paced a few steps away and then wheeled back around to aim all that double-barreled fury at him. "Because you're the high and mighty Dexter Brady, and everything is black and white to you, isn't it? You can't relate to the rest of us mere mortals, can you? Your strict moral code requires an explanation about my unfortunate behavior, doesn't it?"

Shame sparked up his neck and exploded across his face like the lit fuse on one of those sticks of TNT in all the old Looney Tunes cartoons. He knew what the right thing to say was, but it was a bitch getting the words out of his mouth. "You don't owe me any explanations. And I'll never force you to do anything you don't want to do."

A harsh sound came out of her mouth, some crude bastardization of a laugh. "No, no! You want to talk? Let's talk! In fact, let's back up to the beginning. You want to know why I fell for Kareem?"

Yes, goddammit. "No," he tried.

Another biting laugh. "You're such a bad liar. Well, here's the story, since I can see you're dying to know. I grew up in a really nice house in the suburbs. My dad is a doctor and my mother is an engineer. I came from a good family. We went on Caribbean vacations and had a maid service and took really beautiful Christmas card photos every year. My friends were all green with envy. And you know what?"

She paused, her words thickening with emotion.

Utterly still, he tried to brace himself for whatever was about to nail him straight through the forehead.

Her brown eyes sparkled with tears, which she ignored. "You know what, Dexter? My father, the respected internist, came into my room at night and spent lots of alone time with me. We weren't reading Dr. Seuss together, in case you were wondering."

"Christ." Taking two quick steps, he lowered himself to a sitting position on the stairs before his knees had the pleasure of giving way. He couldn't breathe suddenly. Couldn't look at her because he was fairly sure he'd start bawling like a baby, and that wouldn't do either of them any good. Clearing his throat, he worked on swallowing the bile. "What about—"

"My mother? Oh, you don't think she believed me when I finally worked up the courage to tell her, do you?"

So much for not being a punk. He rested his elbows on his knees, pressed his thumbs into the corners of his eyes and let the tears come.

His breakdown didn't move her. If it had, she'd have stopped talking. "And guess what happened when I was a senior in high school? I met Kareem. Guess where I met him?"

Still choked up, Dexter could only shake his head.

"In church. Guess what he was doing?"

Raising his head, he felt a sick smile twist his lips. "Giving away Thanksgiving turkeys to needy families?"

Kira's smile was sicker than his. "Close! Ten points for trying! It was Christmas trees."

"Christmas trees," he echoed, fighting that nausea again.

"Christmas trees. So you can imagine he looked pretty good to me even though there were rumors about his business dealings. A young, handsome man who was wild about me and told me I was beautiful even though I knew I was ruined on the inside?"

"Kira—"

"I was a goner. I couldn't marry him and get out of my father's house fast enough."

The right thing to say skipped in circles around him, staying just out of view. "I'm sorry that happened to you," he began.

"Oh, save your pity. There's more."

"Wonderful," he muttered, lowering his head into his hands.

"I know it was stupid. I know I was stupid. But I believed in Kareem. I needed something to believe in. Can you understand that?"

Despite his sudden exhaustion, he was able to sit up straight and look her in the eye. "Absolutely."

She looked dubious. "Really? So can you also understand that I fell apart when Kareem was arrested and found comfort where I could when he was sent to prison?"

Comfort. Was that what they were calling it these days?

"Yes," he said, and he meant it. He really did. But his heart was wounded and raw, his mind was full of writhing images of Kerry enthusiastically comforting Kira, and his poker face hadn't gotten any better in the last several minutes.

"That's what I thought." Those eyes of hers went as hard, cold, and remote as a North Atlantic glacier. Shoulders squared, she went to the front door and opened it. "Get out of my house."

"Come on, baby. Time for some chow."

Kira opened the passenger-side door for Max, grabbed his leash, and waited while he yawned, stretched, and finally hopped out. Maybe, since she didn't have anything else to do on this fine Saturday evening, she'd give him a bath later. That could be fun, right?

Anything to keep her mind off Dexter.

After their painful parting scene earlier, she and Max had gone for a romp in the dog park, where they'd met a delightful boxer, a talkative husky, and a floppy-eared hound whose baying was so powerful and relentless she had to fight the urge to look around for a chain gang of escaped convicts.

Now she and Max were back home with provisions for the night, which included carryout Thai (her favorite), a half gallon of rainbow sherbet (Max's favorite), and *Best in Show,* a mockumentary about the quirky world of dog shows, and one of the funniest movies ever made. She needed the laugh to block out the endless, looping vision of Dexter's wounded eyes as he walked out.

If they were finished before they even got started, then that was his fault, she reminded herself. His loss, and she would not obsess about his choices. She'd been fine without him for this long, and, despite the yawning ache that had settled in behind her breastbone, she'd be fine again. Because she was a survivor, just like the one in that Gloria Gaynor disco song—"I will survive! I will survive! Hey, hey!"—and just like Oprah, who'd survived rape and incest and was now a woman who could move mountains and a beacon of hope to twisted messes like Kira.

Okay. Enough about Dexter Brady.

"You ready for some chow?"

Max's answer was a tongue-dangling smile and a wagged tail as he waited for her to grab the bags of food from the backseat. Shutting the door on her little ride, which was perversely still going strong, even though she now had the money to replace it, she started up the walk to the porch.

"Huh? Are you hungry? Is my little Maxie ready for some—"

She froze, the plastic bags and leash sliding out of her boneless hands to the ground, her access to the front door blocked by a stack of five long floral boxes, all of them wrapped with beautiful silk ribbon, and all of them identical to the one she'd received and thrown away a little while ago.

For several long beats, her stunned brain flailed around, considering several possible scenarios to explain the additional flowers, all of them centering on a florist who was either an idiot, a drunk, or grossly incompetent. She even reached for her phone, determined to give the manager or owner of the outfit the verbal foot up the ass, but of course they'd be closed this late in the afternoon on a Saturday.

Why would this happen? Was someone trying to torture her for some sick—

The answer hit her. She realized, in a white-hot flash of anger, both that she was being stalked and the identity of the stalker.

Chapter 23

The apartment building was shabbier than Kira had expected, which was something of a jolt because she hadn't expected shabby at all. Set on a busy street in an area that, judging by the abundance of pony kegs, check-cashing businesses, and cell phone stores, wasn't in danger of gentrification anytime soon, the redbrick structure featured a crumbling concrete staircase to the front door, overgrown bushes, and white shutters prone to dangling at odd angles.

The raggedy brass lock on the front door looked as though it hadn't kept anyone out since the Eisenhower administration, not that it made much difference with a battered volume of the Yellow Pages serving as a prop to keep the door open.

Still fuming, she went inside.

The lobby consisted of a wall of metal mailboxes, a black-and-white linoleum checkerboard floor, and an open elevator that she didn't dare enter unless she planned to spend the rest of her life stuck between floors.

Number 102 was easy enough to find, situated as it was between the elevator and the fire door leading to the staircase, which had to be the noisiest place in the building. Well, no. Other candidates for noisiest place in the building included number 100, which was vibrating with music, or number 104, where an angry baby screamed over the cooing voice of its mother.

What a dump. After all her years of undying devotion and loyalty, Kareem hadn't provided for his mother any better than *this*? Hadn't he given her, say, a shrink-wrapped block of cash to be used in case of emergency or his untimely demise? What was the world coming to when drug kingpins didn't leave their mothers nest eggs?

Raising her fist, she pounded, letting her impatience run free, and then, when that didn't produce an answer within three seconds, pounded again.

The door suddenly swung open. Wanda stood there.

If seeing her former mother-in-law's building had been a shock, laying eyes on the woman herself was a blow directly to Kira's solar plexus. She stared, her righteous anger draining away.

Saggy-skinned and hollow-eyed where she had always been pleasantly plump, Wanda looked as though she'd crammed fifty or sixty years of hard living into the last six months. She'd always been sleek and sharp, outfitted in Nordstrom's finest clothes, with glowing skin and bright nails from her weekly mani-pedis, but now she wore a faded green tracksuit that had left its best days behind years ago, and her short hair was curled but had the mashed look of a do that hadn't been combed in the last day or several.

The woman who'd been critical of Kira's every wardrobe, makeup, and hair selection for years now looked as though she'd just arrived home from a long night spent sleeping on a park bench.

It got worse. The proud posture that used to propel her from room to room like a queen in training with an invisible book on her head had given way to the stoop-shouldered slouch of a woman who couldn't find a reason to give a damn about anything the world had to offer. Her eyes held no life, only shadows.

They stared at each other. Kira studied her eyes for a sign of the old spitfire and found none. That was too much, even for Kira.

"My God, Wanda," she blurted. "Are you sick?"

The concern seemed to sting Wanda's pride. Straightening, she drew the halves of her hoodie together and ran a self-conscious hand through her hair. "I'm fine." Her rusty voice didn't sound like it'd been used much lately. "What are you doing here?"

"I want to talk to you."

Without waiting for an invitation, Kira edged through the door and into the apartment, which seemed to consist of a kitchen with a sit-at Formica counter, living room, and, she was guessing, bedroom and bathroom in the back. She turned in a slow circle, taking it all in. Other than the blaring TV, the most striking feature in the living room was . . . Kareem.

It was a shrine, with every inch of wall covered with snapshots of Kareem. As an adorable and chubby-cheeked baby; in his seventh-grade football uniform; as a proud five-year-old who'd lost his first tooth; oh, look—there's Kareem graduating high school.

"Why weren't these destroyed in the explosion?" she wondered, aghast.

"I got them from my sister."

Of course she did.

Kira grabbed the remote from the coffee table and clicked off the TV (Wanda could stand to miss a repeat of *Law & Order* this one time), and tried to ignore the oppressive weight of Kareem's piercing gaze bearing down on her from every angle as she gathered her thoughts.

To her surprise, her mission had suddenly changed. The flowers weren't important; saving Wanda from this self-imposed decline was.

"This isn't healthy, Wanda."

Wanda blinked, clearly losing the struggle to understand Kira's heresy. "He was my son. I want to remember him."

"There's a difference between remembering him and worshipping him. You have to let him go before you waste away to nothing."

"Let him go?" Wanda's lips peeled back in a snarl. "Like you did? Well, it was easier for you, wasn't it? You never loved him like I did, did you?"

There it was. All that animosity, back in all its glory.

Kira rubbed the back of her neck with rising frustration. Jesus. Why had she said anything about the pictures? If Wanda chose to wallow in her precious memories until she wasted away and died, that was her business, wasn't it? And why did Kira feel the compelling need, even now, to defend herself to this woman who hated her enough to stalk her with flowers and memories?

"Oh, I loved him. Even when he didn't make it easy, I loved him."

This only seemed to feed Wanda's irrational anger. Her face grew steadily redder with what had to be a serious spike in her blood pressure. "You're not fooling anybody, Kira. You only married him for the money. I always knew that. And when times got tough, you forgot about the 'or worse' part of your vows, didn't you? You turned your back on him. I never did."

So much for staying above the fray. This woman's view of reality was so sickeningly skewed Kira couldn't let it go unchallenged. "*When times got tough?* He ran a drug empire, Wanda—"

Wanda crossed her arms and widened her stance, stubbornly believing in her fantasy world, despite all evidence to the contrary. "Nobody ever proved that."

"You know he did!"

Wanda shook her head. "I never saw him do anything illegal."

"Oh, my God."

This conversation was so surreal and bewildering that Kira had to back up a step and regroup. She may as well have been trying to prove Einstein's theory of relativity in a discussion with Max.

"He attacked me, Wanda. You were there that night—"

"I didn't see *anything*," Wanda insisted, pressing a hand to her face, which was now losing color. "I didn't see—"

Kira lost it. White-hot rage erupted out of her, spewing shrapnel in every direction. "He raped me! You saw the blood—"

"You drove him to it!"

Kira flinched, too stunned to respond.

It wasn't the accusation that was so disturbing. It was the fact that Wanda had allowed her grief to unhinge her to the point that she had no problems blocking out what she had seen and heard that night.

Well, Kira decided. Fair enough. How else could a

woman who'd raised a monster manage to look herself in the mirror?

So Wanda was delusional. Fine. This was America, and that was her right. But some terrible weakness inside Kira wouldn't let her go until she'd wrung at least one small confession out of the bereaved mother here. One small flicker of acknowledgment that Kareem hadn't been a saint—that was all Kira needed.

"I'm wondering, Wanda," Kira said, calmer now. "If Kareem was such a fine specimen of humanity, why didn't he leave you, his beloved and loyal mother, a little money to live on? He had bank accounts all over the world. You know he did. So why did he leave you to live like this?"

The remaining bit of color in Wanda's cheeks leeched away. "You get out of my house. Don't you ever come back here!"

"How do you live with yourself?"

Wanda marched to the door and flung it open with a bang that rattled the thin walls. A vein was now pulsing visibly in her neck. "The thing you need to understand, Baby Girl," she said, making pointed use of Kareem's nickname for her, "is that Kareem was everything and you are, and always will be, nothing. I don't have to tolerate you now that he's gone, and I don't want to ever see you again. *Get out.*"

Get out. Right. Excellent suggestion.

Drained, Kira was at the threshold before she remembered the purpose of her visit. "I won't come again. But I'm going to live my life and I'm not going to apologize for it. If you have a problem with that, then you should keep it to yourself." She paused, making sure she had Wanda's full attention. "Don't send me flowers again. I don't need you playing head games with me."

Wanda's eyes widened. "What flowers?"

Kira rolled onto her back with a low murmur, lured closer to consciousness by the slow glide of fingers across her eyebrows and over her cheek. Beneath the luxuriant softness of her fluffy duvet and cotton sheets, her body felt weightless, pliant, except for the tightening coil of need in her belly. She undulated and arched, seeking more of that addictive touch, ceding control to the desire and letting go with a serrated sigh.

Dexter.

He was here and she was his, and that was as it should be.

"You came," she breathed.

The answering whisper was so faint it might have come from somewhere inside her.

"I couldn't stay away."

There was no need to open her eyes, no need for hesitation or shame. In a sleepy strip tease, she slipped the linens down and away, revealing her body in its filmy cotton nightie and demonstrating what she needed him to do by first doing it herself.

She ran her fingers down the sensitive curve where her neck met shoulder, and then along the gentle slope of her breasts, which were swelling with a sweet and insistent ache. His fingers followed, adding to the pleasure by running across her pebbled nipples—back and forth, sure and unhurried—until the coos overflowed her throat and poured out of her mouth. . . .

Yes. God, yes.

She smiled, reaching for him, needing his weight pressing her into the mattress and his relentless thrust between her legs, and if she just—

Her hands closed around nothing.

Everything became . . . wrong.

Scrambling into a sitting position, she thunked her spine against the headboard, clearing away the remnants of her dream with the sharp finality of a popped balloon.

She was, suddenly and jarringly, awake.

Awake. Bewildered. And, increasingly, scared.

The room was cool and quiet, illuminated only by the soft blue glow of her alarm clock and the negligible trickle of moonlight through the slats of her wooden blinds. Two thirty-five. Nothing was out of place, but the air felt heavy. Pregnant. And the shadows—chairs, armoire, desk—seemed clearer somehow. More menacing.

Panting, she looked wildly around, desperate to identify the thing—*what was it?*—that made such an exquisite dream—had it been a dream?—into something shapeless and threatening, but there was nothing that she could see.

Nothing to blame for morphing the gentle hands on her body from Dexter's into Kareem's.

Yet she couldn't stop shaking. Couldn't regulate her pulse.

Was it the man's voice? There had been a voice, hadn't there?

And he'd said . . . he'd said something to her, she was sure of that, but the voice hadn't been right for Dexter, had it? Only Kareem had that mellow, sardonic bass. And it was Kareem's presence working in her mind and here in her precious bedroom sanctuary, a presence so strong she'd swear she caught a trace of his earthy cologne.

She'd been dreaming, though, and, after the day she'd had, it made perfect sense that Kareem's malignant memory would storm into her mind like barbarian hordes attacking some defenseless castle.

Just a dream, you crazy woman. Nothing but a dream.

The thought comforted her until she heard the approaching jingle of Max's tags from the hallway, which was fine. What wasn't fine was the faint, almost indistinguishable sound—*was it a sound, or was it her imagination? Was she going insane, or, worse, already insane?*—of a door clicking closed.

Chapter 24

Dexter's heart sank the moment he saw Mom, and any hopes he'd had of experiencing a pleasant visit with her this evening died a fiery death. Having seen no sign of her in the activity room, where the other seniors were gearing up for a craft project that seemed to involve a lot of popsicle sticks and colored pom-poms, he walked down the hall and found her in her private room, sitting in her wheelchair and glaring at the splashing fountain outside her open window.

That familiar expression—flat-lipped, narrow-eyed, and generally surly—boded ill for him, and his footsteps slowed accordingly.

She was mad at the world, just like he was.

Today's shitty day was an exact replica of the last two, the movie *Groundhog Day* come to life in an endless loop: a savage tension headache, snarling at underlings who'd done nothing wrong, and, yes, wishing he could smash everything in sight, all because he didn't know what to do about Kira.

Oh, but there'd been one notable incident this afternoon, hadn't there? His old buddy Jayne had poked her head in his office and he, a decorated career law-enforcement official with a spotless record and a reputation for being so uncompromisingly honest and honorable that even Gary Cooper's Marshal Will Kane from *High Noon* could look to him for guidance, had stared his longtime friend in the face and lied.

It went something like this:

Jayne: "Sorry if I overstepped the other day."

Dexter, scowling: "No problem."

Jayne: "Are we cool?"

Dexter, still scowling: "You bet."

Jayne, looking unconvinced and wary: "Great. Are you, ah . . . okay?"

Dexter, attempting a smile that made his cheeks hurt: "Peachy."

Jayne: "You haven't heard from our favorite confidential informant, have you?"

Dexter, thinking fast and hard while trying not to blink or fidget: "Kerry Randolph? Why do you ask?"

Jayne: "He's gone off the grid. He didn't show up for a scheduled meeting. I think he's fled the jurisdiction."

Dexter, slipping on his *wow, what a surprise!* mask: "Oh, shit."

Jayne: "Did you know anything about this? Did he say anything to you?"

Dexter, eaten alive by guilt and shame, yet still willing to lie and lie again if that was what Kira needed him to do, and to hell with his honor and professionalism: "Nope."

So now here he was, hoping for a moment's comfort from dear old Mom, and maybe, if he was really lucky, a passing moment of lucidity, and Mommy Dearest looked like she wanted to rise up out of that chair and bash his skull in.

Still, he tried.

"Hey, Mom. How are you doing today?"

When he'd crossed the room and leaned down to give her the usual kiss on the cheek, she turned her head and strained away from him, a rejection that still hurt even though he should be used to it by now.

"What do you want?"

This is the dementia talking, he reminded himself, and his head was fine with that. His heart, meanwhile, was crushed.

"I'm here to see how you're doing."

That gaze, almost feral with its hot suspicion, swung back around then. "Bullshit," said the woman who'd never let a vulgar word pass her lips until after she was felled by a stroke. "You don't care about me."

"Mom," he began.

"Screw you," she snapped. "You get the hell out of here. And take your flowers with you."

That was when he saw the bouquet and, simultaneously, felt ice replace the breath in his lungs. They were familiar, those flowers, and he sure as hell hadn't brought them. Sporting pinks in every conceivable color under the rainbow, the bouquet included roses, hydrangeas, and all the other unidentified flowers he'd seen in Kira's birthday bouquet.

"Where . . . did you get those, Mom?" he asked carefully. "Who brought them?"

Mom, petulant as a three-year-old at bath time, crossed her arms and poked her lips out. "You did. And you can take them with you."

"It wasn't me. I need you to try to remember who—"

"Don't you lie to me, boy," she shrieked. "Don't you lie to me!"

The shrieking was always a prelude to a full and usually paranoid meltdown, and this time was no different. By the time he'd rounded up the harried nurse and had Mom sedated and settled into bed for the night, he was fighting frazzled nerves and emotional exhaustion, and he needed to go home for a beer and a shower.

But those flowers.

When the nurse was tucking the covers up around Mom's shoulders, he pointed to them and asked, "Who sent those?"

The nurse cocked her head and gave him a funny look, making that icy sensation leach past his lungs and into every far corner of his body.

"The aide said it was a handsome black man. I thought that meant you."

"No," Dexter said slowly. "It wasn't me."

The suspicion wouldn't get out of Brady's head.

Actually, it wasn't even a suspicion. That was giving it way too much credit.

It was, at best, a fleeting thought. A vague unease. A niggling doubt that was too far-fetched to ever see the light of day. If he had any sense, he'd put it out of his mind—forever—and focus on something job-related and productive.

Like catching drug dealers and allied bad guys.

"You in for lunch, Brady?"

Except that this doubt was as relentless as a beaver felling trees and building his dam. As insidious as a colony of termites eating its way through a log cabin. As horrifying as the slice of a dorsal fin through the water while children played in the surf.

Anyway, it was impossible. Of course it was.

"Brady? You going to keep picking lint out of your navel, or are you coming with us for lunch?"

Startled out of the gathering darkness inside his head, Dexter blinked and realized that the rest of the world was still there. The stack of paperwork on his desk still demanded attention, phones were still ringing outside his office, and Grant, one of the best special agents on his team, was still leaning against the door, eyeballing him as though he suspected him of cracking up, and waiting for his answer.

"Nah. Bring me back something."

"Such as?"

Dexter shrugged. "Surprise me."

"Great," Grant said, turning and heading out the door. "One fruit plate special coming up. Extra cottage cheese."

Dexter snorted. "You bring me back some shit like that and you're fired."

Grant spared him a wave over his shoulder and kept going.

Dexter, meanwhile, stared at the report that needed his signature and saw only that same fucking doubt. The flowers to Mom had set this wheel in motion. Who was the mysterious visitor who'd brought them? Why hadn't any of the dozens of employees in that freaking nursing home gotten a better look at him? Mom didn't get that many visitors; why hadn't they noticed some new guy bearing flowers?

The disturbing thing was, he and his mother didn't

have any family in town, and anyone who came to town for a visit would also check in with Dexter.

The flowers themselves . . .

Why wasn't there a card?

Why hadn't his calls this morning to several of the local florists turned up any information?

Why were his mother's flowers the same as Kira's flowers?

That was why this doubt had him in a stranglehold.

There were too many unanswered questions, and he didn't believe in coincidence. What had the villain said in the James Bond movie *Goldfinger*?

"Once is happenstance. Twice is coincidence. Three times is enemy action."

Enemy action.

It was just a doubt. He knew that. But he had a few questions that he wanted to put to rest. So he picked up the phone and dialed the number of the coroner's office.

Two mornings later, her cell phone buzzed just as Kira was dragging her tired and crabby behind out of bed for work, and she fumbled it on without checking the display. Max, who'd been sleeping on his little bed in the corner, raised his head to give her a disgruntled look through sleepy eyes.

"Hello?"

"Hey. It's me. Kerry."

"How are you? Where are you?"

"I'm at my cousin Ernie's house. Outside Dayton. He's a truck driver, so he doesn't mind letting me crash here."

"Is that safe?"

"Safe?" Yeah. Dumb question; she knew it even before she heard his little snort of amusement. "You're kidding, right?"

She got up, holding the phone with one hand and making the bed with the other. "Are you doing okay?"

"I'm having a grand old time. A laugh riot."

Tiptoeing through a minefield had to be easier than this. She struggled, thinking hard for something upbeat to say to him, something that didn't involve her rejection or his dismal prospects for living a normal life.

"So . . . no more threats?"

"Not a peep."

"That's good, right?"

He hesitated, and she could almost feel his frustrated shrug. "Who knows? I almost liked it better after the threat. This silence works my nerves. I don't know which direction to look."

"But you're sober. I can hear it in your voice."

"That's my Kira. Always looking for a bright spot."

That made her smile. "I see several bright spots. You're alive. You're sober. You're still speaking to me. Seems like a pretty good day to me."

"Don't get too excited. I took a little field trip to the liquor store last night. I'm staring at a fifth of Jack right now."

For some incomprehensible reason, this news didn't disturb her. "But you won't drink it. You promised me, didn't you?"

"Yeah, I promised. There's nothing I wouldn't do for you. As you know."

Man, he just killed her. Every single time. "The only thing you need to do for me is take care of yourself. Okay?"

"Anything for you, Kira." He sighed, the sound as exhausted as a ninety-nine-year-old man at the end of a long day. "I gotta go. I don't want to miss the *Today* show."

Sudden reluctance made her clingy. She knew she couldn't save him—not from his enemies, and certainly not from himself—but that didn't make it any easier to let him go.

"Stay in touch, Kerry."

Forever passed before he answered. "Bye, baby."

She hung up, tears collecting tight and hot in her throat, and went to take her shower.

She was brushing her teeth ten minutes later when her cell phone rang again. Startled, she checked her watch as she hurried back to the nightstand, thinking that it might be the hospital calling with a shift change.

"Hello?" she mumbled around a mouthful of toothpaste.

"Hi." Oh, God. It was Dexter. "I want to talk to you."

Surprise made her swallow the toothpaste, which would make for a serious stomachache in a few minutes, but she didn't care about that now. "Ah . . . Okay. Were you thinking about lunch, or—"

"We've lost enough time over this stupid argument. Come on out. I'm in the driveway," he said, and hung up.

In the driveway? No freaking way—

A quick glance out the window assured her that there was, in fact, a way.

What, now? He had to come *now*?

Cursing, she paused long enough to tighten the belt of her silky robe before she scurried down the steps and out the front door to meet him where he stood leaning against the driver's side of his truck. Apparently he didn't have any court appearances today, because he was deliciously casual in his blue Oxford and khakis. He didn't smile, but his cool gaze flickered over her, lingering on the robe's short hem and her bare thighs.

She stopped three feet from him and waited, every inch of her body tying itself up into excruciating knots.

"Hi," he said.

"Hi."

"Have you cooled off yet?"

Cooled off? Would that include the anxious, stomach-churning hours she'd spent regretting her harsh words and wondering if she'd ruined what might have developed into a beautiful relationship?

"Yes."

"You've got a hot temper," he said flatly.

The observation stung even though it was perfectly true, and she puffed up accordingly, feathers ruffled. "I do not—"

"You need to keep it in check. I'm not the enemy."

"Yeah?" Every second that he stood there, studying her with that indecipherable expression, agitated her a little bit more. "Well, I'm not going to stand by while you judge me, Dudley Do-Right—"

"I was not judging you, and if you'd let me get a word in edgewise, I'd've explained that to you." He paused, scrubbing a hand over a cheek that was growing redder by the second. "I was, ah, jealous."

This was no surprise; she'd pieced this much together using her brilliant skills of deduction. The surprising thing was that he'd admitted it. Men, in her experience, rarely if ever admitted any vulnerability.

"You—*what?*"

He eased closer and his voice dropped, becoming as warm and thrilling as a stroke of velvet across her skin. "The thought of any other man touching you, even if it was years ago, makes me want to smash something."

"Oh."

"But I'm a big boy and I know you had a life before I came along." His lips twisted, as though it was a major effort to force the tricky words out of his mouth. "And anything you did to survive your . . . ah, marriage is, ah, fine by me."

The corners of her mouth began to creep up in a smile. "Thank you for telling me that."

"You're welcome."

"You know, Special Agent, I probably wouldn't be so defensive with you if I knew you'd made a bad decision or two in your life."

His brows contracted. "I've messed up before."

"Really? Library fine? Jaywalking ticket? Broken taillight?"

"One time I snuck into the kitchen and ate half the batter from this pound cake my mother was making for some church thing."

They laughed together, but then, without warning, his smile was eaten up by the sudden heat in his eyes and urgency in his voice.

"You should know by now that I want you as is. You do know that, don't you?"

The relief was so fierce and overwhelming that she couldn't blink back her tears fast enough. "You have no idea how happy that makes me."

He wiped the drops from her cheeks—gently, sweetly—and then raised her hand to his mouth for a lingering kiss. "So we're on for tonight, then?"

"Tonight?"

"The houseboat. Eight o'clock. We'll have a dinner cruise."

Chapter 25

Breezin', which was docked at the far end of a marina on the Ohio River outside the city, swayed gently atop the sparkling gray water. Much bigger than she'd expected, it was white with white railings, large windows with fluttery curtains, two levels, and seemed to be large and sturdy enough to cruise them all the way down the Ohio to the Mississippi and New Orleans, if they decided to go. With a ridiculous and unshakable grin plastered to her face, she walked up the gangplank and, not being sure about the correct procedure for boarding a boat, called through the open window and hoped Dexter heard her.

"Are you there, Captain? Permission to come aboard!"

After a minute and the sound of hurrying feet, Dexter appeared at the door, his eyes widening with surprise. "Hi."

"Hi."

That seemed to max out her limited speaking abilities, but the flush in the apples of her cheeks intensified, burning white-hot. Beneath her skin, meanwhile, her flesh felt as though it was shimmering with awareness—of him; of the water and the breeze; of the night's possibilities—and she wondered if she'd glow once the sun disappeared past the horizon.

God, she was a mess. Had been since she saw him this morning.

Being in his presence again didn't help her composure. If anything, the sight of him made her thoughts scatter like fall leaves in the path of a high-powered blower. Not that he was dressed up or anything; he wasn't. Wearing only a white T-shirt and khaki cargo shorts, he had a checkered dishcloth slung over one powerful shoulder and a wooden spoon held aloft with something red—spaghetti sauce, probably— dripping from the tip.

He stared, his bright gaze skimming all of her, from tank top to flowered skirt and fancy flip-flops, in one sweeping glance. He didn't smile, and yet she had the feeling that nothing could have pleased him more than her arrival, not even the secret to eternal life gift-wrapped with a hot double-cheese pizza and season tickets to the football team of his choice.

After a long pause, he checked his watch and told her what she already knew: "You're early."

"Yeah," she admitted. "Forty-five minutes."

The corners of his eyes crinkled. "Hungry, are you?"

"I missed you," she blurted.

Way to go, genius. There was nothing like being needy and clingy to kill a promising relationship, so this was probably the beginning of the end—

"Yeah?" There was a distinctive husky note in his voice now. "Since this morning, you mean, or—"

"Since this morning, yeah." Since he showed no signs

of screaming and slamming the door in her face, bolting it against her, she decided to go for broke. "And in the last week, since you picked that ridiculous argument with me."

He snorted with laughter.

"And for the last six months," she added softly. "I missed you."

"I missed you, too."

Intense pleasure went directly to her head, intoxicating her, and she lapsed back into a full simpering smile before she caught herself and toned it back a little. "Yeah?"

"A lot."

"So . . . I don't need to wait out here until eight o'clock?"

He held out a hand to help her onto the boat. "Absolutely not."

"Nice boat."

"Come see it."

Their bare arms brushed as she stepped past him, sending sparks along nerve endings that had been dormant for too long. The logical next step would be for her to look around the boat a little. She could already see that it was more like a cheery and spacious condo decorated in—what else?—a nautical theme, with a little entry area, stairs, a living room with wicker furniture and, yes, a galley kitchen. And then maybe she should ask if he needed help setting the table or anything.

Instead, she lingered, caught in his body's powerful gravitational pull.

He smelled good.

Having worked up a light sheen of perspiration in what she assumed was a steamy kitchen, he had the delicious clean sweat scent of a man whose grooming routine has exactly three steps: shower; apply deodorant; get dressed.

It worked for her.

She stared, fascinated by a dewy spot between the hard knobs of his collarbones, and might have stayed there until the apocalypse if he hadn't cleared his throat and snapped her out of it.

An awkward shuffle followed, during which they tried to decide who should go in which direction. Since he was bigger, he won. He steered her by the arm down the few stairs and into the galley kitchen, which was really nice, with white counters, a full-sized fridge, and a stove.

No wonder he and his parents had loved it so much here.

Dinner was well underway, she saw. A pot of marinara sauce bubbled over on the stove, filling the boat with one of her favorite aromas—garlic, and lots of it. Inside another pot, several large pasta shells were draining in a colander.

"Manicotti?"

"Ah, yeah." His flustered gaze flickered between her and the spoon, which he seemed to have trouble using. A beat or two passed before a lightbulb apparently went off over his head, and he gave the sauce a cursory stir. "I hope you like Italian."

"I love Italian."

God, she'd edged back into his space again, leaning over his shoulder under cover of watching his cooking techniques, so close that her nose could skim the soft cotton of his shirt. Her twitchy hands longed to run over the heavy cords of his arms, but sudden paralysis kept her from reaching for him.

They were supposed to be taking this whole thing slow and smart, and anyway, men were supposed to make the first move. It was a rule. If she were smart, she'd stop thinking about moves being made, first or otherwise, and focus on, say, slicing the veggies down at the other end of the counter into a salad.

Only the smart thing felt unnatural, like walking across ceilings, while touching Dexter felt as inevitable as her next heartbeat.

He seemed to know it. His stirring arm slowed down until he gave up on the sauce altogether. Letting go of the spoon, he turned the burner off and gripped the oven handle until his knuckles went white, bracing himself against a force that was stronger than either of them.

His gaze remained down, stubbornly fixated on the digital clock's blue numbers, and he let out a serrated sigh that seemed to go on forever.

"You sure don't make things easy, do you?" he murmured.

Surrendering to the urge, she took that one last step, the one that brought the front of her body up against the back of his, making both of them shudder. She ran her hands up those arms—hard, silky, hot—and her lips up the side of his neck to his ear, where she whispered, "That's what I'm trying to do," she told him. "Make things easy."

He grinned, smothered the grin, and then gave his head a firm shake. The tension in his muscles tightened, and she could almost hear the whining hum as his body strained past his control.

"This is too important, Kira. I don't want to ruin it by taking it too fast."

"Look at me."

He didn't want to. Still staring at that clock, he put it off as long as he could, and if her body hadn't been twisted into so many knots, she would've admired his control. After a millennium plus a lifetime, he straightened and turned, nailing her with a heavy-lidded gaze of deepest brown.

"What could make you walk away from me?" she asked.

He answered without hesitation. "Nothing."

"Then what are we waiting for?"

Something in his face softened, as did his voice. "Nothing."

They stared at each other, the connection between them strengthening and growing into something un-breakable, and she thought, with wonder, that there was every possibility that she was falling in love with his humor, quiet strength, and integrity.

Falling in love . . . with him.

Doubt never had a chance against something this right. Being with him, now, like this, was one of the smartest things she'd ever done.

"Touch me," she told him.

Linking their fingers and moving as though they had all the time in the world, he led her out of the kitchen, up the stairs and down a narrow hallway, to the bedroom.

A breeze and the sun's dying rays streamed through the windows, making the curtains sway and turning the bedroom into a secret hideaway where the outside world could never intrude. The view beyond was of the glitter-ing crystal river, and only passing birds would see them if they cared to make the effort.

With a firm but gentle grip on her hands, Dexter walked backward into the golden glow, tugging her into the light and releasing her hands only to capture her face between his palms so he could angle her head the way he wanted it.

That accomplished, he studied her with rapt attention.

The air in her lungs slipped away into the night, leaving her breathless and light-headed, with both desire and trepidation.

She felt exposed, teetering on the emotional equivalent of a bridge over a glacial crevasse with the wind at her back and no hope of rescue if she fell. What if his scrutiny turned up all of her flaws in high-definition clarity and he didn't want her anymore because—let's face it—who would?

What would she do then?

No detail escaped the skim of his gaze, which started with the wispy-fine hair at her forehead and temples, slid over her brows, lingered forever on her eyes, and then dropped, riveted, to her lips. Once his eyes had blazed the trail, his thumbs followed suit, running across her overheated skin as though she were newly blown glass, too precious to handle.

God.

She couldn't breathe . . . couldn't breathe . . . couldn't breathe for so long that her chest began to heave with the effort, and the rubbing friction of her bra over her tightening nipples was the sweetest torture imaginable. Desire spiraled low in her belly, agitating her. Making her so slick and engorged that she had to rub her thighs together to relieve some of the ache.

"Dexter," she began.

"Shh." His heavy brows contracted, warning her not to dare distract him from his tour of her features, and she tried to stand still. But his hands were now double-teaming her, fingers massaging her nape in the back and thumbs circling the column of her neck on either side, and there was no way to keep her growing frustration from pouring out of her mouth on mewling little cries and confessions.

"Dexter." Her head fell back, too heavy and weightless to stay upright, but she struggled to keep her eyes open, determined to see his emotions play across his shadowed face even if she couldn't read them. "I want you. I want you . . . want you."

But his attention had shifted to covering every far corner of her skin with a kiss, and he didn't seem to hear her. This time he started low, licking her neck from base to chin with one languid sweep of his hot tongue, stealing a sharp cry of surprise from her. Her jawline got a nip; her earlobe, a hard suck. Those murmuring lips— what was he saying?—traveled over the arch of her forehead, from temple to temple, and then, finally, zeroed in on her mouth, hovering.

"Yes," she whispered. "Please—"

His turbulent gaze flickered up to hers for one excruciating second. "You're beautiful," he murmured, and then gave her some of what she needed. The kiss was short and unbearably deep, nothing but the slow glide of his tongue into her seeking mouth, and then, too soon, its withdrawal as he scraped her lower lip between his teeth.

Helpless to do otherwise, she surged to her tiptoes, reaching for him and digging her blunt nails into his back . . . his shoulders . . . anything she could grip to bring him close and keep him there, but he was already breaking away, stepping to arm's length so he could focus all that relentless attention on a new part of her body.

"Turn around," he told her.

She did, manic now with anticipation. Every second that her legs held felt like a major miracle, and that was before those strong hands went to her shoulder blades and worked down her spine for one of those penetrating massages that bordered on pain and yet relaxed her into warm clay.

When his warm mouth settled on her nape, she sighed and surrendered in a way she never had before, passing into a dimension between full consciousness and rapture, where only the miracle of his touch existed and she didn't have to please anyone or do anything except feel.

He made love to her with his mouth, swirling his tongue back and forth and around, sweeping her top over her head and dropping it to the floor when it got in his way. At his silent urging, she held her arms up in the air while he stroked and kneaded them from wrist to shoulder and then, to her dazed pleasure, ran his restless mouth into the curve between her neck and shoulder, latched on, and suckled.

"Oh, God." Helpless tears streamed from her eyes because he was unraveling her, deconstructing each part of her body and reconstructing it into something new and wondrous. Reaching up, she ran her fingers into the coarse silk of his hair, holding him right where he was so he could do this forever and she could die, exactly like this. "God, don't stop. Don't ever stop . . . *don't stop.*"

A croon of deep approval rumbled in his chest and vibrated through her as he finally—finally, finally—

wrapped her in those strong arms and brought her up against the hard length of his body. It was a thrilling shock. Heat flamed between them front and back, searing her as though a forked lightning bolt had embraced her.

The unyielding length of his erection rubbed against her butt, and his thrusting hips set a slow rhythm that was as primal as drums on the Nile. His hands covered her breasts, weighing . . . caressing . . . rubbing . . . circling them through the satin of her bra cups before his fingers flicked the front clasp free and her bra was falling down her arms, exposing her swollen flesh to the summer breeze.

He paused, his thumb poised over one beaded nipple, and her thudding heartbeat filled her ears, drowning out the quieter sounds of her panting breath and his whisper in her ear.

"Should I squeeze these nipples, Kira?"

"Yes."

"Hmm?"

"Please." She strained and writhed against him, giving her body's needs free reign, and the words poured out of her mouth because there was no room for hesitation or embarrassment between them. "I need you to touch me. I need it. I need—"

Why be subtle? Covering his hands with her own, she arched her back, thrusting against his palms and forcing him into a rougher grip. He was an enthusiastic learner, rolling her nipples hard enough between his skillful fingers to make spasms of pleasure shoot through her belly and incoherent noises pour out of her mouth.

All the while, that dark velvet voice kept murmuring, inside her head now. "That's right, baby. Show me what you want. I'll do anything you want. Anything for you. Just show me, okay? Show me."

Mindless now, she turned within his arms, needing both his tongue and his erection inside her. Blind urgency drove her on and she searched for relief, lifting her open mouth to his and wrapping one leg around his waist.

He approved. Planting his hands on her butt, he used his curled fingers to dig into her flesh and bring her sweet spot up against the concrete of his groin. They both cried out, pouring their passion deep into each other's urgent mouths. The kiss was raw and wet, frantic and endless, and they nipped and sucked at each other until she tasted the coppery tang of someone's blood.

The primitive chanting continued; there was nothing she could do to stop it. "I want you so much, Dexter," she said against his lips, caught up in the frenzy of tasting and needing him. "I want you inside me. I can't wait. I can't wait. Please. I want—"

The relentless begging seemed to drive him over some invisible edge. Beneath her fingers, she felt the powerful flex of his back and shoulders as he used those hands on her ass to heft her up high. Needing no encouragement, she wrapped both thighs around his waist as he swung her around to the bed, yanked the comforter out of the way and lowered her to her back against the cool sheets.

Outside, meanwhile, she heard the low rumble of thunder in the distance, and she could almost laugh because the storm out there would never match the one growing within her.

He stared down at her, his jaw hard and his eyes a blaze

of blackest crystal in the lengthening shadows, and she knew, with a sudden burst of wonderful clarity.

"You love me, don't you?"

"I've always loved you," he said, sweeping his T-shirt off and tossing it to the floor before he lowered his head to gorge on her body.

Chapter 26

Wait a minute. Did they forget the ketchup?

Kerry paused outside the front door of his cousin's tiny house, juggling a Coke and his keys in one hand and a greasy bag of burger and fries in the other. From what he could see, the clowns at the drive-through had ignored his request for ketchup, salt, and extra napkins, but he blamed himself for the dry burger he was about to eat.

Had he checked the bag before he pulled away from the window? Had he remembered that the cupboard was bare and he had a better chance of being awarded the Medal of Honor than finding ketchup in his fridge? No, he had not. He'd been so anxious to get back into the semi-safe confines of his new little home away from home that he'd forgotten the Leo Getz rule from one of his favorite movies of all time, *Lethal Weapon 2*:

"They fuck you at the drive-through."

Yeah, he was fucked. Ketchupless and fucked.

Fucking idiots.

Fumbling everything into his left hand, he unlocked the door with his right and stepped into the evening darkness of the living room, wishing he hadn't promised Kira he wouldn't drink that Jack. He was in the process of swinging the door shut behind him when terror clamped a vice grip around his throat and tightened the screws.

He was standing on a crackling sheet of plastic that had not been there half an hour ago when he left to get dinner.

Instinct made him drop, roll, and lunge back to standing as he yanked his piece out of its ankle holder and flipped off the safety, determined to face his attacker like a man. A worthless man, yeah, but still a man.

Useless moves? No question. He would die tonight, and there was no getting out of it. Hell, it was almost a relief. That didn't mean he had to make it easy for the motherfucker, whoever he was.

He was gripping the pistol with both hands, getting his feet under him and looking for somewhere to aim in the shadows, when there was a movement beside him and a sudden, white-hot slice of pain in his side. Stunned and wheezing, he dropped again, to his knees this time, and felt the sickening warmth of his blood as it drained from his body and hit the plastic with a steady patter that sounded a lot like the rain outside.

The gun fell out of his hands, and he squinted into the darkness, wondering what had happened because he hadn't heard the sound of a shot.

Had he . . . Had he been *stabbed*? With a knife?

Who did he know who rolled with a knife rather than a gun?

But he knew, of course, even before he saw the hint of white in those dark eyes . . . the gleam of his satisfied smile . . . the cold glint of a blade that was made for gutting deer and other large animals, not people. Only someone who truly hated him would bother to get up close and personal enough to slice him and feel the primal thrill of blood on his hands.

This was, in other words, pleasure, not business.

The voice, as smooth and smug as ever, only confirmed it.

"Did you miss me, Kerry, my brother?"

Kerry loosened his jaw, gasping in a futile effort to get enough air into his mouth and down to his heaving lungs. Summoning more strength than he'd known he possessed, he grabbed the back of the chair and stood up, sagging against the wall and pressing hard against the side to keep his guts inside his body, where they belonged. Not that it mattered, because he would bleed out soon, but he had a couple of things he'd like to accomplish before he did.

"I can't say that I did, man. Where you been?"

Kareem, always willing to brag about his thrilling exploits, was only too happy to answer. "Outside Miami. I've got people."

"Of course you do." Another gasp. Another searing flash of pain lighting up his body. Another ounce of his strength, gone forever. "What brings you back now?"

Kareem stilled, all his delight at being in the catbird seat leaching away in favor of a cold fury far beyond anything Kerry had ever yet seen him display. "Funny you should ask," he said, examining the blade from every angle and running his thumb along its fine edge. "I have a few questions for you, so I hope you don't die too quick."

"I hope so, too," Kerry said. Kareem didn't seem to appreciate the humor. He moved closer, bringing his black malevolence with him, so much that Kerry felt the chill down to the last cell of his body. Or maybe that was just the blood loss making him shiver. "How did you find me?"

"You can discover all kinds of interesting shit when you buy your wife's cell phone, and of course you and I hung out at old Cousin Ernie's house back in the day—did you forget?—but I'm the one asking questions now." He leaned in, as though he wanted to be close enough to smell any lies that might come out of Kerry's mouth. "What made you flip on me and tell the feds about the warehouse?" There was a wounded note in his voice, as though he couldn't quite understand why Kerry hadn't chosen him to be on his team for a kickball game. "Didn't we grow up together? Didn't we ride our freaking Big Wheels up and down the street together in the neighborhood? Didn't I bring you along with me when my business grew? *Wasn't I good to you?*"

Kerry's knees were shaking now, giving way on him so that he slid down the wall inch by inch. But the longer he kept talking, the longer he stayed alive, so he prayed to God for help, and then asked God not to spit in his eye because he didn't want the help for himself.

"Maybe I got tired of being a parasite, K.J." The use of Kareem's childhood nickname during this final conversation seemed eerily appropriate because they *had* meant something to each other once. They *had* been brothers. "Maybe I didn't like the way you shot Yogi in the back of the head. Maybe I didn't like what we became."

Wrong answer, apparently. Kareem's face twisted in the darkness, becoming grotesque, as though Picasso had rearranged the features on a demon, and he raised his arm and brought it down with a vicious slash.

Kerry's cheek screamed, and the scream ran across his chin and then lower, across his neck, leaving a gaping cut so deep Kerry could swear he felt part of his soul leak out of his body.

He cried out and, hearing his own voice, cursed Kareem for toying with him like a cat with a cricket when he could just as easily have finished the job with that stroke.

"Bad answer, my brother." Kareem walked right up to Kerry now, close enough for a good-bye kiss—close enough for those merciless eyes to be the only thing Kerry saw as he died—and held the tip of the knife at Kerry's jugular. "Try to do better with this question, because this is the thing I really want to know: did you think you could get away with fucking my wife?"

Jesus.

Kerry worked on keeping it together and prayed that his poker face held out better than his knees, but the little bit of oxygen he'd been getting into his lungs now seemed to be blocked by blood coming from God knew where.

He choked and spat. Prayed again.

Because maybe Kareem was only guessing about what had happened between Kerry and Kira. Maybe he didn't really *know,* and Kerry was too scared and fucked up at the moment to remember what Kareem might have overheard him say to Kira on the phone. If Kareem was only guessing about their affair, then Kira's life was in Kerry's hands and hung in the balance right now, and the only question was this:

Was Kerry a good enough liar to save her life?

If Kareem *knew* that Kira had slept with him, or if Kerry admitted it now, then Kira was dead, too.

Kareem's pride demanded it.

So Kerry locked his knees, arranged his features into his most disbelieving expression, and used his peripheral vision to track the distance between him and his pistol on the floor and, more important, between him and the phone on the side table.

Then he looked Kareem in the eye and faced down the demon, pretending he had the courage for the job.

"Fucking your wife?" he echoed. "What the fuck are you talking about?"

After a long, considering pause, Kareem raised the knife again.

Wrung out and undone, the delirium of being claimed by Dexter—touched by him, kissed by him, loved by him—threatened to swallow Kira whole. He was relentless, refusing to let her get a move in edgewise, shoving her hands away every time she tried to do more than grip his arms or shoulders.

Every part of her body was branded with his hands and anointed with his kiss. He nibbled and licked his way down her neck to her breasts, claiming each nipple by sucking it hard into the hottest part of his mouth and then scraping it free with his teeth. She pleaded with him to stop and to never stop, tears streaming down her temples and wetting the pillow, and he ignored her incoherent cries the way he ignored her fumbling hands.

At last he moved on, rubbing his sculpted and bristly cheeks over her heaving belly, tickling and scratching her until she twisted beneath him, nearly choking on her laughter.

"Stop," she said in her fading voice, but he was moving south again, biting the meaty inside of one thigh, and then the other, and was in no mood to grant favors.

"No."

There was only so much her overwhelmed senses could take, and he wasn't even inside her yet. "You're killing me," she complained when he nuzzled that prickly jaw in the sensitive crease between her thigh and her sex, and he raised his head to stare at her with a flash of merciless amusement.

"It's your fault for coming early. I was going to shave."

They shared a breathless laugh, and then the laugh turned into a stare, and his stare turned his eyes to black smoke.

"I love you," he said again, reaching for her hands.

There was an *I love you, too* on the tip of her lips—how could she not? What woman alive wouldn't fall crazy in love with Dexter Brady if given half a chance?—but she withheld it because it was too soon, too scary, and this was too much of a blessing from God for her to go screwing it up with any confessions, and, anyway, he was focused on her fingers now.

His touch transformed every part of her into an erogenous zone, and her hands were no different. When she ran her thumb over his tender lips, he pulled it into the hot suction of his mouth, making her nipples throb and her sex ache. He moved swiftly, sucking on some fingers, scraping others. They all received his attention.

She was melting into the mattress, floating in languid sensation, when he shifted his body lower and scratched his nails over the thatch of springy hair between her thighs and licked her engorged nub. With a cry, she jack-knifed, trying to keep her body from flying apart, at least until he was inside her.

"Don't," she began weakly. "I can't take it."

"I think you can."

Hadn't he taken enough without ever even entering

her body? Would he leave her with nothing that was still the same when he was done with her?

"Dexter, please," she said, because she knew he was a kind man. A fair man. "What are you trying to do to me?"

Unsmiling, he raised his head. "I'm showing you that there's only me. There was no one before me, and there will never be anyone after me. I want to make sure you understand that."

He held her gaze for several excruciating beats, pinning her motionless with that piercing gaze, his fingers stroking her slick cleft, holding the place where his mouth had left off. When she didn't protest, he lowered his head again, and she saw the quick flash of his pink tongue in the second before he latched onto her.

She came, her ecstasy ringing through the room on a single note of astonishment that lasted forever, or at least as long as the sharp spasms that wracked her belly.

Limp and dazed, she had only a vague awareness of his quick movements as he reached into a nightstand drawer for a shiny green package, ripped it open with his teeth, and sheathed himself. But then he was using one of his solid thighs to wedge her legs open wider, settling his weight on top of her, and the world came back into vivid focus.

Reaching between them, he gripped his penis and rubbed it against the thick, creamy, waiting folds of her flesh while he stared her in the face, a question in his eyes.

In answer, she bit the side of his neck and scraped her nails up his back.

Hard.

He groaned. Shuddered. With a dark shout that sounded like triumph, he drove inside her, seating himself to the base, stretching her beyond anything she'd experienced before.

One second of agonized waiting followed, while he braced himself on his elbows and she dug her nails into the tight globes of his ass and twined her legs around his, getting ready.

Then he opened his mouth across hers, thrust deep, and set a relentless pace that had their cries mingling with the patter of rain as it started to fall outside their window.

Chapter 27

The bitch got him.

How do you like those rotten apples?

Kareem had had the last word in the end—he always had the last word— but that didn't lessen the pain any. So much for all his strategizing about plastic sheeting, a swift, clean execution (with a little torture thrown in, of course, but mostly swift and clean), and expeditious disposal of the body.

It'd never occurred to him that he'd be injured and that his blood would mingle with Kerry's. He'd never thought—not for one fucking second—that he'd be forced to leave behind all that evidence.

Hell, it was worse than that. Nothing had gone his way since he came back to Cincinnati, and it was going to be harder, if not impossible, for him to escape unscathed again. How was he supposed to carry out the rest of his plans when his ass was so hurt he could barely put one foot in front of the other?

What was the world coming to?

It was time for him to face the fact that the stakes were higher than they'd ever been before and he might go down with the ship rather than torpedoing it and watching it sink from a safe distance.

Maybe he was losing his touch. Maybe God had turned his face away from him again, the way he had when Kareem was convicted of money laundering a few years back.

Maybe Kareem was on his own.

Ah, but he still had his mama, he reminded himself. A man could always count on his mama.

If only he could get to her.

Loosening his grip on the railing long enough to swipe some of the burning sweat out of his eyes, he counted the remaining steps in this piss-smelling back staircase. Four steps to go . . . Three steps. Shaking with exhaustion, he willed himself to keep going, propelled only by the thought of collapsing on the bed when he reached Mama's apartment.

Two steps.

Last step.

It took him several seconds of panting and resting before he gathered the strength to tackle the heavy steel fire door, which squealed open like the entrance to a crypt in some old Vincent Price movie. More strength was wasted keeping it from banging shut and waking the dead, and then he was standing outside Mama's apartment.

He hadn't been seen and could almost believe he would make it back out of the building without being seen, but then he glanced over his shoulder and saw something that stopped his heart cold:

A connect-the-dots trail of bright red drops of blood ran back down the hallway and disappeared on the other side of that fire door.

They could be wiped up—the floor was a pitted and

stained black-and-white linolcum tile—but he had been here and there was the proof. He could almost feel the scratch of a noose tightening around his neck, and he was beginning to think about Bonnie and Clyde and the benefits of going out in a blaze of glory.

It wasn't like he had anything left to lose.

He knocked on the door.

No answer.

He knocked harder, praying that only his mother woke and came to investigate, but he'd seen paper towels thicker than the walls in this dump and didn't hold out much hope.

A third round of knocking produced a muffled thump and shuffling footsteps inside the apartment, and then he heard the click of a lamp and saw a strip of light under the door right before the chain lock jangled and the door swung open.

Mama stared at him, her sleepy eyes uncomprehending.

She looked exactly the same, with the familiar powder blue housecoat, matching foam slippers, and black netting holding her bobby-pinned curls in place. But she was stooped and frail now, with lines and wrinkles mapping the skin that had been so smooth the last time he saw her up close. For the first time he questioned the wisdom of coming here for help. *What could this old woman do for him now?* he wondered, the sour taste of disappointment filling his mouth. But he had nowhere else to go and no one who cared about him like she did.

He waited, knowing what was coming.

Her jaw dropped. Her face paled. She looked away. Blinked. Looked back again. Raised shaking hands to his face. Touched him like a blind woman trying to see with her hands. Swayed on the spot and gripped his arms to keep from collapsing to the floor in a heap.

Then it came—the *Oh, Jesus* chorus she'd been wailing at his funeral, in full stereo effect. He swooped inside, shutting the door and helping her into a chair before she could really get started.

"Oh, sweet Jesus," she sobbed, rocking back and forth with one hand on Kareem and the other raised to the ceiling in gratitude. "Thank you for bringing my son back to me, Jesus, thank you, thank you—"

"Mama," he tried. "You've got to be quiet. I don't want the whole world to know I'm here. Shh, Mama, please—"

There was no point. The chanting continued, louder than ever, interrupted only by her wet kisses, rained all over his face and hands. "Thank you, Jesus," she said, over and over until he wanted to scream with the irritation, which was almost as strong as the frustration and pain. "I knew you'd bring my precious son back to me. Thank you, Lord. Thank you—"

If she had any questions about his sudden resurrection, she didn't ask—at least not yet—which was one of the things he'd always liked best about Mama: she didn't ask. She was like one of his high-priced defense lawyers in that way, instinctively understanding that some doors were best left closed and double-bolted.

But he didn't have time for this hysteria shit.

He had work to do before it was too late.

Grabbing her by the shoulder, he gave her a good shake. "*Mama*. Pull yourself together. I need your help."

Those hands of hers went right back to his face, stroking and caressing, but her streaming eyes narrowed down for a critical look at him for the first time. Judging by the sharp intake of breath, she didn't like what she saw.

"What's happened to you, boy? What's happened to your face? What— Oh, Jesus, so much blood! What's happened to you? We need to get you to the hospital—"

"No." He shook her again and kept a hard grip on her arm so she'd shut the fuck up and focus on listening rather than babbling. "I'm not going to any hospital. No one can know that I'm still alive. *Do you understand me?*"

"But—" she floundered, jaws still flapping. "But you'll bleed to death—"

"No, I won't. That's why I'm here. You're going to stitch me up."

"Stitch you up?"

For God's sake—had she turned into a parrot while he was gone?

"Stitch. Me. Up. Let's get this over with."

Her eyes went round and wide. "With what? I'm not a doctor!"

"Get your sewing kit," he said grimly.

They stared at each other while more of his blood flowed, and the situation would have been funny if it wasn't so fucking serious. He hadn't worked, planned, and suffered for all these months, finding a way to be free from Johnny Law, only to come back to Cincy at his moment of triumph and bleed out on his mother's flowered sofa.

There was no goddamn way.

"Mama," he roared, shaking her a final time.

That snapped her to attention. She nodded, once, becoming the hardheaded and focused woman that he needed her to be. Some of the rising panic eased back from his chest, letting him breathe.

"Let me see," she said, going to work on his clothes.

He submitted, biting the inside of his cheek while she peeled back his shirt and revealed the tiny hole in the front and the mangled and raw meat from the exit wound in the back, all that remained of his ruined left shoulder.

Dexter propped his head on his elbow and watched her sleep.

Ridiculous? Yeah.

Sappy? You betcha.

Was he a pussy-whipped punk? The world's biggest.

None of that kept him from yawning back the sleep and keeping his tired eyes open so he wouldn't miss anything about this remarkable night.

She slept on her belly, nowhere near a pillow, with her head turned toward him and her fingers curled into a loose fist beneath her chin. Her breathing was deep and easy, her brow smooth and untroubled, her lips swollen from his kisses. Already he could see marks appearing across her shoulder and down the side of her neck, remnants of his stubbly face, which he now rubbed with regret.

Actually, no. He didn't regret it. She was his woman now, and he was just caveman enough to appreciate the visible proof.

His woman.

There was no end to his delight in her. The smell of lilies on her skin, the way her hair curled around her ears, her small but amazing breasts, the junk in her perfect round trunk, the smooth silkiness of her long legs. Her tears, her warmth, her passion. All of it astounded and humbled him, swelling his heart until it threatened to crack open like the first overripe watermelon of summer.

He should cover her with the sheet before she got cold;

she was his responsibility now—his treasure—and he planned to take excellent care of her. Except that then he wouldn't be able to admire the tantalizing side of one bare breast, the slope of her toned back or the swell of that ass.

Anyway, if she got cold, he planned to warm her right back up.

As though she felt the weight of his gaze, her lids flickered and then slowly opened, revealing those sparkling brown eyes, and her mouth curved into the sexiest smile he'd ever seen. Color flooded her cheeks and he felt a responsive kick low in his belly as he, too, remembered everything they'd said and done.

"Hi," she said.

"Hi."

She studied his face, running her gentle fingers over his brow. "You're very serious."

"I'm a couple of quarts low on fluids."

That made her laugh as she rolled onto her side and propped her head on her hand, and he was pleased to see that there was no shyness in her, no scurrying for cover as they watched each other by the light of the nightstand lamp, which he'd turned on a minute ago.

She was so freaking incredible, there was no room in his mind to absorb it all. Sweet happiness glowed in her face; had he had anything to do with that? Lower down, meanwhile, her perky breasts were still swollen, her nipples dark brown with engorgement, and lower than that, the ruddy folds of her lips were slick and fragrant with arousal.

She tied him up in knots, this one did.

"You wore me out," she told him.

There was that caveman tendency again, making him want to thump his chest and swing from the rooftops.

Instead, he contented himself with reaching out and dragging her closer, so he could settle his stiffening penis into that nest of hair between her legs and his hand on her very fine ass.

"Yeah? You look okay to me."

"I didn't say I wasn't okay," she said.

He grinned with pure male satisfaction.

Screw it. He was a caveman. Just call him Krong.

"We didn't eat your dinner," she said, slipping her hand between them to grip him tight, peeking up into his face to see if he'd stop her this time.

He didn't.

"You were my dinner," he told her.

Making a distinctly feline sound—somewhere between a mewl and a purr, she eased closer, running her tongue across his lower lip and then slipping it deep inside his oh-so-willing mouth. He went from zero to sixty, hardening inside her milking hand as though it had been ten years rather than ten minutes since his last orgasm.

With a lingering suck and a nip, she pulled back just enough to look him in the eye while her hand worked its magic. "You were right," she said, her thumb now running around his swollen head—around and around until need spiked in his belly. "It was way too soon for us to make love. The relationship is ruined now, isn't it?"

Jesus, she was going to make him come, right now, and she was asking questions like that?

"Maybe if we . . . try really hard we can . . . put it back together."

"You think?" she asked sweetly, giving her wrist a little twist that nearly shot him to the ceiling. That was it. Game over. With a primal growl he was all over her, snatching her to her back and kissing her with frantic, openmouthed urgency—basically eating her face.

She kissed him back, laughing, and then, suddenly, nothing was funny. He saw the sudden flare of panic in her eyes and it touched his heart. "What is it, baby?"

"I'm so happy. I can't even— I don't have the words for it."

Christ. She was going to make him bawl like a baby if she kept this up.

"Being with you is so easy. That's a sign that something's wrong, isn't it?"

He stared at her, thinking about where she'd started from and where she was now. As far as he was concerned, tonight was only the beginning of a lifetime of happiness that he fully intended to give her.

"Nothing's wrong." Cupping her face, he leaned in to press a reassuring kiss to her forehead. "I told you before: it's supposed to be exactly this easy."

"God, I hope so."

"Now I have a question for you." Down below, he covered her hand with his, tightening her grip until his breath caught in his throat. "Where's Max? Do you have to get home and check on him or anything?"

"Oh, didn't I mention? He's at the kennel tonight."

"Thank the good Lord," he said, hooking an elbow behind her knee to spread her wide as he settled between her thighs. "I never made my way down to your feet, did I? Remind me to do that."

Chapter 28

The dream continued.

Kira's warmth was in his bed. Her scent was in his nostrils. Beneath the fluffy softness of the comforter, her sleek curls trailed across his belly, tickling him. Arousing him. He sighed and rolled onto his back, his movements as easy and languorous as a soak in a spa after a massage. She came with him, settling the silky smoothness of her body between his legs. Stroking her hair, he waited, his breath suspended in this exquisite moment.

Her hands slid up the inside of his thighs, and lingered, teasing. He shifted his hips, the hot rush of blood to his groin making him impatient. Urgent. When she laughed in response—a triumphant, purely female sound of delight —her breath's humidity nearly sent him through the roof.

With an indistinct murmur, she took his rigid length between her hands and licked him. Her slick tongue traced a slow circle around the sensitive head of his penis, hitting nerve endings he hadn't known he'd possessed. His fingers tightened convulsively, tunneling down to her scalp to bring her closer. He caught himself and loosened his grip, afraid he'd hurt her before this was all over with, but her need seemed to match his.

Easing that clever mouth to one side, she swirled that tongue around the meaty part of his inner thigh, sucked it deep into her mouth, and scraped it with her teeth—just enough—as she released it, the same thing he'd done to her earlier.

He cried out, every muscle in his body tightening to piano wire, and held her head in a death grip.

She didn't complain.

After another easy nuzzle, she stuck out her tongue, ran it slowly . . . slowly . . . up his entire length and then, without warning, took him so far inside the wet suction of her mouth it felt as if she was swallowing him whole.

Something snapped inside his head, breaking through the restraints that kept him human and turning him into an animal driven by his basest urges, pure and simple.

Nearly mindless now, he thrust as deep as she could take him. Maybe it was too much, but, Jesus, she had to know she was driving him out of his freaking skin. Another smug female laugh answered him, and the corresponding vibrations heightened the sensations until his breath stalled and passing out seem like a real possibility.

"Kira." It took the last molecule of his control to tug gently on her hair and issue a gasped warning. There had to be a special place in heaven waiting for him for stopping at this crucial juncture. "Baby. If we're going to stop, we need to stop now."

The covers shifted and then she appeared in the muted light of the lamp. Rumpled hair, flushed cheeks, gleaming eyes—she was exactly the way she'd appeared in all of his dreams: heart-stopping.

Looking up, she let him see the wet pink glisten of her tongue as she circled it around his head again, while her hands, meanwhile, milked him with a relentless rhythm.

"Now why would I stop?" she wondered.

There was one arrested moment when she held his gaze, and then she put that mouth on him again, finishing her work and making him come with a hoarse shout that could probably be heard for miles up and down the river. When she was done, she crept back up the bed, taking her place at his side and smoothing his chest as his lungs heaved for air, as though it hadn't been her damn fault that the top of his head nearly blew off.

He gathered her up and held her tight, relishing the tight buds of her nipples against his side and her legs wrapped around his.

Sudden panic flared, robbing him of words.

Never before had he had so much to lose, and all of it was right here in his arms.

Before Kira, his life had been fine.

A little boring, a little lonely, but fine.

There would be no after Kira for him. It was that simple. To live, he needed food and water, shelter and clothing, air to breath, and Kira. Without any of that, he could not go on.

He stared down at her, tracing her features. Raising her heavy lids, she blessed him with a drowsy smile that claimed the last little bit of his heart that wasn't already hers.

"Are you trying to ruin me?" he asked.

"Yes," she said simply, but, when she looked at him like that, he realized that being ruined was the best thing that could ever happen to him.

* * *

So the question was: what should she cook for dinner?

Kira wove her way through the crowd at Findlay Market the next morning, awake and alive in a way she'd never been before, her senses open to the sights, smells, and sounds that the world had to offer her in such blessed abundance.

Yeah.

She'd done a spectacular swan dive into the sappy pool and was doing a few laps.

She grinned to herself, that same simpering grin she'd been trying to smother for the last several hours, and passed it off as a particularly cheery hello to a young mother who went by with a curly-haired and chubby baby on her hip.

The hot flush that she'd been sporting broke past the confines of her face and spread to every far corner of her tingling skin, and the tender area between her thighs renewed its sweet, throbbing ache, no doubt wondering, as she was, how soon she could feel the breathtaking thrust of Dexter Brady moving inside her body again.

Dodging around an elderly couple, she edged through a glass door and into the nearest bakery, smiling at everyone and seeing nothing except Dexter . . . his hands . . . his mouth . . . the perfect triangle as his wide shoulders narrowed to that flat belly, all of him sinewy and cut, strong and powerful . . . and the sprinkling of hair between his nipples that trailed down and then flared out, guiding her to . . .

Wow. There went that hot flush again, prickling in her scalp now. The only surprise was that she didn't smell the acrid singe of her own hair.

Okay, so . . . dessert. She studied the massive glass display case, mesmerized by the choices. Cheesecakes of every description, chocolaty or fruity, slices or whole. Cakes with so many layers of filling they were marvels of modern engineering. Pies and crumbles, cookies and brownies.

What would Dexter like?

Dexter.

God. What had she ever done right in her life to deserve a man like him?

After the rape, she'd spent hours . . . days . . . weeks worried that she'd spend the rest of her life dreading intimacy and cringing at a man's touch. Hah. Dexter was so different from Kareem, so entirely *other,* that there'd been no need for fears and trepidation. No room for them between them.

Nothing could have prepared her for last night, and she was no virgin. She and Kareem had screwed like athletic bunnies in the early days of their marriage, as though every room and flat surface had to be tried, at least once, and every conceivable position given a test run. With Kerry, there'd been stolen moments, poignant and desperate.

Great sex, all of it.

But never had a man worshipped her the way that Dexter had. Never had a man used her so thoroughly, wringing every last drop of pleasure out of every square inch of her body and taken such joy in doing so. Never had she reveled in giving everything she was—everything she had, everything she could offer—to a man, until last night.

He had, in short, taken her apart and put her back together again, making her a more confident woman in the process. More than that, he'd proved his point beyond any doubt: nothing that'd happened to her before this counted; neither of her other relationships mattered now or would ever matter again.

Right on cue, her cell phone vibrated in her pocket, and she pulled it out, checking the display. It was him, of course. Trying to step out of the way before she was trampled by a customer who was shouting at an employee behind the display case, carrying on about his urgent need for some schnecken, a rich German pastry that was pretty much a stick of butter with some sugar thrown in, she ducked into an alcove in the corner near the window.

"Hi."

"Are you thinking about me?" he asked.

Again—wow. They'd have to try the phone sex thing one of these days, because the low murmur of his voice in her ear was more than enough to make her breasts swell and her honey flow.

"Of course I am."

He grinned; she could hear it in his tone. "What are you thinking?"

"I would tell you, but I don't want to melt the phone."

"Nice answer. But how am I supposed to go down to the office when I can't get my pants zipped?"

"It's Saturday. Why are you going down there at all?"

"I won't be long. I just need to, ah, check on a couple things."

"Is there a story there? Should I be worried?"

"Absolutely not. You let me worry."

That wasn't quite the answer she'd hoped to hear. "Are you telling me there's something to worry about?"

"I'm telling you that if you ever feel threatened, for

any reason, like, say, you see one of Kareem's associates or something like that, I want you to go back to where we were last night and I'll find you there, okay? Not that I think you will, but I just want us to have a plan. A plan will make us both feel better. Okay?"

Now he was really scaring her. "Okay, but—"

"More importantly, I want you to pick up some stuff for my dinner and be waiting for me in two hours. That's as long as I can go without touching you. Got it?"

Geez. He was right. Now they had a plan, in case they ever needed one, which they wouldn't, and she could relax. When would she ever stop looking for disaster around every corner? Why couldn't she embrace the sunshine and give herself permission to be happy? Hadn't she earned it? She smiled, wrestling those nameless fears back into the dungeon, where they belonged.

"Got it."

"You drive safe, okay? I don't want anything to happen to you."

"No? Why's that?" she wondered, blatantly fishing and hoping he'd say it again so she'd know he'd meant it last night.

"Because I love you," he said softly, and hung up.

"Bye." Happy tears welled in her throat and burned the insides of her eyes. Taking a deep breath, she blinked them back, forcing herself to focus on the matter at hand: dessert.

When she opened her eyes, her gaze snagged on a man outside the window, standing under the awning of a cheese shop in the next block.

He was staring in her direction, alert and still when

everyone else—all the people walking up and down the sidewalks between them—were animated and purposeful.

Ice water replaced her spinal fluid, creeping up her back inch by inch, spreading numb terror. He was . . . watching her.

He looked like . . .

No. She blocked the thought, refusing to let it form and intrude on her newfound happiness. She was stronger than that memory and would not be blindsided by random reminders.

But her lungs had seized up, and clammy sweat was now trickling down her sides. Over the dull roar of the crowd inside the shop, she heard the relentless crackle of the brown paper bag she held in her shaking hand.

The man was featureless. A shadow of black amid the bright hubbub, probably due to some trick of the distance between them and the sun's rays as they fell on his awning. His race was a mystery, his clothing only an assumption. He might have been twenty-one or eighty-five, but it didn't matter.

The sight of him struck the kind of terror in her belly that she had never felt outside her husband's presence.

She stared, paralyzed down to the last drop of blood in her body.

Without warning, a woman overloaded with bags and balancing a white cake box between her hands plowed into Kira, knocking her off balance and making her stumble.

"Oh, I'm so sorry," the woman began, bobbling the cake box. "I wasn't looking where I was going, and I don't know how I'm going to get this cake—"

Kira heard none of it. The second she regained her

footing, she put her palms on the glass and looked out, desperate to find the phantom again, to watch him move into the light so she could see with her own two over-wrought eyes that he bore no resemblance to any night-mares from her past and she didn't need to be so—

He was gone.

Chapter 29

Dexter stared at the e-mail, the shit-eating grin he'd been sporting since he spoke to Kira a little while ago fading into frozen disbelief tinged with the beginnings of blind terror.

What had started out as a quick and probably unnecessary trip to the office to make sure all possible loose ends had been snipped and tied had unexpectedly turned into a scenario with nightmare potential that he did not, even now, want to consider.

All because of two lines from the coroner's office:

The dental assistant who provided us with the records in question was killed in a car accident nearly six months ago. Will follow up with the dentist on Monday.

This unacceptable answer was not what Dexter had prepared for. He'd thought that the coroner would say that the records had been double- and triple-checked, that they'd been certified beyond all human doubt and that Kareem Gregory was, therefore, the crispy SOB currently occupying the grave in Spring Grove, so Dexter could therefore go about living happily ever after with the beautiful widow.

Instead, there was a glaring loophole in this whole scenario, a trail he could not follow.

The person who'd provided the dental records that allowed for a positive identification of Kareem's body was now dead and could not be questioned.

But . . . this could be nothing, right? The coroner would follow up on Monday, they'd discover that there were no discrepancies in the records or anything, and conclude that Kareem's death and the assistant's death had been nothing more than a . . . coincidence.

Too bad he didn't believe in coincidence.

He thought of Max's disappearance and the prowler Kira'd thought she'd seen.

He thought of her birthday flowers.

He thought of the threat to Kerry, which, in fairness, could have been sent by any one of a million different thugs and/or enemies.

He added all these things together and came up with one conclusion:

Fuck.

Resting his elbows on the desk and his forehead on his fisted hands, he tried to choke back the primal fear and use the brain God had given him. Think, Brady. *Think.*

Okay. Let's assume that Kareem somehow escaped the explosion.

Ridiculous, but let's assume it anyway.

Let's further assume that he managed a switcheroo in no time flat and substituted some poor chump in his place.

Absurd, but let's run with it.

Who was the chump?

How had Kareem wiggled out of the ankle monitor and gotten it onto the other guy?

Where the fuck had Kareem been all this time, and why was he back now?

What did he want?

Stupid question there. If Kareem was alive, he wanted what he always wanted:

Vengeance against his enemies. Power. Kira.

Not necessarily in that order.

Dexter stared, unseeing, at the e-mail. Dread, meanwhile, slithered up his spine like a chilled snake, and sweat collected across his forehead.

And then his cell phone rang, flashing some unfamiliar number.

Shit.

"Yeah?" he barked.

"Dexter? This is Amy from Pine Lake. You didn't take your mother out, did you?"

"My mother?" he asked stupidly, his brain struggling to shift gears.

"She's gone."

Kira left Findlay Market and went straight home. Simmering anxiety was hot on her heels, trailing her like an overzealous shadow, and her fingers were ten useless popsicles, despite the day's heat. She did not buy any of the luscious desserts on display, nor did she pick up grilling steaks from the meat counter.

It was all she could do to weave her way through the crowd to the parking lot and the relative safety of her car without erupting in shrieks of paranoid hysteria. It was a blessing from God that she arrived back home unscathed, because she drove with her gaze glued to the rearview mirror, making sure the ghost hadn't followed her.

That's all it was. A ghost. It had to be. Because if the choices were between losing her mind and seeing ghosts, or being perfectly sane and seeing a man who should be dead but wasn't, she'd take insanity any day.

Insanity was her friend.

She couldn't stop shaking. Her blood ran cold with it; her hands vibrated with it; her teeth clacked with it. Six months and dozens of hours in therapy later, and she was as big a mess as she'd ever been. Maybe she should ask her shrink for a refund.

She crept into her kitchen, trapped between numb paralysis and abject terror, afraid of the creak of her feet on the floorboards, the hidden places behind her furniture, and, most of all, of what might happen next.

Maybe her hallucinations would extend to purple scorpions climbing her walls, and wouldn't that be fun?

Maybe she wasn't hallucinating at all, and Kareem was in the house with her, right now, waiting for her.

There was a yap and a scurry, and Max scrambled through his doggie flap from the backyard, eager to greet her even if she was coming unhinged. Grateful for the distraction, she stooped to scoop up his wriggling body, and that was when she saw it:

The insistent red flash of the message light on her answering machine.

She stared at it, Max's head tucked under her chin, and tried to convince herself that her screaming intuition was wrong, and whatever she was about to hear was not the warning sound of danger headed straight her way.

Creeping up on it, as though the machine was a fanged fire-breather who must not, at all costs, be disturbed, she pressed the button.

The machine's indifferent male voice announced the message:

"You have one new message, sent yesterday at eleven P.M."

Had the message been there when she came home from Dexter's this morning, then? Had she missed it in her afterglow euphoria?

And then, from the other side of hell, came another voice. The faint, choked, and mangled voice of what was left of someone she'd once known.

"Kira? Pick up the phone." There was a muffled thump . . . a pause . . . an animalistic wail of despair that froze the marrow in her bones. "Kira! For God's sake, pick up the phone! *Kir-aaa!*"

"No."

Gripping Max tighter as her knees gave way, she slid down the wall and landed hard on her butt. Max whined and twisted free, trotting away and coming back to cock his head with concern when the silent sobs doubled her up.

"No. No, no, *no!*"

Hysterical now, she punctuated each *No* by slamming her palms on the hard tiled floor, until the sting of pain shot up her arms and through the top of her head. Where was she when this happened? Where was God?

God didn't deign to answer.

The message, meanwhile, went on. There was an endless pause, during which she heard excruciating gasps and horrible gurgling breaths, as though someone had caught a fish and clipped a microphone on it while it tried to drag air rather than water over its gills.

The suffering went on, both in the message and inside Kira, and she couldn't sob hard enough, couldn't cry enough tears for this kind of pain, and couldn't get the sound out of her soul.

After long seconds, Kerry's breathing seemed to even out, and then to slow to a seething rattle.

"Kira." That voice was a whisper now, a dying man's echo as he left the world. "He's alive. He—"

"End of messages," interjected the machine's mechanical male voice, and the machine clicked off.

That was it.

Kerry was dead; no one could survive what she'd just heard. Despite all her hopes and prayers, she hadn't saved him from being slaughtered like an animal and dying alone and in terror.

And Kareem—brilliant, malevolent, vindictive Kareem—was alive, and his so-called death had only been a trick to catch them all unawares. And why had he done that? It was so obvious now, so sickeningly, painfully obvious. He'd done it to avoid jail and, more important, so that, when he was ready, he could come back, terrify and torture them and then, finally, claim his pound of flesh.

And somewhere, in the darkest corner of her soul, she'd known all along that Kareem would never be gracious enough to just die and leave her in peace.

I have to get out of here, she thought, scrambling to her feet and choking back the rising hysteria that wanted to claim her. Now. She had to grab Max and her Glock, and then she'd meet Dexter at the boat—had he known Kareem was alive when he suggested that rendezvous point?; had he suspected?—and then she could tell him about Kerry and they'd figure out what to do next—

Oh, God.

What was that?

Sitting on the baker's rack, just as pretty as you please, was a tiny robin's-egg blue box with a white satin bow. From Tiffany, of course. Kareem's favorite jeweler. Where else?

How many times had he gifted her with boxes like this over the years? For Christmas and her birthday, their anniversary, and just because. Every time, she'd squealed with excitement and fallen all over him with delight.

This time, she stared at it as though it was a roadside bomb with a hair trigger wire.

And then, inexorably drawn, she crept toward it. Picked it up. Discovered the heavy linen envelope underneath.

Kira, it said, in Kareem's bold scrawl.

Hands shaking, she opened it and pulled out the card.

Did you forget, my wife? Forever and a day.

The hysteria roared back, flooding her throat with sobs and laughter—Jesus, he was so predictable, it really was funny—and her eyes with tears.

Her fumbling fingers refused to coordinate with each other, so it took her forever to untie the ribbon, work the box open, and peer inside and see what further delights Kareem had waiting for her on this nightmare day.

It was the diamond engagement ring—the real one— that she'd tried and tried to find in the last days of her marriage. The one that Kareem had secretly replaced with a fake so she couldn't sell it and have the money to leave him.

Kira stared at it in utter disbelief.

And then she screamed.

Chapter 30

"I don't understand this!" Dexter finally lost his temper and, along with it, his determination to remain a shrewd and levelheaded law-enforcement officer during this crisis. Screw it. He'd lapsed into the darkest nightmares of his childhood, and he wanted his mommy back. Right now. "What kind of Keystone Kop operation are you people running here? And when are we going to be able to look at the security tapes?"

After a search of his mother's wing of the facility, during which he, the director, and about a dozen nurses, aides, and other employees had searched every room, bathroom, closet, nook, and cranny of this godforsaken place, they'd all converged back here under the awning outside the lobby to compare notes and wait for the arrival of a couple of units of the Cincinnati police.

Maybe they could explain how she'd vanished into thin air and wave their magic wands to get her back. There'd been some early discussion of her simply wandering away from the unlocked floor, but this theory had died a quick death because it'd been four months since she sat in that wheelchair and never got out, and even then she'd relied heavily on a walker.

Mom had been kidnapped, vaporized, or abducted by aliens because there was no sign of her in any direction that he could see.

He was betting on kidnapped, and a sickening knot of concrete had settled in his belly because he didn't think he'd ever see her alive again. Was Kareem somewhere nearby, watching him right now, laughing at his growing panic? Was this the price Dexter had to pay for bringing that monster to justice, or was the greater vengeance still to come?

The director, a whisper-thin woman who'd always exuded confidence with her somber suits, sensible shoes, and no-nonsense expression, wrung her hands like she was wringing the water from her delicates. He did not take this to be a good sign.

"She hadn't been gone that long when we noticed she was missing. Five minutes at the most—maybe less."

Dexter was in no mood to be gracious. "Five minutes is all it takes."

The aide who'd left Mom alone to answer a page at the other end of the wing reappeared from down the hallway, towing a guy in white behind her—the janitor, maybe.

"Craig saw something," the aide said triumphantly.

Craig, a middle-aged guy with graying temples and an eager to help expression on his face, nodded. "Some black guy was pushing her down the hall. I thought he was her son or something."

"I'm her son," Dexter told him. "What'd he look like?"

Craig shrugged. "I only saw him from behind. Looked

young. Dark pants. Dress shirt. About your height, I guess. Nothing special."

"Where were they?" Dexter demanded.

"Back hallway near the beauty salon."

Dexter was already heading in that direction. "Show me."

Craig led the way and they were there in less than a minute, a nondescript corridor that dead-ended in the double glass doors leading to a small courtyard they'd already searched. But it wasn't the courtyard that held Dexter's attention this time. It was the freight elevator.

"Where does this go?"

"The basement and the roof."

The roof.

Guided by instincts that sharpened by the second, he punched the button and stepped inside the massive car when it came, all but oblivious to the others as they piled in after him. After a short ride up—the place only had three stories—the doors slid open to reveal a short and dark hallway and a fire door with a blaring red exit sign over it.

Dexter charged off the elevator and banged through the fire door, blinking against the sudden blinding sunshine. He glanced wildly around, his heart sinking with disappointment.

There was nothing up here, and he'd been so sure. Industrial exhaust fan for God knew what . . . air-conditioning units . . . nothing but— Jesus.

There she was. Sitting in her chair, her back to him, her head drooping with sleep, with the wheels one inch, if that, from the edge of a thirty-foot drop.

Dexter froze and flung out a hand to stop anyone else from running up to save her. In his mind's eye, he saw it

all with a bowel-loosening burst of clarity: Mom startled
awake, disoriented and combative, arms and legs flail-
ing. Mom, who'd never hurt anybody and had been
beloved by everyone who knew her, going over the edge
and dying with a splat on concrete rather than peacefully
asleep in her bed with her family by her side.

Huh-uh. Not gonna happen.

He crept forward, sparing a glance over his shoulder
to give everyone the *shh* symbol. Which was unnecessary because they'd fallen into a hushed silence, and
the loudest noise for miles around was the excruciating
crunch of the gravel beneath his feet.

Without warning, Mom's head lolled. She snorted,
startling herself awake, and looked around with a slow
stiffening of her shoulders and an involuntary mewl of
fear that stopped his heart.

It was now or never.

Springing forward with a burst of speed he hadn't dis-
played since his DEA training days, he covered the remaining ten feet between them in point-two seconds,
grabbed the chair's handles—he hadn't expected the
brake to be on, and it wasn't—and pulled her back to
safety, which caused exactly the kind of disorientation
he'd feared.

"You stop that!" Her hand lashed out and caught him
squarely in the jaw, loosening a couple of his molars if
he wasn't mistaken. "What you trying to do to me, boy?
You leave me alone!"

When the stars cleared from his vision, Dexter sank
to his knees in front of her, leaning in to hug her around
the waist, even if she bloodied his nose for it.

"I love you, you cranky old woman. I love you."

Mom wasn't feeling the affection. "Get off me!"

Planting her hands on his shoulders, she gave him a hard push, and as he was settling back on his haunches, he felt the rough scratch of cardboard against his chin.

There was cardboard in her lap.

No, not cardboard, he realized with rising dread. An envelope made from that heavy, expensive ivory paper people used for wedding invitations and birth announcements. There was a name on the front, written in blue ink by someone with perfect penmanship:

Dexter.

His hands shook as he opened it, a fact that would embarrass him later, if and when this nightmare day ever ended. Taking a deep breath, he read the single line on the embossed card:

I can take away anything you love.

"No." Frantic with a fear that made what he'd just gone through seem like an hour-long, full body massage, he stared at the card and tried to figure out what the fuck he should do now, because Kira hadn't answered any of the texts or returned any of the messages he'd left for her in the last hour, and he was beginning to think he'd never see her alive again. "No!"

Only when she let herself and Max onto the quiet boat did Kira's heart rate slow to anything approaching normal. The shaking in all of her frigid limbs hadn't stopped, though, but that was the least of her worries at the moment. She set her purse and Max (now in his carrier because she'd never had him on a boat before and didn't have time to chase him away from the edge of the deck to keep him from jumping into the water) next to the sofa and checked her watch again.

Almost time for Dexter to meet her there.

Thank God they'd had this date already arranged; she hadn't dared call him from either of her phones. What if Kareem had them both tapped? Hell, with Kareem, that was probably a foregone conclusion, along with a video camera of some kind, probably stashed in her light fixture or some such.

Max whined, wanting to be let out, but she ignored him in favor of adrenaline-fueled pacing.

It all made sense now. Max's disappearance. Her phone being off the charger—that was probably when Kareem put a listening device in it. The flowers. Even the dream of someone touching her, she realized, shuddering. That was Kareem. It was all Kareem.

That'd been him at Findlay Market earlier, too, and—

Footsteps sounded out on the dock, growing closer, and Max did his little warning rumble to let her know someone was coming.

Dexter!

Oh, thank God.

Thank God, thank God, thank God—

With a happy cry, she raced back up the four steps to greet him in the entry area and threw the door open.

It wasn't Dexter, though.

It was Kareem.

"Hello, wife."

Forcing his way inside and using a vicious backhand so lightning-fast it almost didn't register with her vision, he sent her tumbling back down the steps and to the floor, where she landed with a brain-jarring thud.

It took a minute for the disorienting flashes of light and ringing in her ears to taper off enough for her to know which end was up. Giving her head a shake in a largely futile attempt to clear it, she struggled to her hands and knees, willing her eyes to focus. When they finally did, she saw his legs looming over her, right in her face, and his expensive loafers were polished and scuff-free, his dark slacks perfectly creased.

The sight of those legs in that easy, unconcerned stance, as though he was in line at Starbucks, staring at the overhead menu while he made his selection, enraged her. Galvanized her.

Why was this man still alive, walking the earth with his evil?

Worse, why had she let him catch her off guard *again*?

This was it, she decided. Screw it. Maybe he would kill her today—hell, he probably would—but she intended to take a pound of his bloody flesh with her when she went.

A primal sound burned its way out of her throat, part war cry and part furious roar, and with it came a burst of suicidal strength. With a little help from God, she intended to take this fucker's head off before she died.

Letting her thighs do all the work, she leapt out of her crouch and caught him around the waist (he emitted an *oof* of surprise, and that damn sure sounded like music to her ears), making him slam into the wall with a force that caused one of the framed photos to fall and shatter.

A high-pitched bellow came out of his twisted mouth, and she realized, with dawning clarity and hope, that it had nothing to do with being taken by surprise. He was . . . injured. His left shoulder was, in fact, now oozing blood through his tan silk shirt like some violent ink blotch.

If he was hurt, then she had a chance.

A small chance, but a chance.

The Glock. If she could just get to her Glock.

They staggered, mirroring each other as they both tried to get their feet under them. His face contorted with an animalistic black rage, Kareem lunged for her just as she dove for her purse on the floor. Kareem was quicker. Hooking her with his good right arm, he brought her down and they crashed to the floor together with enough force to knock every molecule of oxygen out of her crushed lungs.

For one terrible second, she stared up into the feral glitter of his eyes as he straddled her, gasping for air and wondering if she was looking into the face of her own death.

But the maneuver took something out of him, too, and he cried out, cursing and favoring that shoulder.

Kira made her move, bending her knee and slamming it into his back with everything she was worth.

Pay dirt.

He screamed and fell off her, giving her enough room to roll to her belly and try to escape with a military crawl. It didn't work. Blessed with the reflexes of a young Muhammad Ali, he grabbed her ankle with his good hand and yanked her back while she kicked desperately, trying to connect with his face.

Survive, Kira. All you have to do is survive until help comes. It doesn't matter if he breaks a few of your bones. Just survive.

She kicked again and felt a satisfying crunch beneath her foot, but it came at a high price: his big hand clamped down around that ankle and twisted, wrenching it until, through the searing pain that shot all the way up and out of her head and through her ears, she heard a snap.

Agony caught her in a death grip, trying to hold her under until she drowned in it. Yelling with rage—he would not do this to her!—and fighting for consciousness, she reached overhead, stretching out across the floor and grappling for something—anything, God, anything—to use against him.

She found it, waiting for her on the lower shelf of the coffee table.

With a guttural cry, she twisted back around and jammed the serrated branches of a basketball-sized piece of petrified coral into his face and neck until the thrilling trickle of his warm blood flowed over her fingers.

He shrieked with the kind of bloodcurdling sound she hadn't realized a human could make.

That was her moment. She broke free, scuttling backward on her butt and dragging her useless leg with her, heading the last four feet in the direction of her purse and the Glock, but he'd recovered already and, worse, had a weapon.

The six-inch length of a killing blade gleamed in his hand.

"No," she whispered.

Despite the sliced and bleeding side of his face, a smile touched his lips. "Yes," he said. "Oh, yes."

Chapter 31

Being attacked and beaten was one thing. She could deal with that. Being shot? No problem. Quick and easy. Bring it on.

The sight of that hunting knife made her throat seize up with dry sobs. "Please don't," she said, still creeping backward on her butt. "Please don't cut me."

He wasn't doing much better, but at least he'd reached his weapon. Using his good arm, he levered himself to his knees to loom over her, swiped some of the sweat and blood off his face, and widened that malevolent grin.

"What should we talk about before I kill you, Baby Girl?"

She made sounds. Terrible sounds. Laughing and sobbing, all mixed together, so choked and manic it took her several long beats to gather her thoughts and activate her voice.

"Why aren't you dead, you son of a bitch? Did they kick you out of hell?"

He didn't seem offended. If anything, she amused him. "I was in Miami, getting my face done. Not that you can appreciate that now that you've sliced most of my skin off, but I thought they did a pretty good job."

He angled his head this way and that, presumably so she could admire the remnants of his narrower nose, sharper cheekbones and brand new chin cleft.

Sweat dripped into her eyes, but she blinked and swiped it back, determined to keep him talking for as long as possible.

"Why'd you do that, pray tell?"

"Well, you see," he said conversationally, "it was all part of my plan. I blow up the house to keep the feds from getting it, I die, I hide out in Miami for a while and get a new face, and then I come back, take care of a little business, and then ride off with you into the sunset. Somewhere that Johnny Law can't catch me. Brilliant, wasn't it?"

"How did you do it?"

"Do you know how easy it is to tamper with a gas line if you don't care if it looks like arson?"

"Apparently I don't. Go figure."

"I slipped out the back. I wasn't planning on you showing up. Good thing you didn't stay too long, eh?"

"Did you care about Jacob Radcliffe dying in your little inferno?"

The question seemed to baffle him. "Why would I care about that piece of shit attorney who couldn't keep me out of jail to save his life?"

She stared at him, speechless with horror. This was what evil looked like up close. No horns. No fangs or forked tongue. Just a man without a conscience.

"Who died for you?"

He gave his good shoulder an irritated twitch, as though he didn't want the interesting parts of his story to get lost in favor of meaningless details. "He worked for me. Nobody important."

Kira struggled to make her lungs work, each breath a conscious effort. "Did he know he was going to die for you that day?"

"Nah. I just told him I needed him as a decoy while I slipped out for a while. He was already in the house that night when you showed up, waiting in the den. Did I mention I had two ankle bracelets, both programmed the same? He wore one, I wore the other one. Easy as pie when you've got the money to pay a few people."

Impressive. Why hadn't she thought of that back when she was so certain he hadn't died? "And did you pay off the coroner, too?"

"Oh, no. Just the woman in the dentist's office. But then she had to go, too. Can't have loose ends dangling. It's bad business."

"You were at the funeral, weren't you? I felt you there."

"Damn straight you felt me there. You almost knocked me over. I was the man with the cane. Remember?"

She did, vaguely. "Why didn't anyone see you?"

"Probably because they didn't expect to. And I had sunglasses on with my hat pulled low and my scarf up high."

Kira flashed back to Wanda's devastation that day, her sobs and her agony at the loss of her only child. She was no fan of Wanda, certainly, but she hadn't deserved that. And to think that Kareem was there the whole time, just like she'd thought, watching the show.

"You're sick." She laughed and cried, staring up at the ceiling and wishing she could see God. She really needed to ask him whether he'd meant to create such a perfect monster when he produced Kareem. "Why did I never see that about you?"

Wrong choice of words, apparently. His satisfied smile faded away, leaving only his malignant stare. "Don't move one more inch—"

She froze, her palms planted on the floor behind her, just a foot from her purse, if that.

"—and think about the names we want to use on each other because I can think of a couple for you, you fucking ho."

Kira didn't dare breathe.

She wondered if Dexter was on his way.

She prayed that he was, and that she'd live long enough to tell him how much she loved him. Why hadn't she said it when she'd had the chance?

She prayed harder that he'd stay far away from this boat and this monster. That he'd live, even if she died today.

"Huh, Baby Girl?" Her silence only seemed to enrage Kareem, who lowered those heavy brows into a fearsome frown. Holding the knife higher, between them, he examined it in minute detail, angling the blade so it reflected the light, mesmerizing her with terror. Would the steel be cold? Hot? Would he slice or stab her? How long would it take for her to bleed to death? "Cat got your tongue?"

Kira didn't answer.

"You want to tell me why you fucked Kerry, one of my lieutenants? Or maybe you want to start with why you fucked Brady, the DEA agent who brought me down? Which one do you want to start with?"

There was no way to answer this, and Kira didn't even try.

"Answer me, you little bitch," Kareem roared, lunging for her.

Oh, God. She was such a liar.

She wasn't strong. She was afraid of pain. She wasn't ready to die. Not like this.

Screw it. If no rescue was coming and her time was up, then he'd kill her anyway. He might as well kill her while she was reaching for the Glock.

She crept backward again, and her hand just closed around the blessed braided strap of her leather purse on the floor when Kareem caught up with her. Dropping the knife by his side, just out of her reach, he used his good hand to grab her hip and yank her to her back.

Her skirt rode up, well over her thighs, stopping her breath.

Moving with slow deliberation, his flat gaze locked on her face, he straddled her.

No. Not that. Not again.

"No!" Enraged, she pummeled him with her fists, which seemed to have no discernable effect. "Don't you touch me! *Don't you touch me!*"

"Why not?" Those fingers crept north, to the waistband of her panties, and began to work them down her legs as she thrashed. "If you can fuck my lieutenant and my DEA agent, then you can fuck me, too, right? I am your husband—"

"No," she screamed, kicking out at him with her one good leg, and that was when she saw it.

A flash of movement at one of the windows.

Surprise and hope filled her up before she could stop them, and they must have shown on her face because Kareem turned just enough, twisting so he could put a knee on her throat while keeping his hand on her crotch.

"Is that you, Brady?" he called. "Did you come to watch my reunion with my wife?"

No. Kira writhed and spluttered, trying to speak, to warn. It wasn't supposed to happen like this, and she didn't want Dexter to die with her. "Run, Dexter!" she shrieked in that one second before the weight on her throat threatened to crush her windpipe. "Run—"

Dexter appeared in the window, his face mangled with rage and fear, his pistol fisted between his hands and pointed at Kareem. "Let her go, Kareem!" he shouted. "Let her go or I swear I'll take your head off!"

Kareem laughed. Taunted. "You'd better think again, motherfucker. I'll crush her throat before you can squeeze the trigger."

Oh, no, you won't.

With one hand, Kira hauled off and drove the flat of her palm up and into his nose, determined to hear it break. It did. With her other hand, she twisted, grabbed the knife, and embedded it to the hilt in Kareem's thigh just as the crack of a shot from Brady's gun roared over their heads and splintered the wall behind them, showering them with paint and plaster.

Howling, eyes wild and bulging, Kareem grabbed the knife, pulled it out, and kept coming at her like the indestructible demon seed she knew him to be.

But Dexter was here now, and she didn't have to die. She wasn't going to die. Only Kareem was.

Twisting again, she grabbed for her purse. Missed, and had a wild flashback to that horrible rock-climbing wall. If she could do that, she could do this. So she adjusted her angle and grabbed again, this time closing her fingers around the precious metal of the Glock, which she pulled out just as Kareem raised the knife to her throat.

"No!"

Hands fisted around the muzzle, she swung like Babe Ruth going for a homer, pistol-whipping Kareem in the temple with all of her adrenaline-fueled might.

Something cracked.

Yeah. She wanted more of that.

She swung again, and again, hysterical and oblivious to everything but the need to wipe this vermin off the face of the earth, forever.

He fell, collapsing to the floor like an anvil dropped from the Eiffel Tower, but she kept going, swinging and shouting.

"I told you I'd kill you with this gun if you didn't leave me alone, you bastard! I told you I'd kill you! I told you—"

"Kira! Stop, baby! He's gone! He's gone!"

"No!" she cried. "He's never gone! He's never—"

Dexter was there, suddenly, catching her arm and wrenching the gun out of her hands. "He's gone. Look. See? He's dead. You did it. You did it."

She looked.

Kareem lay sprawled on the floor next to her. His brown eyes were open but glazed, and the side of his head was a bloody mess, but that wasn't enough. She grabbed his neck, feeling for a pulse. There was none. That wasn't enough. She held her palm over his ruined nose, waiting to feel his breath. Nothing.

Bewildered, she looked to Dexter for confirmation.

"He's dead?"

"He's dead, baby."

"Really dead?"

"Really dead."

She stared at him. Looked, one last time, to Kareem.

Then she fell apart, sobbing with relief. "Oh, my God," she cried. "Oh, my God."

Being careful of her leg, Dexter gathered her close, rocking and soothing her. "It's okay now, Kira. You did it. He's gone."

"He killed Kerry."

"Kerry's not dead."

"What? But I thought—"

"Jayne found him last night. He's alive. Critical, but alive. She called me a little while ago."

"Oh, thank God. I was so scared," she sobbed. "I thought—"

"It's okay." Dexter rained kisses all over her face and neck, smothering her with love. "He's not going to hurt you again—"

"No." Pushing back a little, she wiped her face and tried to get control. After several hiccupping breaths, she managed it. "I was afraid I'd never get to tell you—"

"Tell me what, baby?"

"How much I love you," she said helplessly, and then, because once wasn't enough, she said it again. "I love you. I love you."

Dexter snatched her up again, burying his wet face against her neck and holding on as though he meant to keep her there forever. "I love you, too."

Laughter came then, shining through her tears, and she grabbed his cheeks, bringing his face up so she could kiss his smiling mouth.

"You still love me?" she murmured against his lips.

"I'll always love you."

"I never meant to be this much trouble."

This time, he laughed. "You're worth it, baby. You're absolutely worth it."

Epilogue

One Year Later

"Come on, baby. You can do it."

The wind spiked just then, rustling through the trees all around them, and Dexter took a second to breathe deep and enjoy the earthy smells of pine needles, the damp ground, and sunshine. It was cool but not chilly, and he took everything in: the way the ridge gave way to a sea of purple wildflowers on the one side, and a splashing and craggy creek on the other; the white-tipped mountains in the distance; the sweet ache of hard work in his straining leg muscles; and Kira.

Kira most of all.

"I like Telluride," she told him. "Good choice."

"Yeah? You don't wish you were lounging on the beach in Bermuda right now?"

"Maybe for our first anniversary."

"Duly noted."

"Come on," she said again. "Only a few more steps, old man. You can do it."

Dexter glared from behind his sunglasses and struggled the last few feet up the world's rockiest and most treacherous path. Her sunglasses blocked him from seeing the amusement in her eyes, but he knew it was there by the way her lips curled in a sorry attempt to keep her smirk to a mere smile. When he came within range, she reached out a hand and helped pull him the rest of the way to the top.

"You did it!"

"You know," he said when he'd caught his breath a little, "I was going to ask you how your ankle's doing, but there doesn't seem to be much point."

"My leg is great. How are you doing?"

He raised their joined left hands to eye level, so they could enjoy the way the plain gold bands gleamed in the sunlight.

"I'm happy," he said simply, kissing her smiling lips.

"So am I. We make a great team, don't we, husband?"

Wrapping his free hand around her supple waist, he brought her in closer, for another kiss and a nuzzle.

"We do indeed, Mrs. Brady. We do indeed."

Don't miss
Deadly Pursuit
On sale now

Cincinnati

Kareem Gregory settled deeper into his leather chair and listened to his attorney do so much worthless yap-yap-yapping that he wanted to shove his fist down the man's throat. Every overpriced word that came out of the dumb-ass bitch's mouth only made Kareem hate the man more.

Fucking lawyers.

But for them and their incompetence, he'd be out of this mess by now.

Thanks to them, he was still hip-deep in shit.

What kind of shit? Entrapped by the feds, for one. Arrested on bogus money-laundering charges, for another. All his assets, from his million-dollar estate down to his last pair of diamond cuff links—pretty much everything he'd ever worked for—threatened with seizure and currently being eyeballed by the DEA *and* the IRS. Convicted and sent to a phone-booth-sized cell in federal prison when he had a business to run.

Well . . . two businesses.

His string of auto-customizing shops because, yeah, he liked to pimp rides.

And his real empire. The drug one.

Not that the feds had ever been able to nail him for it, because he was too slick and clever for them and he compartmentalized his organization so that the right hand never knew what the left hand was doing, and only he had both hands.

Only a few people knew he was the top dog, and he intended to keep it that way.

The feds' best efforts had only led to a money-laundering conviction. Even so, he'd gone to prison— and prison was prison.

He was lucky he'd survived one day on the inside, much less a year. Lucky for the fine wool of the suit he now wore and for the soft cotton of his undershirt instead of those coarse prison rags that scratched his skin.

The only good thing a lawyer had ever done for him, despite the tens of thousands he'd paid in legal fees, was winning his appeal. Now, after all the suffering he'd endured, God had finally smiled on Kareem again and sent him a few blessings, no doubt as a sign of greater things to come.

A retrial. Release on bail. The opportunity to crack a few heads and make sure everything ran smoothly within the organization. Renewed success in his hunt. The chance to expand his wine collection and screw every woman in sight.

Well . . . every woman but the one he really wanted.

Kareem shot a quick glance at Kira, his tight-lipped wife. She sat beside him in her designer dress, looking the way she always looked: icy and beautiful.

Funny, huh? The one woman he should be able to have at will hadn't given him any since he was arrested nearly two years ago, and here he was, still sniffing after her. Back in the day, she'd loved him and given him that delicious body enthusiastically and often. She'd been his moon and stars. His freaking sun. Kira wouldn't let him touch her for now, but he'd get her back as soon as they worked out the whole trust issue.

In the meantime, there were plenty of other fish in the sea—damn sexy little minnows, too—and Kareem had several of them on retainer. Why not take full advantage? It made sense to store up a little in case his latest lawyer turned out to be as incompetent as all the rest, lost the retrial, and landed Kareem back in prison.

Not that Kareem had any intention of going back to prison.

Ever.

Which was one of the reasons he'd taken matters into his own hands.

That, and revenge, which was going to be oh so sweet.

"The U.S. Attorney's Office sent over their final witness list. A lot of familiar people on it." Jacob Radcliffe, who looked barely old enough to be out of diapers but was one of the best criminal defense lawyers in the city, flipped through his thick file, found some papers, and slid them across the enormous carved desk to Kareem. "No real surprises."

Ignoring the sudden, slight tremble in his hand, Kareem scanned the alphabetical list for the names he wanted, ignoring the others. He found them right away, and each one jacked his blood pressure up another thirty notches, sent his thundering pulse into overdrive.

Jackson Parker. Ray Wolfe.

Feds.

A searing rage rose up his neck and burned his cheeks before it prickled in his scalp. To think that *he,* Kareem Gregory, a world-class judge of character with enough savvy and street sense to sniff out every liar within a twenty-mile radius, had trusted them. Liked them. Let his guard down around them.

And what had his good faith gotten him? Betrayal by the kilo.

To add insult to injury, those men had eluded him and his inevitable retaliation for months. *Months.*

That, fortunately, was about to change.

"So that's the plan." Jacob showed signs of wrapping this shit up, thank God. "We're going to do our best to get an acquittal this time and make sure you never have to go back to prison."

How touching. As if Kareem would leave his future in this punk's pristine hands. Not in this lifetime. He thought of his plans, which were in motion even now. He thought of the bit of crucial information that had recently and unexpectedly fallen into his lap. He thought about how difficult it would be for his former business associates—Parker and Wolfe—to testify against him at the retrial if they were dead. He thought of their deaths, one of which was imminent.

Best of all, he thought about doling out the punishment these men had coming, and he smiled.

If you betray Kareem Gregory, even if you're a fed, you pay the ultimate price.

Simple as that.

"I'm going to do my best to stay out of prison, too," Kareem told his lawyer. "My very best."

Chapter 1

Lawrenceburg, Indiana

The irritating, nostril-burning smell of cigarette smoke woke Payton Jones from a sound sleep. Or maybe it was Mama's croaking bullfrog voice, or the violent thud as the old bat rolled into Payton's bedroom with enough force to bang the cheap door against the wall, no doubt leaving chip number three million in the puke-yellow paint.

"Gitcher lazy ass outta bed. It's one-thirty in the afternoon."

Payton pushed the covers down and cracked a bleary eye open against the bright sunlight streaming in the window above the headboard. Unfortunately, Mama's wheelchair was parked directly ahead, and Mama, wearing her dirty red housecoat and as unavoidable as a sperm whale in a lounge chair, was in it.

Payton groaned. It was too early for this shit.

Muttering, head pounding due to the nine—or was it ten?—Jell-O shooters that went down the pipe last night, Payton dove under the blankets again. This resulted in a smack on the leg sharp enough to clear the sinuses.

"Jesus." Good and awake now, Payton sat up and glared at Mama. "Who put a bee in your freaking bonnet?"

"I put me a list together, for the grocery." An inch-long strip of ash wavered and fell from the end of the cigarette onto Mama's lap, whereupon Mama brushed it onto the white sheet, one inch from Payton's hip. Payton yelped and swiped it to the floor. "Yer gonna need to stop at Walmart, too, and pick up my prescriptions."

"Why can't Al do it?"

"Because Al's working, like you should be."

"I can't find a job," Payton said.

"Helps when you look for one."

Of all the hypocritical bullshit Payton had ever heard, this running thread about looking for a job was the worst. How a woman could take one slight on-the-job hip injury, turn it into worker's comp benefits into perpetuity, and then have the nerve to complain about someone else not looking for a job was something Payton would never understand.

"I've *been* looking." This, as they both knew, was a lie, more or less, but what was left of Payton's pride required it.

Mama glared, her watery eyes squinched against the cigarette smoke that wafted up into them as she spoke. "You're nothin' but a big disappointment to me, Payton—"

"Shit." Payton got out of bed, stalked over to the closet, and rummaged through shirts and whatnot, scraping the hangers across the bar in the hopes of drowning out this latest recitation on the depths of Mama's disappointment, but the noise didn't help. It never did.

"—a disappointment and a burden. Never gonna amount to anything, as far as I can tell. Dropped out of college. Dishonorable discharge from the army. No job. Out all night at the Argosy, drinking and gambling away the only two cents we got to rub together. What'm I supposed to do with you?"

"Beats the hell outta me," Payton said from the depths of the closet.

Payton had created this whole messed-up situation—no one else to blame there. Living at home in a trailer at twenty-four. Driving a piece of shit car that cost more than it was worth every fill-up. Saddled with the bitch here.

The army had provided two precious years of freedom, but that hadn't worked out in the end.

Blowing through the money from that last job wasn't the smartest thing Payton had ever done, but the blackjack table had been hot that night. For a little while, anyway. Still, betting ten large at once was a bad idea, so there were no real excuses.

Now Payton paid the price every time Mama played that same old broken record—*Payton Screws Up: Volume One*—and every time Mama swore that Payton would still be living at home decades from now.

Payton almost gagged at the thought.

Over near the bed, the bitch droned on, working up a head of steam, when a miracle occurred.

The phone rang, and it was the special ring tone—the Dixie Chicks' "Not Ready to Make Nice"—announcing that this was an important call, the kind that didn't happen often enough. Payton lunged for the leather jacket perched atop the teetering pile of clothes on the chair, fished the phone out of the pocket, and flipped it open.

"This is Payton."

There was a long pause, and then, "Someone's looking to hire."

The surge of gratitude and relief was almost blinding. "I'm available."

Mama watched with sharp eyes, mouth gaping open and cigarette stub dangling from the edge of her bottom lip by what could only be spit. Trying to look casual, Payton turned and stared out the window to that lousy battered blue car, which seemed to lose a foot or more of its body to rust every day.

"I recommended you."

"That so?" Payton now felt a little wary because Lady Luck generally wasn't this good or this timely. "Who needs me?"

"A friend of Travis."

Thank God. A referral from Travis was as good as gold, better than a personalized note from Oprah.

"So . . . you interested?"

Interested? Payton would gladly explore any escape option out of this pit, including an express train straight to the molten center of hell if one pulled up.

"Yeah. I'm interested."

Mount Adams, Washington

"You're wasting my time."

Amara Clarke gave the assistant prosecutor sitting across the table from her a pointed look, just for emphasis, and waited for the inevitable comeback, which didn't arrive immediately. Good. Maybe now she could eat her dinner in something resembling peace. Amara took a quick, desperate bite of the now lukewarm but still delicious chicken and noodles in her bowl, the only food she'd had since the brief recess at one this afternoon.

Katie O'Farrell watched her as she sipped her coffee, glowering and no doubt framing her rebuttal.

Amara didn't bother to hide her impatience; she had dinner to eat and work to do. Flapping a hand at her open laptop, she hoped Katie would take the hint and scram.

"Let's wrap this up. I need to write my closing, and so do you. And I'd like to get home before ice glues my car to the street."

A sheet of rain drove into the window at the end of the booth, chilling the air inside the diner and making the ominous *pings* that could only mean sleet. Amara shivered, cold down to the marrow of her bones. If only she was home in a bubble-filled tub, breathing in the scent of lavender and letting Calgon take her away. She had better hopes of discovering a cure for cancer by tomorrow, but a girl could dream.

It was nearly ten and she was running on fumes. Her thirty-six-year-old body had started feeling the strain of the trial, which ended its second day today: tired, gritty eyes, empty stomach and a weird combination of sleep-deprived exhaustion and caffeine-driven agitation.

There was no explaining her case of nerves, even to herself. She ate prosecutors for breakfast, lunch and dinner. Thrived in the courtroom like an orchid in a greenhouse.

Why was she so antsy tonight?

The cook, whispered that insidious little voice in the back of her head.

No way, she thought, knowing she was a damn liar.

Taking another bite of noodles, she shot him a glance through her lashes. Being discreet was an unnecessary exercise, though, because he rarely looked at her. When he did look at her, it was with an unfathomable darkness in his eyes that made her feel like something he'd throw in the Dumpster out back.

Jerk.

Standing over at the grill on the other side of the long counter, flipping burgers or whatever it was he did, he had his white-T-shirt-clad, broad-shouldered back to her. This, fortunately, spared her from his cool-eyed disdain, but unfortunately treated her to an unimpeded view of the world's greatest ass, which was encased in faded, baggy jeans but still clearly tight and round.

Her face flamed. She looked away, irritated with her surging hormones.

That ass and that man, whoever the hell he was, had ruined the Twelfth Street Diner for her and, along with it, her trial rituals.

In the old days, she'd finish up after a long session at court and bring her laptop here to her favorite booth, where the hanging lamp over the table provided a soothing light, and the view of the arbor in the park across the street was more relaxing than watching the Travel Channel at home.

She'd order the pork chops and work late into the night, the comings and goings of the other regulars keeping her from the absolute loneliness she felt within the four walls of her house. She'd been well fed, content and as relaxed as a criminal defense attorney ever got.

All that had changed three months ago when *he* showed up.

Realizing she'd lapsed into staring again, Amara looked away, cleared her throat and tried to focus.

Katie O'Farrell, who was a friendly acquaintance even

if she was Amara's current courtroom enemy, lowered her cup and clanked it on the table with unmistakable irritation. "You can't seriously believe I'm wasting your time. The jury's not with you. You should be glad to hear my offer."

"Oh, please."

"In case you didn't notice, you didn't make any dents in Detective Curtis today."

Amara *had* noticed, but she hid her scowl. Detective Curtis had emerged from her withering cross-examination smelling like a June rose, yeah, that was true.

It was also true that the *we hate you and the horse you rode in on* vibe from the jury didn't bode well for her client, Greg Kinney, accused low-level drug dealer and fumbling college student in his spare time. Poor dumb Greg stood better than a fair chance of spending some quality time in the pen, where he probably belonged.

Luckily for Greg, though, he had a U.S. senator for a father, and Daddy Dearest had enough money and sense to hire a good lawyer. Enter Amara.

She wasn't about to let Greg go down without a fight, no matter how stupid he was.

"Excuse me?" Amara slipped into full battle mode, her excess adrenaline fueling her outrage. "I'm supposed to have my client plead guilty and pack his bag for prison on the basis of your little hunch about which side the jury's on? Is this a joke?"

Katie shrugged. "Your client'll never get two years from the judge if he's convicted, and you know it. This is a decent deal."

Maybe. Probably. But Amara hadn't given up yet, nor would she. Tomorrow she'd deliver a closing argument to rival Clarence Darrow's in the Scopes Monkey Trial. Then she'd let the jury decide.

"We're not pleading out."

Katie, practically snarling now, put her elbows on the table and leaned in. "Are you holding out for one year? Is that what this is about? Because—"

"I'm not holding out for anything."

"—I'm not recommending one year. I know how you operate, Amara—"

"I'm not *operating*."

"—so don't even try it."

"I'm not trying *anything*."

Amara didn't bother trying to keep the annoyance out of her voice. What'd a person have to do to be left alone around here? Why couldn't she eat and work without harassment? "I don't want a deal of any kind, I'm not holding out for a year, and *I am not done with my noodles*."

A thick, muscular, brown arm had reached down to take her bowl, and Amara spoke without thinking. Her unnecessarily harsh tone registered with her brain a millisecond before the regret did, but by then it was too late.

Oh, God, it was *him*.

Flushing hot enough to ignite her own eyebrows, she slowly glanced up. Towering over her stood six and a half feet of masculine perfection and irritation, a man so unspeakably virile he'd make Zena and her band of Amazons look like petite-size zeros.

Thunderstruck, Amara stared like an idiot, her mouth hanging open.

This was the closest she'd ever been to him and she almost needed a shield or lead blanket to deflect some of his unholy chemical effect on her. Things had been bad enough from a distance, but now she could smell him, too, and oh, what a thrill that was. Sandalwood, spices and the fresh, healthy musk of a man who spent hours over steamy pots and pans. Just his scent alone was enough to peak her nipples and get the honey flowing between her thighs, but she still had to assimilate the face and the body.

Like that was possible.

The body was something she'd fantasize about for years to come. A pristine white T-shirt—how did he keep it so white, working in a kitchen?—stretched across broad, square shoulders and a rippling slab of chest and abdomen. One of those starchy chef's aprons, the kind Martha Stewart wore, had been folded down and tied around his narrow hips.

He had light brown skin and haywire curls the same sandy color. The brows, though, were dark and moody. So were the flashing eyes, which right now were expressing something fierce, like his fierce desire to dump the bowl of noodles on her head.

His five o'clock shadow had gone to seed a week or so ago, but that only added to his attractiveness, his air of surly attitude teetering on the edge of outright menace.

Looking at him gave Amara the kind of violent visceral response she'd never in her life had for anyone else. She wanted him. Had fantasized about his tongue in her mouth and her legs around his waist. Would love to have his scent and stubble marks all over her skin. Needed the slow, deep thrust of his body inside hers.

And then she needed it again. And again.

If he smiled or crooked his finger at her, she, Amara Clarke—defense attorney extraordinaire and fiercely independent woman who prided herself on never needing anyone, didn't believe in casual sex and hadn't had a

date in three years or sex in four—would probably
follow him into the back room, or the bathroom, or his
car, or the nearest hotel, and let him do whatever he
damn well wanted to do with her.

Yeah, she wanted him *that* much.

Their gazes locked and the cook looked her in the eye
for only the second or third time ever. His dark brown
gaze, so frigid it would no doubt cure the global warming problem if only someone would provide his transport
to the Arctic, raked over her face and, in those fleeting
milliseconds, one thing was perfectly, brutally clear:

He hated her.

He believed she was a snotty bitch who thought he
was a peon well beneath her notice, and he despised her
for it. There was no aspect of her that he liked; probably even the buttons down the front of her dress offended
him. She had no hope of redemption against such absolute loathing, no possibility of him ever finding anything whatsoever worthwhile about her.

So it was no surprise when he slammed her precious
bowl back on the table, turned his broad back on Amara
and spoke to Katie.

"Who's the chocolate bunny?" He jerked his head in
Amara's direction. "You should teach her some manners."

Oh, man. He was blessed with a naturally low, deep
and sexy voice, the kind of voice that would keep a
woman up all night with a vibrator in one hand and the
receiver in the other if he worked for one of those phone
sex hotlines.

Katie didn't miss a beat, smiling up at him with
Nancy Reagan-esque adoration. "Amara can't be taught.
But I'm happy to be your bunny if you, you know, need
one in vanilla."

He grinned at Katie, and Amara seethed with something ugly, almost like jealousy, but then his words registered with her brain. That was a compliment, right? Chocolate bunny? It was also a condescending endearment offensive to anyone with a pair of ovaries, and of course she hated it on principle, but . . . did that mean she'd caught his eye?

"Where's Judy?" Katie wondered, referring to their waitress.

"Went home sick," Jack told her, still favoring her with the brilliance of his smile.

Amara tried to recapture his attention. "I—I'm sorry."

He glanced over at Amara, his jaw tightening.

"I just . . . I'm really hungry and the noodles are really good, so—"

The irritation vanished and he faced her, one corner of his incredible mouth creeping up into the wicked half smile of a man with one thing on his mind, and it wasn't food. To her utter astonishment, he gave her a pointed and assessing once-over, nearly searing the bodice of her dress off her body with the intensity of his gaze.

That look was about the rudest thing she'd ever experienced in her life.

It was also the sexiest.

"Why didn't you say so, Bunny?" he murmured. "I made the noodles. And I'm happy to let you taste anything of mine whenever you want."

If there was the teeniest doubt in her mind that he was trying to be as obnoxious and insulting as possible, the tiny wink he gave her cleared it up. Amara gaped at him, stammering. Her skin felt so hot it had to be purple by now.

Turning to Katie, who was also drop-jawed, the cook

flashed a pleasant, dimple-revealing smile, the kind he sprinkled liberally on everyone else in the universe, but never Amara. "More coffee, Katie?"

Wait a minute.

Amara's belated outrage finally kicked in and, fuming, she eyed her own glass, which held only a couple of melted ice cubes and the sad dregs of a Diet Coke. How come his over-the-top nasty talk had her all hot and bothered? And how about a refill on *her* drink?

"Umm . . . yeah." Katie simpered under his attention until Amara wondered if she wouldn't slither onto the table and undress in an impromptu striptease for his special benefit. The killer prosecutor turned to vanilla pudding right before Amara's disbelieving eyes. "More coffee'd be great."

"How's the trial going?" The cook kept his back firmly turned on Amara and refilled Katie's cup from his steaming carafe. "Another conviction, you think?"

Katie seemed to recover some of her composure, which was more than Amara could do. "Absolutely. Unless I can get Amara to plead out."

Royally pissed off and telling herself it had nothing to do with being crudely propositioned by the world's haughtiest cook or jealousy over his attention to Katie, Amara let her quick temper get the better of her.

"I'm not pleading out," she told Katie, and then glared up at the cook. "I need another Diet Coke, if you can stop flirting with customers long enough to do your job. And my name's not *Bunny*."

Oh, God. There was that look again, that flash of mischief that dried out her mouth and sent shivers chasing over her skin.

"No problem, Sugar. Just let me know what you want

me to call you, and I'm there." With that, he strode back to the kitchen, leaving the women to admire his ass as he went.

"Oh, my God," Katie breathed. "He wants you."

Amara clenched her hands in her lap to stop the embarrassing tremble of her fingers. To think she'd been attracted to that jerk. Hah. He'd cured her of that, hadn't he?

And yet . . .

She felt hot-wired and unreasonably alive, as though someone had strung a power cord along her spine and it was shooting sparks through her body.

"He's only yanking my chain because he's a jackass." Working hard to sound normal, she waved at her laptop to remind Katie of the business at hand. "Can we wrap this up? I really have to get cracking here."

Katie frowned, looking resigned. "So no deal?"

"You know I've got reasonable doubt," Amara said with a conviction she didn't feel. "Otherwise you wouldn't be here doing your Monty Hall routine. Your office shouldn't have brought the charges in the first place, and it wouldn't have if this wasn't a senator's son and you weren't trying to show taxpayers how tough on crime you are. No deal."

Rolling her eyes, Katie slid out of the booth, flipped a couple of bills on the table, and grabbed her things. "See you in the morning, then. Tell Chef Hottie I'll dream of him tonight."

They both laughed, and Amara watched as Katie went through the glass door and disappeared into the night. The diner was empty now except for one of the other regulars, a senior citizen named Esther, who sat at the Formica counter flipping through the paper as she ate her pancakes. Amara was looking back at her screen when the cook reappeared with a new Diet Coke and handed it to her.

"What'd you do to Katie?"

Amara took a sip and tried not to bristle at the implication that she'd driven Katie away, which, she supposed, she had. "She left."

"Drove her away, eh? That probably happens to you a lot, Bunny. You should work on being less abrasive. You might make a friend or two."

Ouch. The mouthful of soda soured to vinegar on her tongue.

Though he couldn't know it and she'd die before admitting it, his barbed arrow hit its mark because people, generally speaking, didn't like her.

Her personality, it turned out, was a little caustic. Not that she was into self-analysis or anything, but it was probably because she'd grown up in foster care. Maybe she'd developed a defense mechanism to keep people away, not that crowds were knocking down her door trying to get close.

Anyway, that was how she was wired. If she wanted to get something, she got it, and if she wanted to say something, she said it. Sure, this turned some people off, but she didn't have time to smooth over people's hurt feelings. Plus, she couldn't easily turn off her defense attorney's fighting instinct outside the courtroom, which resulted in her plowing her way through life. Hazard of the job.

So, yeah, nobody liked her, but it was rude of him to say it.

Incensed, Amara recovered her speaking abilities

and got over the whole intimidation thing. This guy may be a god sent down from Mount Olympus to torment womankind with lust, but he was still an arrogant SOB who needed a smackdown.

"I think you've got the market cornered on abrasive, *Honey*," she said.

Uh-oh. Wrong tactic. Abort—*abort*.

That hint of wickedness came back into his expression, not so much a smile as the disquieting light of amusement in his eyes. Planting his palms on the table, he leaned down, right in her face. "I like the endearment, Bunny. Got anything else for me?"

"My name is Amara Clarke. Use it. *Honey*." She extended her hand, wondering exactly how rude he was prepared to be.

The simple gesture took him by surprise.

For several long beats, he didn't seem to know what to do. For all his smirking bravado, she realized, he didn't want to touch her. His ambivalence was so strong she could almost stick her tongue out and taste it.

Dark eyes sparking, brows lowered, he glared, apparently cursing her to hell and back for all eternity. Then his gaze wavered and he looked down his straight nose to her hand. Finally, as though he'd never participated in a handshake before and wasn't quite sure how the procedure worked, he reached out and grasped her hand in his firm grip.

Holy God.

There was no preparing for the current of electricity that surged through her body when their palms connected. Nor could she explain the flow of blazing heat between them, which was disproportionate to anything a human being should be able to generate.

His expression was, for once, unreadable. "Jack. Patterson."

He pumped her hand twice, an unremarkable, socially acceptable handshake, and then let go. Without another word, he turned and walked back into the kitchen, leaving the door flapping after him.